IN THE DOGHOUSE

A gift of a book, with love from...

Samantha David

The characters and events portrayed in this book are fictitious. Any similarity to real persons, living or dead, is coincidental and not intended by the author.

ISBN: 9798736024063

Cover design by: Letty David
Library of Congress Control Number: 2018675309
Printed in the United States of America

In memory of Dolly, the best dog in the world

CONTENTS

PROLOGUE

Sally tilted her chair back, propped her feet on the desk and wiggled her toes. The ruby varnish on her toes was chipped. How annoying. Damn Flo for taking so much of her time. "Come on, darling," she wheedled down the phone. "Just for me? Pretty please?"

A thousand miles away, Rosie's heart sank. The last thing she wanted was a stranger hanging round the house, upsetting the dogs. "A writer? What would a writer do here?" she said evasively.

"Write, of course. You're miles from anywhere..."

"45 minutes from Aix."

"Exactly. Lost in France. And that place of yours is huge, you've got twenty-five bedrooms, you won't even notice him. It's ideal - isolated, quiet, no distractions. He'll have nothing else to do."

"Most of those rooms are uninhabitable and it's not quiet here. The dogs..."

"Oh, darling!" Sally swivelled her chair so she could look out of the window at the people strolling over Waterloo Bridge. "They're only tiny likkle puppie wuppies!"

"They bark," said Rosie. "They howl, and Spike hates people, he tries to bite them, he's enormous, he's got big teeth." She sighed noisily. If it had been anyone else she would have hung up but Rosie knew that if she did, Sally was quite capable of appearing on the doorstep the next morning with her horrible writer in tow. She pulled a despairing face at a scruffy white lapdog lying upside down on the sofa. Dolly winked, waved her paws, and panted back at her.

Sally steam-rollered on. "Look sweetie, the point is it's a perfect hideaway. No-one will know he's there, no-one will recog... It's the perfect... "

"What do you mean, no-one will recognise him? Don't tell me he's one of your disgusting, arrogant film stars wanting daily massages and boiled egg whites?"

Sally stopped wiggling her toes, swivelled her chair back to the desk and sat up straight. "No, darling! Absolutely not!" She tugged at her short, peroxide hair. "I meant, um, where he lives obviously people know he's a writer so he... people ask him how the book is going when he's trying to go shopping at... Woolworths! So utterly distracting, darling." She could have kicked herself. Woolworths? Did it even still exist? Irritated, she lit a cigarette.

Rosie was also irritated and also sitting bolt upright. "Oh really? And what kind of book is he writing? Not a Hollywood kiss-and-tell, by any chance?"

Sally shook her head until her earrings rattled. "Darling! As if I would! No! Oh come on, Rosie! Anyway he doesn't live in Hollywood. He lives here in London. He's a neighbour of ours as a matter of fact. Would I lie to you?" There was silence. She dropped her voice to an intimate caress. "Sweetie... just give him a chance?" All that earned her was an unresponsive grunt but Sally couldn't afford to give up. "He really needs this break, poor thing. He's divorced, and so lonely."

"You are making it worse."

"No! You're wrong! He's not looking for anyone. I mean, he won't bother you!"

"Oh? And why is that?" Rosie was fast losing her temper.

Sally crammed her cigarette into the ashtray and reached into the filing cabinet for the gin. "I mean," she said, hastily unscrewing the top, "because he's gay!"

"He's divorced and gay?"

"Same sex marriage, darling. Get with the programme." Sally took a large swig of Gordon's straight from the bottle.

"So he'll want to re-arrange all the furniture?"

"No, I told you he's a writer. A gay one, but he doesn't do furniture because... he's short-sighted. Practically blind... not aesthetically aware at all, lives in his own world... won't even notice the furniture." That bit at least was true. "Come on, Rosie. For Christsake, say yes. I really need this, and you owe me!"

"I do? How come? How? Why?"

"Because I smuggled that horrible dog back from Italy for you."

"But that was 25 years ago! We were just kids."

"And if we'd been caught, I could have gone to jail. Stop saying but. I could have been locked up, and I don't even like dogs."

"You were heroic."

"I bloody was, and now I need a favour in return. No danger, no prison, no police, no international smuggling. Just a harmless little writer spending a few weeks in your vast château, finishing his book. You won't even know he's there." Sally took another swig of gin. "Is that too much to ask? Considering the scar that I still have on my leg?"

"You don't!"

"Livid and puckered, my dear."

"I wish I'd never answered the phone."

"Darling! I knew you wouldn't let me down," said Sally, breathing a huge sigh of relief. She put the bottle down. "Right. Now. His name is er, Bernard. Let me find my pen, ah, yes here we are..."

"Bernard? No-one's called Bernard!"

"Michael Bernard. You wouldn't have heard of him. He writes specialist books, you know. Factual stuff on, er, Roman china. Very boring and dull. He'll be arriving on Tuesday, I'm sure I can arrange an early morning flight."

Rosie sighed heavily. "Which airport? I suppose he wants collecting? What time?"

Sally realised it wasn't the moment to mention a private plane. "No, that's all right. I'm arranging transport. He'll make his own way from the airport in a hired car. I should think he'll be with you sometime between lunch and supper."

"Oh goodie. I'll spend the afternoon loitering at the lodge gates."

"Perfect!"

"I've got nothing else to do," pursued Rosie, but the shaft went wide.

"I'll send you a cheque to cover expenses," said Sally crisply. "Don't argue. Rather you than the taxman, dearest."

"I don't need a hundred quid. The state I'm in it won't make any difference..."

"Oh, we can stretch to more than that," drawled Sally, screwing the top back on the gin. "How about three grand to start with? I'll arrange a transfer this afternoon. You do have an IBAN number don't you, or do I have to pay you in little lumps of muddy gold?"

Rosie choked. "Three grand? Are you mad? What?" She was just short of 4,000 euros to finish paying the annual property taxes on the château. If Sally was serious, the taxe foncière nightmare would be over for another year.

"For God's sake Rosie. I know you're broke and honestly, I'll just write it off as a business expense. It's nothing. But I really need you to put up with this guy; you don't have to train him or groom him, or whatever you do with those ghastly canines. Just house him, and feed him from time to time. And keep him sober, OK?"

Rosie was still absorbing the implications of a large cheque. "Sally, you don't know how much this..."

"Just shut up and listen."

Rosie stopped trying to speak and started taking notes. Her head was spinning. Finally putting the phone down, she looked at her daughter in the doorway, flicking her hair impatiently.

"Larrie darling," said Rosie, feeling numb with financial relief. "Home from school already?"

Larrie was trying her best to look angelic. "Can I go out, Mummy?"

"Riding? No. Do your homework."

"Mummy! No, please!" Larrie scowled and stamped her foot. "There's no point anyway. Horses don't speak German!"

"Viennese Lipizzaners do. Go on, get a move on."

"Who was that on the phone?"

"Your godmother, Sally. She's sending one of her writers to stay with us."

Larrie's eyes lit up. "Because you owed her a blood bond?" she said, with gleaming eyes. She advanced on her mother wielding an imaginary dagger.

"No, just a favour."

"Ah ha! Blackmail!" Larrie leaned over the desk. "If you refused, she'd sell incriminating photographs of you naked on the beach."

"Naked photos of me? I should cocoa. He needs somewhere to write and in return Sally's paying the taxe foncière."

"She is! What, all of it?"

"No, that would be mad, and I've already paid most of it. Anyway, he's coming on Tuesday."

"I bet he's hiding out from Interpol!"

"You monkey," said Rosie but she wasn't really listening. She was already mentally sorting bed linen looking for a sheet that wasn't torn, mended or stained. "Go and do your homework."

"So who is he, then? Is he a maniac? Is he going to burn the place down in the middle of the night? Will I have to tie my sheets together and escape out of my bedroom window? He'd better not try riding Sobie or I'll kill him."

Rosie laughed. "You've been reading too many adventure stories! He's no-one. Just some lame-duck writer friend of Sally's. She always seems to have at least one of them on her books. I shouldn't think he'll want to go riding. Apparently he's withdrawn, half-blind, divorced, gay and only interested in Roman coins."

"So what is he writing?"

Rosie laughed. Larrie was so transparently trying to do anything to avoid opening her schoolbooks. "German homework, mostly," she said, shaking her finger in Larrie's face. "Go on, skedaddle!"

Defeated, Larrie stamped off to her bedroom and Rosie's gaze wandered over the bookcases, untidily stuffed with every book ever written on canines, to the fireplace painted crazy ice cream colours by Chris when he was about Larrie's age, the thick curtains, the sofas and armchairs, the side tables, the sheepskin rugs, the flowers and jugs and general cosy clutter of her favourite room.

Eyeing Rosie from the comfortably collapsing sofa, Dolly yawned and put her head on her paws. No walkies yet.

She wouldn't let Sally's writer in here, she decided. He could have the yellow bedroom. It was big enough to work in, it had its own bathroom and it was in the modern wing of the château. She would ask Chris to help her put a bigger table in there. A writer would probably have loads of papers. And he'd want wifi. She wondered how Spike would take to a new man in the household.

Dolly's beady black eyes gleamed. She yawned, deliberately making a noise like a rusty hinge. Her tongue curled out of her little pink mouth and she stretched her fluffy bottom into the air, staring fixedly at Rosie.

"All right! I'm coming!" said Rosie getting to her feet.

Trotting at her side towards the door, Dolly wagged happily - after walkies it would be time for din-dins.

CHAPTER ONE

"So Muma, what's this I hear about a writer?" said Chris, passing his plate over. "One of Aunt Sally's young boy protégés, is he? Why does she want to send him here?"

"He's a murderer and he's on the run from the law," said Larrie waving her fork at her older brother. "His pockets are full of blood and he walks the ramparts when the moon is full..."

"Don't talk such nonsense, and take that salad out of your pocket," said Rosie. "I've told you before, don't filch food off the table for that wretched horse. Now eat up, and stop telling stories about the poor man." She tore a chunk off a stale baguette.

"Poor, is he? Hasn't he got any money either?" said Larrie, obediently pulling a large and very crumpled lettuce leaf out of her pocket and putting it back on her plate. "I thought all Sally's gang were rich."

"He can't be that rich," said Rosie. "Or else why is he coming here? I mean if he was rich he'd go to some posh hotel in Cannes, wouldn't he? In fact,

I don't know exactly why Sally was so keen to send him here. She knows it's a mess. Perhaps it was just her way of doing me a favour?"

"She's paying the foncière," Larrie told Chris. "As a bribe. Because he's a bandit. On the run. From the mafia."

Chris rolled his eyes at his younger sister.

"Sally says he's intellectual, weedy, and into stamps," said Rosie. "Apparently he also has impaired sight, so you mustn't leave stuff around. Especially not on the stairs, or he'll break his arm and we'll never get rid of him. And don't make fun of him either. He's sensitive. What's the betting he gets sunburn?"

"What does that mean?" said Chris. "Sensitive? You mean he's gay?"

"Well he's not riding Sobie!" said Larrie, shoving a lump of dry bread into her pocket. "I don't care how sensitive he is!"

"Better make sure Spike doesn't take a dislike to him," said Chris. "Or you'll have a lawsuit on your hands."

Hearing his name, Spike lifted his massive, scarred face off his paws, sat up and nudged Rosie's elbow with his huge wet nose. She absent-mindedly gave him a piece of cheese rind and, on the other side of the room, Dolly instantly woke up and bounced off the sofa. She was followed by three big dogs who rose up as one from beside the Aga, playfully biting at each other's ears. And then a pair of large marmalade tomcats uncurled themselves from a sagging armchair and wove their way between the chair legs meeping for treats.

"Muma, didn't you say we shouldn't feed the dogs at the table?" said Chris severely. "You've set them all off now."

"You're totally right darling," said Rosie dipping a chunk of stale bread into the lentil sauce. "Be nice now, don't snatch. Spike! Sit!" Spike's huge bottom obediently sank to the ground and he plonked one massive paw on her lap. His big eyes were pleading and sincere.

"Muma!"

Rosie popped the dripping bread into Spike's mouth. Drooling, and jerking the stump of his tail, he retreated to a basket beside the solid fuel stove. Bustling into his place, Dolly gave two sharp yaps and a twinkly wink. Every inch of her white fur was demanding her rightful share of crispy bread and lentil sauce.

"Muma!"

"Oh darling, it's only a little bit and she's so cute. Look at her little nose all wrinkling up!"

Dolly panted loudly, her bad breath sweeping over the table like a wind from a rotten cabbage patch. Larrie held her nose. "God, she stenches!" said Chris, pushing the cats off the table. "So exactly when is this effete Roman mole of Aunt Sally's arriving?"

"Tuesday. And Sally said she'd transfer £3,000 to begin with," said Rosie. "Isn't that nearly 3,000 euros?"

"Probably more," nodded Chris.

"That's what I thought," said Rosie. "I can pay the last of the taxe foncière."

"But what about his expenses?" said Chris. "How are you going to pay for them?"

"Oh well," said Rosie vaguely. "I don't suppose he'll eat that much."

"That's what you said about Spike."

"How much is she sending exactly?" said Larrie. "Exactly three thousand euros, or a bit more? Can I have a new saddle pad? Eglantine's got one for Pompom. Pink and green. Heinous, but it is really thick because he's got a cronky spine but that's her fault cos she's always galloping him on the road and she's got a seat like a coffee grinder. So can I, Muma?"

"Can you what? Gallop on the road? Certainly not."

"And no saddle pad either," said Chris. "Whatever this scribbler is paying, once the foncière is paid there won't be enough to kit that equine tractor of yours out like a bloody Grand National runner."

"A new kitchen fridge would be useful," said Rosie, thoughtfully scraping round the lentil dish. "If there was any money left over. I could put the old one in the kennels. The fridge in here has moss growing on the door, and I'll soon have to buy coal for the winter because there's none left."

"He won't be paying that much," said Chris getting up and putting the kettle on. "By the time he's eaten and drunk everything he can get his hands on, broken a few things, nicked a few more and run up a huge phone bill ringing some wannabe publisher in Toronto five times a day, there'll be nothing but bills, whatever Sally sends."

"I'll hide the phone," said Rosie. Chris was frighteningly acute at times. Most of the time, actually. Far too grown-up for his age.

"Where's he sleeping?" said Chris. "Do you want a hand sorting it out?"

They inspected the yellow room in the east wing the next morning while Larrie was at school. It wasn't too bad; the wallpaper was still more or less sticking to the walls and there were no holes in the floor. In fact, the parquet in there was rather pretty. They opened the windows to let the sunshine in, and dragged in various bits of furniture to replace the stuff which was too old or broken to be of any use.

"What do you think, Chris?" said Rosie gazing round the room. Although it was brilliantly sunny and hot outside, inside it was cool and dark because Rosie had half-closed the shutters of the three tall French windows like a row of hands in prayer. Apart from the four-poster, there were various dark oak chests and wardrobes and a large glass-topped dressing table. They had added a large desk near the window, but despite the additional furniture, it still looked as if someone had just moved out.

"It's fine," said Chris, his dark eyes serious in his pale face. "I mean, it's not precisely luxurious but it's correct - the curtains match the armchairs and the wallpaper isn't new but at least there is wallpaper. I know what you mean about our side, but we have 12th century stone floors and the windows don't close properly. The bit we live in is medieval."

The east wing was the most recent extension to the château, having been constructed in the late 18th century using romantic grey stone. It had elegant turrets at the corners and a massive front door surmounted by slim pillars. The facade overlooked a large inner courtyard covered with grey gravel in the middle of which was a long-dry fountain. The main reason Rosie hardly ever used the rooms was because of the high ceilings which made them so hard to heat.

"You're right," said Rosie. "He'll be better off here. Less noise too. Thank you darling. You've been a real help."

Chris slid out of the room in the direction of his studio and, picking up a large wickerwork basket of cleaning stuff, Rosie also left the room, Dolly pattering at her heels. At the end of the corridor the landing formed a slight gallery with another door which was locked and bolted because the west wing was truly derelict, with gaping holes in the roof and weeds growing out of the windows.

Rosie walked down the shallow stairs. She hardly ever came this way, it was far quicker to go down the back stairs, but she just wanted to check, and a good job too because the cats had caught a large rat and were sitting over its remains looking bilious.

"Oh no!" she said. "Not here and don't be sick! Out cats, out!"

Rolling her eyes to the ceiling, Rosie noticed a black cobwebby rope slung between the tarnished chandelier and the wedding cake mouldings. She would have to get the big stepladder out. She picked up the remains of the rat in a cleaning rag and shooing the cats along, went back through the rambling corridors to the utility room. She had a mass of things to do. Unwelcome guest or not, she had to exercise the dogs and catch up with the horrible accounts. She hated paperwork, and sending out invoices was just as awful as getting them from other people. She never knew what to charge. In the kitchen she let the dogs out and went off to find towels for the guest room.

Dolly was about to follow but then she heard a strange noise. Not the dilapidated hairdryer noise of Chris's crème-de-café Renault 4 with the seats smelling of firewood, and not Rosie's fire-spitting, rattlesome pickup, Johnny, either. Johnny was in disgrace for sicking up all his oil anyway, so Dolly knew it couldn't be him. No, this was a noise she'd never heard before and didn't recognise. It was the satisfied growl of a powerful engine in perfect working order. Following the noise, she followed the path round to the courtyard, and saw a sports car pulling in through the gates.

Turning the engine off, Flo climbed out of the scarlet Porsche, and stretched his long legs. Half a mile down a leafy tunnel, a pair of tall, wrought iron gates - this had to be it. Christ, it was grim: a formal pile of grey stone presiding over a large square of gravel, and a long-dry fountain. No neat box-hedges, no symmetrical clumps of topiary and instead of window boxes bursting with flowers and colourful sun-blinds, the entire facade was hung with louvered grey shutters, most of which were closed. There was no sign of a welcome mat, a luggage trolley or a uniformed lackey.

He shuffled through Sally's instructions again. How peculiar. He crunched across the gravel and up the shallow steps to the front door, calling "Hello?" But still it didn't open, no-one came running, there wasn't a sound, not a movement, not a thing. It was almost as if he wasn't expected. He tossed the thought aside. Absurd. Of course he was expected. He was always eagerly expected.

He pushed the bell and stood back, waiting for the double doors to be flung open, but nothing happened. A few moments later he pressed it again, more insistently. Then he saw a small white dog peering through a doorway in the courtyard wall. The dog yapped at him before suddenly turning away and trotting off. A canine bell-hop, he thought. Unusual. Whatever.

He flicked the keys at the car and crunched across the courtyard. In contrast to the air conditioned car, the heat was stifling and he really wasn't in the mood, but he didn't have much choice so he followed the dog round the side of the house. A hurried and extremely haphazard attack with the nail scissors had ruined his carefully cultivated hair and he'd replaced his contacts with a pair of cheap, deeply unflattering glasses which obscured his high cheekbones. He thought the disguise would serve. He had no qualms about deceiving his hostess; Sally was probably paying her handsomely and in any case she would probably recognise him immediately, in which case he would simply persuade her to play along. All he had to do was lie low and besides Sally said she'd briefed the woman: "All fixed, heart. And don't forget you're Michael Bernard, okay? I haven't told Rosie who you are, although I shouldn't think she's heard of you in any case."

"What do you mean? Hasn't heard of me?" Flo knew that was impossible.

"Behave yourself," said Sally. "And don't forget to take a laptop. And don't try anything on with Rosie because she's immune, permanently off men. So don't bother turning on the charm or doing that famous smile thing. And try not to act like you're completely up your own arse. She won't take crap from anyone, least of all you. Just be sincere and nice. Try and be humble."

"Why? What have I done?"

"I told you, she's off men. Permanently."

Humble, just channel Uriah Bloody Heep, he thought, noticing the weeds growing through the path. A woman emerged from the vegetation behind him wearing blue overalls and a headscarf. Was this her ladyship?

"Hullo," he muttered as humbly as possible.

"You," she said, pointing at him. "You search Rosie?"

She must be garden staff, he thought. "Er, yes," he muttered, keeping his famous brown eyes on the ground. The woman made a slight disgusted pout and jerked her head sideways. He raised his eyebrows. She waved her hand in the direction he was going and shouted a long string of obscenities in French.

"Right, fine," he said, the amazingly fluent creativity of Nicole's invective going straight over his head. "I'll just go this way then." The woman turned away with a shrug and disappeared back into the garden leaving Flo to continue round the side of the house, shamelessly peering through all the windows. Some of the rooms contained solid 19th century furniture and proper carpets, but others seemed to have been ravaged by wolves, with bitten cushions on unsavoury sofas and hairy old rugs on the floors. Was Lady Fitzwilson redecorating?

He turned the corner and found himself on a long elegant terrace shaded by a series of majestic plane trees. Suddenly, just inches from his face, a dog's jaws reared up, snapping, snarling and barking. He leapt backwards. A powerful boxer with pearly white teeth and sharp claws was barking hysterically at him and shivering with fury. Flo realised the bloody animal was about to spring at his throat and began to sweat as he backed cautiously away.

"Spike!" exclaimed Rosie, coming out of the

back door. "Play nicely!"

The boxer stopped barking immediately.

"Good boy," said Rosie, patting him on the head. "Who's my baby?" The dog rolled over onto his back, displaying obscenely large genitalia.

"Jesus Christ!" said Flo, wiping his forehead. The dog glanced calmly up at him as the patting continued and the stump of his tail twitched from side to side.

"Noo, noo... Spikey is a good boy!" cooed Rosie reassuringly. "If he does that to you again, just ignore him. That's the best thing, you know. Just take no notice. Did he frighten you?"

Flo was about to say the bloody animal ought to be shot but changed his mind. No point in antagonising the natives. "Scared the pants off me, if you want to know," he confessed, giving her one of his famous crooked smiles.

Their eyes met and Rosie's stomach shivered. It was the strangest sensation. She'd never felt anything like it; dizzy, hot and cold all over, weak knees. Her breath was ragged and her heart was pounding. Irritated, she tried to pull herself together. What an inconvenient moment to have a fainting fit!

Flo watched her with satisfaction. Even with a ruined haircut his sex appeal was intact; no woman could resist him. No woman ever had, and no woman ever would. His presence was obviously having the usual devastating impact. Feeling better, he stepped back slightly to lessen the effect on the poor woman.

It must be indigestion thought Rosie, crossing her fingers that she hadn't picked up a stomach bug. She shook her head to clear the dizzy sensation and forced herself to focus. The new dog had a good coat, she thought, dark chestnut curls, good conformation, short back, long legs, broad shoulders. She liked handsome dogs. Firmly in control of herself, she shifted her gaze to his face. His expression was quizzical and intimate. It had made every woman Flo had ever met swoon, but Rosie merely raised her eyebrows. He looked to her like a dog with a good basic temperament but no real education. She fingered the training clicker in her pocket. She might be able to do something with him.

"Is this Château Moission?" faltered Flo. He couldn't quite understand what was going wrong. He had perfected his smile years ago and knew it worked. It was world famous, after all. His smile said he understood and shared every thought she'd ever had; his eyes, half closed against the sun and crinkled at the corners, said he would never look at anyone except Rosie, and the little breeze which had sprung from nowhere and was ruffling his curls was saying, "It's all true, I'm unaffected, sincere and completely unselfconscious. And I think you're marvellous. In fact I've never met anyone like you before."

Another wave of dizziness hit Rosie and she swayed on her feet. She'd never had indigestion this badly before. And then suddenly she realised what it was... She was bit young, and she hadn't realised it could hit you so suddenly, smack out of the blue, but it was clearly the menopause. What else could it be? She made a mental note to see her GP. Her heart thumped uncomfortably as his melting brown eyes gazed into hers, and with annoyance realised she'd have to get into the shade and cool down. Damned hormones.

Flo wrinkled his forehead, gave a lopsided smile and cocked his head to one side. It was a gesture which had filled cinemas and graced the front cover of every magazine worldwide. It had earned him so much money that he had thrown it all away. He couldn't help it. Even when he was trying to be humble, his famous sexy charm was just second nature. She wasn't bad, he thought, even without make-up. With make-up she'd be stunning. He might as well flirt with her. It would make her day, after all. He reached out to kiss her hand, but she slapped him away and moved out of reach.

"Basket!" she snapped. "Down!" No manners at all. He definitely needed training. "Name?"

"I'm looking for Lady Fitzwilson," he said, the smile draining away from his face.

"That's me," she said giving him a smile and a click for obeying. "And you are?"

Flo could hardly believe his ears. Hadn't she recognised him? He blinked. What had Sally said? The woman was off men. Was that actually possible? He felt as if the world was turning backwards. "I'm Sally's writer-bloke," he said finally.

"You don't look much like a writer," she observed.

Stung, he held his hands out, and Rosie raised her eyebrows. He'd obviously been very well groomed, probably by a professional. His nails were all the same length, perfectly clean and neatly filed. Not a mark, not a callous, not a scratch. He had obviously never been for a country walk in his life. He didn't even look like he could use a computer. He must be Sally's bloke.

"You'd better come in then," she said. "Would you like some tea? Bic-bic?" Without waiting, she led the way into the house and Flo followed, ducking through the door behind her. The kitchen was huge, all scrubbed antique oak and cream paint, and after the blazing sun outside, it was deliciously dim and cool, but Flo only noticed that the paint was peeling in places and the window frames were rotting at the bottoms.

"We keep all the windows and doors shut," said Rosie, shutting the kitchen door. "Do sit down. I know it's not desperately hot in September, but it keeps the heat out, along with the mozzies and the dust. So please don't open the windows." She pointed at a chair. "Sit!"

Flo found himself obediently sitting at the long kitchen table while she filled the kettle. She was lithe and slim, wearing faded jeans and a frayed white cotton bodice. In the kitchen, she looked less pale than she had before. Golden, in fact.

"There should be some biscuits," she said,

from the other side of the table. "Unless Chris has eaten them all again."

"Chris?"

"Yes, my son. He's nineteen, nearly twenty, but still eats everything he can find. I have a daughter too. Larrisa. Twelve. Didn't Sally tell you?"

"No," he said, ruffled. "No, she didn't. She didn't mention dogs either. Just you and the château. Warned me not to move the furniture."

"Oh," said Rosie, pushing a mug of tea in his direction. "Do you want to move the furniture?"

He had no idea what to say and just watched her absent-mindedly pulling the knotted hair at the nape of her neck.

"I suppose you can if you like," she conceded at last, "but only in your own room, I'd sooner you didn't move anything in here. But can I ask you something?"

"Yes, ask me anything," Flo smiled. She'd just recognised him. Not surprising, really. And now she was about to ask him about his latest film. And obviously she was going to apologise. The world started moving forwards again.

"Don't you fall over if the furniture keeps moving? With your bad sight?"

"I'm not blind!" he snapped, snatching the cheap glasses off his face.

"No, of course not," she said quickly. "It's just that Sally said..."

"What? What did Sally say?"

"Nothing," she said, revising her opinion of

his temperament. He was obviously not as meek as she'd thought. She had a sudden image of him kissing the back of her neck, and decided to call her GP first thing in the morning. She was clearly having hallucinations. With an effort she gave him a bright smile. "Right, well. Welcome to the Château de Moisson. We're delighted to have you, although we don't have any particularly interesting antiques or Roman coins for you to play with."

"Roman coins?" he said, baffled.

"Your book? About Roman coins?"

"Fascinating stuff," he said quickly. "Gripping. Nothing like a Roman coin to get the pulses racing."

She didn't believe him, and Flo looked away. There was a battered solid fuel stove at one end of the room with a collection of dog beds beside it, a large wooden dresser to one side and a series of cupboards and shelves. There was also a white stone sink, a 50s Kelvinator and a large pile of dog blankets on one of the shelves. Counting round the table, he estimated that it would comfortably seat a dozen people although the seats were falling out of most of the chairs. At the other end of the room was a pair of huge shabby sofas covered with paisley shawls and cats. The room obviously doubled as a place for outdoor staff to relax. A sudden prolonged clattering noise from the direction of back door made him twist round in his chair.

"Oh dear," said Rosie. She hurried to the back door where he could hear her laughing. "Oh Dolly!

What have you got there! No, I don't want that in the house. Yuk! Disgusto-dog! You're stuck, you silly girl, stop wriggling! Oh God, that's revolting!"

Flo tilted his chair back onto two legs and craned his neck to see what was going on. His hostess was crouching down beside a muddy cat flap trying to free a rabbit and a fluffy white dog, both of which seemed to have got stuck halfway through. "Oh I like rabbits!" he said, just as Rosie succeeded in pushing the dog back out of the door and pulling the rabbit's head into the house. It was just a rotten head, attached to a slimy bit of skin, two hind legs and a tail. The smell was indescribable. Flo reared away, holding both hands over his nose. Rosie bundled it up and took it off into a side room and then he heard bin noises and a running tap. The fluffy white dog poked its head through the cat flap again and barked loudly. "Come in, Dolly!" said Rosie, opening the back door.

The little dog trotted into the kitchen and sniffed around the floor. "No!" said Rosie, sitting down at the table. "It's all gone. No bunny. Nothing for you at all!" Dolly scrambled clumsily up onto Rosie's lap, turned round twice and sat down. Breathing heavily, her chin on the edge of the table, she focussed her beady black eyes and gave Flo an evil grin.

"She's a bichon," said Rosie shying a packet of biscuits over the table. "Pretty close relation to the poodle, but calmer and different coat of course," she said, scratching behind Dolly's ears. "Not that she's pure-bred, poor thing, but she's mostly bichon. Do take a bic-bic!"

A gale of evil-smelling dog-breath swept across the table, almost knocking Flo unconscious. "Why?" he choked. "Dogs, I mean, what's the attraction?"

"Ooooh, Dolly's my baby-heart," she cooed and then because he didn't say anything there was silence. "You can rely on them," she said finally. "Dogs won't let you down. They don't lie and they don't pretend. They don't know how. Look at Spike. Hopeless case really; rude, aggressive, unfriendly, but at least he never pretends to be anything else. I mean, he's always revolting. With everyone. So you can rely on him."

"To attack people?"

"Yes, well. We're going to have to stop him doing that..."

She was obviously completely nuts, thought Flo. How was she going to train Spike? And why would a beautiful woman spend her whole life shut up in a remote castle with a pack of filthy hounds? Especially when, with her looks, she could easily find someone... "How did your husband die?" he asked abruptly.

"He didn't," she replied. "He left. Years ago. Now, if you don't mind, Mr whatever..."

"Flo... Michael. Michael Bernard."

"Flo?"

"My friends call me Flo. It's a nickname from school... I looked a bit girlie back then."

"Well you don't look girlie any..." She went bright red. "Look, nice to chat but I've got to feed the dogs now, and I'd better check what Larrie has done about the horse nuts and there's supper to make, so, perhaps I could point you towards your room? I'm sure you can find your way, can't you?"

Flo wasn't used to being dismissed and his hackles rose. How dare the woman prefer feeding some horrible pack of hounds to entertaining him? "I can leave if you prefer," he said shirtily. "I don't have to stay here if you don't want me."

The words made Rosie's stomach drop. She didn't want him in her house, but she couldn't afford to let him leave, and sooner or later he would find out why. So she took a deep breath and confessed: "Well, if you want the honest truth, you've got to stay because I've already spent the money Sally sent to pay for your keep. I wrote a cheque for the taxe foncière this morning. So if you go, and Sally asks me for her money back, I'll probably end up in prison or something. Which means you can't go whether I want you or not. Want you here or not," she corrected herself.

Flo blinked. She didn't find him good-looking or sexy or amusing. The only reason she was giving him houseroom was because Sally had written what sounded like an obscenely large cheque.

Rosie stood up and put the mugs into the sink. "I know it's not ideal for you," she said. "I can tell you don't like kids and we've already established that you're terrified of dogs..."

"No, I bloody don't like dogs!"

She turned round to face him. "I'm sorry but this is the doghouse. I have a lot of dogs here. What you've seen is just the tip of the iceberg. I also have two teenagers, and they always come first. And I can't keep any of it out of your way, although I can try to keep them out of your room. I suppose. Maybe."

"I've never been so bloody..."

But there was no stopping Rosie. Now she'd started, she was determined to finish. "I also have a leaking roof, a car with no brakes, a fridge with moss growing in it, and more debts than you can even begin to imagine. That's why I'm so grateful that at least the taxe foncière is paid. So if for some insane reason you might be able to sit upstairs and finish your book, I will do my best to make sure you're not disturbed. And I promise I'll stay completely out of your way. I won't come near you. I guarantee it. You'll have absolute peace and quiet. But you'll have to take us as we are. Dogs, kids... the whole damn thing. I'm sorry, but there it is! But please don't make me pay the money back."

He gazed at her angrily, his hair springing into untidy tufts around his forehead. She gazed back, thinking that he really did look rather lost. An uncertain dog is a barking dog, she thought, and waited for him to start shouting. How had such a well-bred specimen become such a lost dog?

"Mummy!" exclaimed Larrie, bursting in through the back door. "Call the vet! Quickly! Sobie has eaten his hoof pick!"

"What? Eaten his hoof pick? That's impossible, darling!"

"Sobie?" said Flo.

"Short for So-Big, he's a horse," Rosie told him out of the corner of her mouth.

"No, Mummy, he has!" insisted Larrie, hopping from foot to foot in the doorway, her face drained of all colour. "Honestly!" I left it in his manger, and now it's gone! He must have eaten it while I was putting his tack away!"

"Have you put a sweat rug on him?" said Rosie, putting the milk in the fridge. "Sorry about this, Mr..."

"Of course he's got his rug on!"

"I'll have to go and sort it out," said Rosie, and Flo stood up. "Sit!" she ordered. She took an apple out of the fruit bowl on the dresser, and pushed the palm of her hand towards his face. "Stay!"

Dolly at her heels, she followed Larrie out of the kitchen to the stables thinking that Sally was a comprehensive liar. Flo obviously didn't have a sight problem, wasn't the slightest bit shy or effete, or gay or any of the rest of it. Judging by his hands, the only true thing she'd said was about being a writer. She realised he wouldn't stay and Sally would want her money back so she'd have to find another way of paying the tax bill. Perhaps she could sell something? Maybe the piano would fetch enough to keep them going for a while?

"Mummy, oh help, Mummy, just think! He's

going to get it hooked up in his guts!"

In the loose box on the other side of the yard, Sobie was swaying from side to side, balefully knocking at the bottom half of his door with one gigantic hoof. He was at least 17 hands tall, a gleaming chestnut giant of a horse with huge dark eyes, a black mane and tail, one white sock and a pale blaze on his forehead.

"You see, Mummy?" said Larrie, with tears welling up again.

"Calm down, darling," said Rosie. "Hello boy, how are you?"

Sobie banged his massive head down over the edge of the door and nudged Rosie's hand greedily. "Have you fed him, Larrie?" she asked, cutting the apple into quarters with her pocket-knife.

"Mummy no! If I feed him, the hoof pick'll get lodged, Mummy. Lodged!"

"Darling, I honestly don't think he's eaten a hoof pick," said Rosie, feeding Sobie another chunk of apple.

"Do you want me to have a look?" asked Flo coming up behind them. "I used to do a bit of riding, years ago. Hello boy," he said, squinting up at the horse's great head and proffering his palm. "How are you?"

Sobie blew on his hand, whickered and then lowered his forehead onto the man's shoulder. Flo scratched his forehead gently.

"I thought I told you to stay," said Rosie.

"Don't just stand there talking!" said Larrie in

a rising panic. "Help him! Please!"

Realising that she was on verge of hysterics, Rosie opened the stable door and they all shuffled into the loose box, which was big enough to have housed at least three normal-sized horses, and furnished with an ocean of fresh straw, a gigantic bucket of water, a large salt lick and a hay net capacious enough to have satisfied an entire herd of elephants. Reaching up on her tiptoes, Larrie hung on Sobie's neck calling him baby heart and little duck, and Flo kicked the straw.

"What are you doing?" said Larrie, her voice rising and her face like beetroot. "That's not going to help!" Tears sprang into her eyes. "Oh Mummy, he could die!"

"Oh, I don't think so," said Flo bending down. "Is this the missing item?" He stood up with his hand out. There was a hoof pick in his palm.

"Well done," said Rosie.

"Oh!" said Larrie, hanging her head. "That's my... You think I might have dropped it?"

"Who knows," said Flo giving it back to her. "Maybe the brute spat it out."

"How dare you! He's not a brute. He's my baby!"

"Well, he hasn't eaten a hoof pick anyway," said Flo, and if Rosie hadn't been permanently off men, she'd have patted him. Or at least scratched the top of his head. As it was, she absent-mindedly gave him a click.

Leaving Larrie promising Sobie hot mash,

Rosie and Flo walked back to the house with Dolly wagging at their heels. Dolly always enjoyed a visit to the horse kennel; muckheap smell was her favourite perfume. Specially if you rolled in it.

"Do you know a lot about horses?" said Rosie, curiously.

Flo was just about to say yes, when suddenly he realised how fast the topic would lead him onto dodgy ground. "No," he said. "Not much, really. I just had to research them once, for a par... a part of a book! And I spent a bit of time at some stables in um..."

"Oh," said Rosie, and realised with a small shock that she'd actually hoped he knew something of practical value. How ridiculous. "Well, never mind," she said with false cheer. "Shall I walk you back to your car? I assume it's that red thing in the courtyard?"

"Yes, it's a Porsche," he said. He looked down at her as she stood beside him, wiping her pocketknife on the back pocket of her jeans.

"Is that the best place to park it?" he said, and he could hardly believe his own ears. What was he thinking?

She looked up surprise. "Why? Are you staying, then?"

"Well maybe a couple of nights if you can put up with me," he said and even as he said it he could have kicked himself. Was he mad? She didn't even like him!

To hide her relief about the taxe foncière,

Rosie shrugged. With Dolly still at her heels, she led Flo through the kitchen into a long flagged corridor and up a shallow flight of steps leading to yet another door. "This way," she said, opening it and stepping into an echoing, musty-smelling hall. "Until you learn your way around, you'll probably find it easier to walk round the outside," she said. "But this is the door to the east wing." Flo judged that they must be in the part of the house which overlooking the courtyard. It didn't seem at all inhabited.

"We mainly live in the back part of the house," said Rosie.

Flo gazed at the formal high ceilings, the mouldings decorated with cobwebs, and felt like he'd just walked off the set of a 16th century pastoral romance and onto the set of a gothic novel complete with bats and a midnight shutter banging in a storm.

"You'll have silence all day long in this part of the house. And no dogs," she said firmly. "I promise I won't come near you."

"But..."

"Sally said you needed peace and quiet. You are a writer, aren't you?"

They were at the foot of a wide curving staircase leading up from what had obviously once been an impressive reception hall. Now however, the checkerboard tiles were cracked and the wallpaper was faded.

"Come on, Dolly. Heel! Up the stairs we go! Leave that alone. I think she must have smelt a rat.

The cats brought one in earlier. Don't worry, I've thrown it away now. Chris has organised wifi. Or at least, I hope he has. And there's a new bottle of gas in your bathroom so..."

"Gas? What do I need gas for?"

"Hot water. Unless you prefer cold showers? I mean, cold showers are fine," she nodded. "Absolutely. Fantastic. Very cheap."

Reaching the first floor, she flung open a pair of double doors. "Here we are. I made the room up earlier. And I have swept, so there shouldn't be any scorpions. Don't worry, I turned the mattress myself and those sheets were airing on the line this morning."

Horrified, he stood in the doorway gazing at the mismatched, second-hand furniture, the faded carpet and the dirty wallpaper. The place was a complete dump.

"Sally was lying, wasn't she?" said Rosie. "You're not broke and you've never been to Woolworths in your life, have you?"

"It's closed. It went bust. Years ago," he said automatically. How on earth had he got involved in this?

"It did? Oh that's a shame, I rather liked poking around in Woolies," said Rosie, suddenly seeing the room through Flo's eyes.

"Pick and mix," he said walking across the room to the window. "I used to love that when I was a kid. Raspberry Ruffles. Oh, there's my car." He was mentally flicking through his address book wondering where else he could go.

"That's what I mean," she said coming to stand beside him at the window. "If you're a writer, how come you're driving that?"

"It's hired, it's all they had," he lied automatically.

"Well, I hope no-one sees it or we'll have half the village wanting to have their photos taken sitting on the bonnet."

"No! Really?" He turned away from the window at exactly the same time as she did and their arms brushed.

She jumped back from him as if he'd burnt her. "Right, I'll leave you now," she gasped. "I've unlocked the front door so you can bring your luggage up, and then I daresay... supper at eight. On the terrace. Bathroom through there." Without waiting for an answer, she walked straight down the stairs. Dolly skittered along in her wake with her tail turning in mad circles like a helicopter blade. Then a door slammed, her footsteps faded and Flo was alone in his hideous, musty, uncomfortable room. He pulled his mobile out and dialled. Thank God there was network. Sally answered almost immediately and he guessed she'd been waiting for his call. "Have you gone mad?" he demanded.

"Calm down, sweetie."

"It's a fucking zoo! Wild dogs, giant metal-eating horses, apparently there are scorpions, and the woman doesn't even like me. Says she's only putting up with me because you paid some fucking bill or other. Get me out of here! Now!"

"Listen Flo, said Sally in a level voice, "you're hanging by the thinnest of threads. One more drinking bout, one more scandal and the insurance companies won't touch you. You'll never work again. I need you out of the headlines. And the only way that's going to happen is if you're off the radar."

"This isn't off the radar, it's off the fucking planet!"

"Look, I didn't want to have to say this, but no-one else will have you."

"What do you mean?"

"I'm all out of favours on your behalf. There isn't a hotel, a hideaway or a rehab unit that will take you. You don't have a friend who can afford the damage. You don't even have a handy mother who will give you houseroom. No-one wants you. No-one likes you enough to take the risk. You're a pain in the arse, Flo. Rosie is my last call. She's the only person I know who is broke enough to bribe. You blow this and I'll have to drop you."

"But I'm... you can't..."

"You haven't got the money. You're broke. There's nothing left to pay people off with."

"What are you saying?"

"I'm saying you've got no choice. You just stay there, behave yourself and let me do my work. There's only one human being on this planet who can get you the Bond contract, and that's me, and you know it. Two outings as 007 and you'll be back on track. The rest will be forgotten. Then once you're out of the scandal rags, I can sell the idea of the new you. The cleaned-up, intelligent, adult you. The hard-working, talented, easy-to-work-with you. Then you can rebuild your career."

"Fuck off. There is no new me, and you can't make me stay here."

"No, I can't. So why don't you do what you usually do? Drive down to the nearest bar, make a big splash, buy drinks all round, get pissed and papped in some French tart's bed..."

"I don't have to stay in France, I could..."

"What? Buy a scheduled airline ticket? Go to an airport on your own? With no security? Are you mad? You'd be mobbed in a minute. Fly to the States? Then what are you going to do? Thump another policeman? Insult another fan? Get some teenager pregnant?"

"This place should be condemned!"

"Rosie is one of my oldest friends. If you upset her, you'll have me to deal with." Her tone suddenly softened. "Look, just give it a week and then if you really can't stand it I'll try and find somewhere else."

"It's a fucking rat-hole, Sally."

"Don't be a shit-head all your life, Flo. Ring me in the morning."

The phone went dead, and he noticed a tall thin boy standing in the doorway.

"The last of the fucking rat-hole residents, at your service," said Chris, icily. He'd have done anything to be able to chuck this simpering urban snob out of the house, but the way things were, he was going to have to put up with him.

Flo smiled winningly. "I was talking about somewhere else!"

But Chris was having none of it. He knew they lived in dereliction, and didn't need his nose rubbed in it. "I'm Chris. Son of Rosie, and your IT helpdesk rep for the duration," he said, without the glimmer of a smile. "Do you want me to get you on-line?"

"Sorry," said Flo. "I didn't realise the door was open." But Chris's expression didn't soften. "I'll just go and get my stuff," said Flo, mentally cursing Sally.

"You do that," said Chris. "I hope you're not expecting any of us to donkey it up here for you."

Flo went downstairs. From the landing, Chris watched him tugging at the front door. "You have to push the top of the door at the same time as you pull the handle halfway down," he said.

"Got it. Thanks," said Flo. He wasn't used to being dismissed by young teenagers and he didn't like it. Squinting against the sinking sun, he flicked the key fob at the car and the lights flashed reassuringly at him. At least something was working. He began lugging a series of expensive suitcases out of the boot onto the gravel.

"You look vaguely familiar. I'm sure I know you from somewhere," said Chris suspiciously.

Flo's heart sank. He really didn't want to have to listen to this kid's opinion of every single performance in every single film. "I don't think so," he said, turning his face away. "I'm sure I'd remember if we'd met before."

"Do you always bring so much luggage? What on earth have you got in there?"

"I thought I'd done rather well. I mean, I probably won't be... but I was expecting to stay for a month or so you know."

"To finish this mythical book of yours? The Roman Coin and the Call Girl?"

"All right," sighed Flo. "Pax, kid. Pax. Okay?"

Chris narrowed his eyes. "I'm sure I know your face from somewhere," he said. "Which of those has your computer in it?" he said gesturing at the cases. "Bring that one first. And no, I'm not carrying anything."

Boiling, Flo picked up a selection of the smaller cases and staggered up the stairs with them. He knew there was a laptop in one of them but he didn't really want the kid messing about with it.

"We set up a desk for you by the window," said Chris gesturing at a large table adorned with a pile of dictionaries, a phone and a printer. "But that was when we still thought you might want to write. Give me your computer." Stung, Flo pulled his laptop out of its case and gave it to Chris. Opening it, he sat down, switched it on and started tapping the keyboard. "Still, I expect you'll enjoy surfing YouTube, won't you?" he said patronisingly. "And you'll be able to Facebook your pals."

"The password..."

"Don't need it. Your security is crap. I'll just

register myself as the administrator, and there we go... yup. Think we have it. It might dip in and out a bit and you'll probably find you don't get much mobile phone reception at night, but that should keep you going anyway." He got up and stalked to the door. "Bathroom's through the other side. Don't go mad with the hot water. The gas bottles are hideously expensive."

"Thanks. Listen..." From habit, Flo started fishing in his pocket for change.

"I'm not a bell-hop and I'm not a waiter," said Chris and stalked away, leaving Flo feeling thoroughly ruffled. He'd only just arrived and already everyone hated him. The gardener, the mistress of the house, and her son... all three of them thought he was lower than a toad, and even the hysterical horse-mad girl didn't rate him as high as her precious nag. What was wrong with them all? He shuddered and then thought gloomily that the supper was also bound to be a nightmare. Probably dog food on toast.

CHAPTER TWO

But when he finally went downstairs, for the first time that day he was pleasantly surprised. The table, outside on the terrace, was laid with a waxed tablecloth and white china; very French, very romantic, with the last of the day's sunlight filtering through the trees making golden dapples and haloes on everyone's faces. There was a short string of coloured bulbs strung between two branches. And there was red wine and water, a basket of fresh bread and some olives on the table.

"Sit!" said Rosie, suddenly noticing him watching them all. God he was beautiful, she thought. Beautiful and sulky. "No, not near me," she said as he came towards her looking like a hopeful spaniel. "Over there, right over there! Sit! I'll just get the chicken," she announced, getting up from the table. "Move, dogs!" she ordered, and the dogs variously yawned, scarpered, and followed her into the kitchen.

Flo pulled a chair out and sat down warily. He looked at Chris and then at Larrie, wondering when they would recognise him, because even if their mother had been a media refusnik for the last twenty years, he already knew that the boy knew his way round a computer and in his experience teenage girls were all glued to gossip rags whatever their parents thought.

It didn't occur to him for a second that no-one at the château was interested in popular entertainment. Rosie didn't have the time, Larrie and Sobie lived in an adventurous wonderland of their own, and Chris looked down on celebrity as a concept, let alone a product. As for being too broke to buy a television, go to the cinema, pick up a trashy magazine, or read a newspaper, Flo had half forgotten that normal people had to pay for this stuff with actual coins out of their grubby little pockets. To him, being broke meant bank managers and agents bullying him into signing contracts worth millions to make films that bored him. He glanced suspiciously at the kids but they had lost interest in him and were playing with one of the dogs.

"What's it called?" he said, gesturing vaguely at the animal.

After a short pause, Chris said, "This is Minnie. You probably can't see her from there, but she's a greyhound. The black Lab is Sooty. The brown terrier mongrel is Tramp and that weird looking lurcher-chap is Rupert. Spike, I believe you already know. And that's Dolly of course." He gave Flo a challenging look across the table.

Flo sighed. "Look I'm sorry for earlier," he said. "Sincerely, truly and in every way. Ok?"

Chris gave him a considering look and then apparently decided to accept Flo's apology. "Yes. That's Dolly, more usually called Maggot or Stenchy," he said, with the flicker of a smile.

"Because she's always rolling in stinky things like horse poo and dead seagulls!" added Larrie with a grin.

"You get lots of dead seagulls round here, do you?" asked Flo.

"Well, you know what I mean," she said and then, going slightly pink around the gills, added, "I don't usually fly off the handle, you know, about Sobie."

Flo looked at her again. Had she guessed? Was she trying to butter him up? But no, she really didn't know who he was; she was just an unspoilt friendly little kid apologising for making a fool of herself. Which was more than could be said for her brother, who was an over-sensitive, stiff-necked little sod.

"Oh, I don't blame you," he said easily. "I mean, stranger things have happened." He gave her a small little smile. Humble, he reminded himself, I'm ever so, ever so humble.

"That's true," said Larrie brightening. "Here, have some wine. I expect you want some, don't you? Grown-ups always have wine." She reached over the table and splashed a generous serving into the tumbler beside his plate. "Bread? We cut it up with a knife because you're here, but normally we just rip it. Unless it's too hard. Then we toast it so it goes crunchy. But it's all right tonight, just a bit chewy. And take some olives. I did them, with extra garlic."

At that moment Rosie came back with a laden tray. "Here we are, salad, cold chicken and rat."

Rat. Oh very funny. Flo rolled his eyes. This time she'd gone too far. Broke they might be but... across the table Chris shook his head and mouthed "no" at him fiercely. Oblivious, Rosie spooned generous helpings of ratatouille onto everyone's plates. "Help yourself to chicken," she said, picking through the serving dish with her fork and putting most of the white meat on Larrie's plate. "Here you are darling, no bones, so I want you to eat it all or there's no pudding."

"This is cold!" said Flo tasting the ratatouille.

"We always have it cold," said Larrie.

"Saves gas," said Chris.

"Don't you want it?" said Rosie. Beside her, Dolly waggled her ears expectantly. She loved cold rat. It made a change from kitten poo.

"Can we get this heated up?" he sighed, picking his plate up and waving it generally in the direction of the kitchen.

"No, we can't," retorted Chris. "We're eating it cold."

Flo shot him an exasperated look over the table but Chris just glared back, his eyes burning in his thin white face. Flo looked at Rosie but she wasn't taking any notice of him, she was feeding chicken skin to her horrible white lapdog. Furious, Flo put his plate down and took a large swig of his wine. It was disgusting; sour, and bitter enough to kill an army. He choked and as Chris rolled his eyes, Larrie ran round the table and slapped his back energetically. "Did it go down the wrong way?"

"How are you settling in? Have you got everything you need?" asked Rosie politely, noticing that Minnie was sitting on a chair next to Chris but deciding not to mention it unless she actually licked the tablecloth.

Flo wasn't used to being denied hot food, glared at, slapped on the back, or forced to sleep in musty lumber rooms and he was about to inform her that actually he didn't have anything he needed at all when Chris kicked him under the table. Flo narrowed his eyes, and Chris swallowed nervously but didn't back down. Suddenly Flo realised he was protecting his mother. Or perhaps his sister.

Fuck, he thought. If only there was a maître d' or a butler or a manager, or even a bloody waiter, he'd wipe the floor with any of them without a second glance. Probably smash the place up too, just to make his point. But for some unfathomable reason, he couldn't bring himself to destroy a thin-faced over-sensitive adolescent with burning eyes and no sense of humour. Even if the brat was asking for it.

Promising himself he would leave first thing in the morning, he said, "everything's fine. Young Chris here has sorted out my laptop and I'm sure he'll instruct me on how to operate the bathroom."

"I'll show him how the bottle works after supper," said Chris quickly. "It's a new one so it should last out. As long as you don't stay too long."

Turning away, Flo took a tiny forkful of aubergine and realised that the ratatouille, unlike the wine, was excellent. He wasn't sure about the chicken. It was all in bits and most of it seemed to be bone. He decided to give it a miss. He'd treat himself to a huge steak in a gourmet restaurant tomorrow.

"Are you vegetarian?" asked Rosie.

Flo shook his head and, forgetting that it was undrinkable floor polish, gulped at his wine, bringing tears of pain to his eyes. He grabbed a piece of bread but it was rock hard.

"Dip it in the sauce," said Chris.

"Give him some chicken, Larrie," said Rosie. "Now, let's see tomorrow morning, what time do you get up? I'll be up early because of the dogs and Larrie has school."

"No, it's Wednesday, Muma. It's only maths," said Larrie, dumping a large portion of chicken bones, a wing and the parson's nose on Flo's plate. "So I'll have to go all the way on the bus, wait for hours, sit though maths and then wait for another hour before I can get the bus home again. It's a total waste of time!" She spooned olive oil and herbs over the chicken.

"That's enough!" said Flo his nose wrinkling up in disgust. If his dietician could see the contents of his plate, she'd have a blue fit.

"That's as maybe," said Rosie, "but you're going to school anyway. Chris, have you got plans?"

"I won't be around much," said Chris. "I've got

a deadline coming up."

Sucking her fingers, Rosie looked vaguely across the table at Flo. "Do you eat breakfast?" she asked. "Because if you do, can you have it with Larrie? At 7.30? Then I can get on."

"We could have fresh croissants, pains au chocolats and raspberry tarts," said Larrie with a sparkle in her eye. "Fresh baguettes and hot chocolate!"

Flo perked up. A decent breakfast would just about hit the spot. "Sounds good," he said. "I love French bread."

"Great! I bet that fancy car of yours has got petrol in it, hasn't it? I bet it even starts with the key. You don't have to push start it, do you? So you could go down to the boulangerie while I'm mucking out, and in return I'll make the hot chocolate. I'm really good at it; I do it with real grated bars! It opens at 6.30 so there would be plenty of time. And I've got 4 euros and if you've got 5 euros, we could even get the liquorice straws!"

Flo shuddered. Bloody awful, horrible...

"Don't be silly," said Rosie. "You won't have time to mess around grating chocolate, and if you miss the bus I'll be really cross. Why not go to the bakery in the afternoon?" She turned to Flo with a smile. "There's no school on Wednesday afternoon," she told him kindly. "You can take her to the bakery after lunch if you like. Then she can show you the way."

"I'll be out riding all afternoon, you know

that!" said Larrie. "Honestly Muma. I don't need to go to maths. I can get the notes from someone else and the teacher's a pillock anyway. He's got hairy ears. Disgusting." A cat hopped neatly onto the table to sniff Larrie's plate, and she gave him a piece of chicken.

"That doesn't make him a pillock," said Rosie. "Don't feed cats at the table."

"But he is! He said that only stupid people need pets, and he said they only have them for emotional comfort."

"Definitely a pillock," said Chris.

Flo watched the cat clawing more scraps off Larrie's plate. No-one lifted a finger to push the animal off the table. What Barbarians.

"So I don't have to go?" she said with pleading eyes. "Do I?"

"Yes, you do have to go and you do have concentrate and you do have to learn something."

"Look, horses don't do maths. Four feet, two ears, one heart..."

"And no brain!" said Chris with a snort of laughter.

"Shut up! The point is I'm never going to need maths in my whole life! Not even if I live to be as old as him," she said, gesturing at Flo.

"Maths is exercise for your brain," said Rosie, but everyone round the table could see that she wasn't really convinced. To cover up, she quickly helped herself to more ratatouille, and slipped a piece of chicken skin to the dogs.

"What do you think, Oh Venerable Guest?" said Chris, raising an eyebrow at Flo. "To calculate or not to calculate?"

Very clever, thought Flo. If I say school is shit, your mother will kill me and if I say schooldays are the happiest of your life, you and your sister will despise me forever. "Well, I've got to return the car tomorrow morning," he said, breaking one of his perfect nails on a lump of stale bread. More than ever, he was determined to leave in the morning regardless of Sally. He didn't give a damn how these maniacs paid their tax bills or fed their horse, or got their insane schoolgirl educated. Tomorrow morning he would drive his Porsche out of their ruined courtyard and leave them behind forever. He had no intention of informing them of his plans however. Why should he? He didn't owe them anything. Once he'd cleared out, Sally could tell them that he wasn't coming back, and as for the money, it simply wasn't his problem.

"You'll be out tomorrow? Excellent!" said Rosie. "So I'll be able to get on!" and then realising that she wasn't being very subtle, she added, "I mean, I've got a lot to do. Now that school's started again I need to get the summer stuff packed up, clean the BBQ, roll the fly curtains up, wash the swimsuits and towels, that sort of thing. It's sloe-picking time and I need to freeze some chestnuts for the stuffing..."

"At Christmas we have so much stuffing that it oozes out of the turkey's bottom!" said Larrie.

"And sausage meat!"

"And there are the last of the pears and quinces to deal with and I was going to attack the rose bushes this week, give them a haircut. Find the wellies. And finish off the rumtoft. It just needs the apricots and it's done."

"That's fruit in alcohol," Larrie informed him. "It sits in the cupboard under the stairs and you mustn't touch it, in case it makes you sick!" She stretched over the table and took a chicken wing off Flo's plate. "It's got cherries, peaches, plums, blackberries apples, and pears in it already. In layers. We're having it on Christmas Eve," said Larrie, pulling the meat off the bones and letting the cat lick the scraps off her fingers. "But I'm not having the juice because I had some once when I was little and I was sick all down the stairs and it dripped onto Chris's head!"

"And I've got a pregnant spaniel arriving," continued Rosie. "Keeps miscarrying. The vet seems to think she'll need a c-section unless she comes here. Personally it's all probably nonsense, but the owner's paying through the nose so that's good. But I'll have to sterilise a run for her. And I've got my puppy class at two. I don't suppose you'll want lunch, will you? After a big breakfast? The kids usually just grab some bread."

She gazed down the table. Larrie and Chris were teasing and bickering across the table about maths teachers and rumtoft. Rosie smiled at them indulgently, and then looked over at Flo. He'd left all his chicken, wine, bread and olives and was picking moodily at the green salad, inspecting each leaf suspiciously before he folded it into his mouth. She leaned forward and said kindly, "Not used to all this chit chat, are you?"

Flo looked up at her. The last rays of the sun were just touching her hair and shoulders making a soft halo around her face. She was completely insane, but she had the beauty of a blonde Madonna, and she was looking sorry for him. Suddenly he felt sorry for himself too. He wasn't enjoying his day at all. He shook his head, and noticing the way his eyes crinkled at the corners, Rosie thought that with a decent trainer, he might show promise.

"Tea?" she said loudly. "Coffee? Come on kids, get moving! Clear the table! Find the fruit bowl!"

Flo watched them all running around the terrace, with the dogs getting in the way and forks falling off the plates. Why on earth were they living in this derelict château without any staff? Rosie had some sort of a title, so she must have some cash behind her somewhere or how had she bought this place? Eccentric. Totally barking. Howling at the moon.

The coffee was cold and the fruit had bruise marks and brown lines on it. The sun went down suddenly. He shook his head, hoping to be offered something else, but no-one cared. They just went on eating and talking and feeding scraps to their pets, and Larrie kept up an endless stream of jokes and nonsense, and then suddenly Rosie stood up and yawned and he realised with horror that although it was barely half past nine, they were all going to bed.

Dogs barked, doors slammed, chairs and jugs were tidied up, dinner plates and dishes put on the ground - "The hedgehogs will wash them up," said Larrie. And then Chris was standing by the kitchen door ready to escort him to his room. Hardly believing his senses, Flo followed him through the musty corridors and found himself outside his bedroom. "You're going straight to bed?" he asked Chris. "Don't fancy a nightcap, do you?" Any port in a storm.

"No," said Chris. "And don't try to make me believe that you want my company."

"Sorry. Look, I really am..."

"It's all right," said Chris. "I'm not threatening to hang you at dawn, just going to bed. And frankly, you look like you could use some sleep too," he said, retreating down the corridor.

Flo wondered where the kid was heading off to - was there some other part of this rat-hole that he hadn't seen yet? But so what. The kid could sleep in a shit-pit for all he cared. He went into his bedroom, slammed the door, dragged a bottle of Scotch out of his luggage, and span the top off. He took a huge slug straight from the bottle, and then another one. Flinging himself on the bed he stared at the stains on the ceiling. The bed was lumpy and the pillow was old and flat. There wasn't a clean whisky glass in the place. He took another long swallow of Scotch.

He dialled Sally's number but her phone was turned off. He gazed at the list of contacts in his phone, and let it fall onto the floor beside him. What was the point? He didn't have any close family; he was an only child and his parents had died years ago, and as for friends if he was honest with himself, he knew Sally was right. He didn't have any real friends; not one of his contacts would give a shit about his predicament, and none of them could be trusted not to leak the story to the press.

He held the bottle up against the light. He'd stop when he got down to the top of the label. A familiar heavy weight settled on his shoulders. The world looked black and uninviting. Tomorrow would be no better. He really needed some distraction. A party, a bar, something... But he was marooned in a dump with a bunch of morons who were all happily trotting off to the land of fucking nod halfway through the evening, and he was stuck with it. Sally didn't want him, and nor did anyone else. No-one had rung him. No-one was missing him, no-one had realised he'd effectively disappeared off the face of the earth 24 hours ago. He drank some more and realised he'd gone way past the top of the label.

"Shit!" he muttered. If he drank it all, he'd have to get some more in the morning, and the press would have a field day if they caught him trying to buy Scotch in a French off-licence, and Sally would go stark staring mad. Again.

Imprisoned, forgotten, fading, broke and

useless, that's what he was. But Sally was turning him over a leaflet. A new leaf. Feeling that he really ought to drink some fruit juice to ward off a hangover, he decided to go down to the kitchen. They didn't have anything else, but even horrible jailors had juice, didn't they? He had another drink to fortify him for the journey.

It took time and he trod in something disgustingly slippery on the way, but he found the kitchen without too much effort and even managed to turn the lights on. Instantly, a pack of dogs surged towards him, yawning and wagging their tails. Then he tripped over a chair and suddenly Spike reared up at him and started barking, and the other big dogs joined in, and they were all weaving in excited circles, while Spike barked and barked.

"Shut up!" he hissed. "Stupid dog! Get down! Stop barking! Shut the fuck up!" He could hear footsteps above his head. The bloody animal had woken everyone up. Spike dropped onto all fours, his hackles rose and he growled menacingly. Flo picked up a chair and thrust it at the wretched animal's teeth just as it sprang at him.

"Stop that!" said Rosie coming into the kitchen behind him. "Spike! Down!" she ordered, going straight past Flo towards the terrified boxer where he stood snarling and spitting. "That's enough now, Spike. I'm here and I'll take over." Spike hung his head, but his eyes were still fixed on Flo, and he was shaking.

What in hell are you doing?" said Rosie, placing herself front of Spike and looking daggers at Flo. She clicked her fingers at the rest of the canines. "You big dogs, basket! Go! Go to bed!" The three big dogs obediently went to their baskets by the stove and once she was sure that Spike was under control, she got a small yellow bottle out of the cupboard and gave him a dose of Rescue Remedy. Very soon he stopped shaking and dropped his great stupid head into her arms. "Come on, baby," she said in a soothing voice. "Let's go find bic-bic in the laundry, eh?" Slipping her fingers under his collar, she walked him out of the room.

Shrugging, Flo went to see what was in the fridge. There must be something in the soft drinks line. The bloody woman was as mad her as her disgusting dogs. At which moment Rosie stalked back into the kitchen. Her voice was low, but each syllable was absolutely clear. "How bloody dare you! If you ever, ever frighten one of my dogs again," she hissed, "You will leave this house! And what in hell do you think you're doing in my fridge?"

He straightened up and grinned at her. "Jus' need sum juice," he said waving a carton at her. "This'll do." She was wearing pyjama bottoms with a baggy t-shirt and no bra. She had pale blue tennis shoes on her feet. Very sexy, he thought, all rumpered, rumpler, rumpled.

"No, you don't," snapped Rosie. "That's Larrie's because she doesn't eat fruit, she only drinks juice. So we save it for her. It's expensive. Put it back!"

"Make me!" he invited, giving her a playful smile.

"You're drunk," she said, taking the juice out of his hand and returning it to the fridge.

"Snot the end of the world," he said, as she closed the door. "C'mere!"

He grabbed her round the waist so suddenly that he caught her off-guard and she staggered against him. For a split second, as his mouth closed on hers and his arms pulled her close, she had an insane desire to respond. But it was just a split second. "Get off!" she gasped, pushing him away.

"Ah come on," he said, relaxing his grip. "I don't wanna marry you for Goss sake! I juss wanna bit of company. Juss one night..."

"Basket, sir!"

"Don't you fancy a fuck?"

"Are you completely insane? I'm not some cheap tart you've picked up in Soho!"

"Sorry..." he said, looking surprised. "It's just sex, ya know. Sex doesn't mean anything, iss just chips ya know. Fancy a few chips now and again," he said, pulling himself up and making an effort to speak clearly. "But no offence meant. I am verily sorry if I've offended you. I give you my word that it won't happen 'gain."

Rosie was genuinely shocked. He really was a dog; even his approach to sex was canine. What a Barbarian. "Go to bed," she ordered. "And don't you dare come down here at night again."

"Muma?" said Larrie from the doorway.

"What's going on?" Standing beside her, Dolly did a huge squeaky yawn and glared at Flo. It was bed-night-time but the new Smelly Man was getting in trouble. Had he sicked up his din-dins?

"Nothing," said Rosie. "Flo was just getting a glass of water."

"Why didn't he go to his own bathroom?" said Larrie looking wide-eyed. "Why is he in here?"

"He's just going back to his room," said Rosie as Flo weaved past them in the direction of the east wing. Rosie locked the door behind him and turned round to give Larrie a big hug. "Come on, baby heart," she coaxed. "Let's go back to bed, you can come in with me if you like. Just for a little while. Dolly, heel!"

"What was he doing?" said Larrie.

"Just being silly," said Rosie. "Come on, let's cuddle up and imagine what Sobie would do on holiday at the seaside."

Larrie was too sleepy to argue and sleeping in Muma's bed was too good to miss so she dropped the subject, but it was far from forgotten. The next morning she went beetling off to Chris's room before he was even out of bed. "He's a Bad Man," said Larrie with round eyes. "I saw him last night in the kitchen and he was walking sideways! I'm sure he was pissed."

"Pissed?" said Chris, blinking at her.

"Pissed, potted, fishy..."

"Fishy? You can't say fishy!"

"I can too," said Larrie sitting on his bed. "He

smelt funny and he looked fishy. And Muma was telling him off."

"Oh really? And what did she say?"

"She said it was nothing, and then she made him go back upstairs and she locked the door behind him. "I'm going to hold him up and shoot him."

Chris sat up and pulled a t-shirt on over his head. "No, you're not. Don't be ridiculous. I'll hold him up. What's the time? You'd better go and get dressed."

"You're not riding Sobie!"

"Not on horseback... I'll just waylay him or something. Put the fear of God into him. And I'm going to google him too." He stretched mightily and yawned. "I know his face from somewhere. I going to find out who he really is."

The sound of furious and sustained barking in the courtyard outside made him groan. "Go on, Larrie, push off and let a chap get dressed."

Flo also groaned, as the barking woke him up and a sledgehammer hit the back of his eyes. Blinking at the grey light, he could tell that it was hideously early, and he knew he wouldn't get back to sleep again. Outside, the row continued. Cursing under his breath, he went to look out of the window. In the courtyard, the gardener woman was yelling her head off and apparently trying to run Spike over with a wheelbarrow. Spike in his turn was barking maniacally and trying to attack her. He stepped out onto the shallow balcony intending to shout at them both, when suddenly Spike bounded away through the courtyard door. The gardener turned on Flo's Porsche and gave the side door a vicious kick leaving a massive dent in it.

"Oy!" he yelled. "What are you doing? That's my car!"

She span round and looked up at him where he stood like a Greek God framed in the window wearing only pyjama bottoms, the white net curtains wafting around his perfect body. Livid with fury, she shook her fist at him and made a big show of spitting on the car. Then she launched into a long string of insults and even if Flo couldn't understand the detail he recognised full well that it was a stream of murderous invective.

He was completely taken aback. He was the sexiest man in the world, everyone knew that. He could do no wrong. In fact, he was right even when he was wrong. It was a well-known fact that he was perfect. People killed each other just to catch a glimpse of him. What on earth did she think she was doing? How dare she? The bloody woman must be completely insane. Bloody Barbarian. Furious, he dragged his jeans on and shot down the stairs, but by the time he'd heaved the front door open she'd disappeared. Gritting his teeth, he stomped round to the terrace and found Rosie sitting at the table. She looked up. Flo had dragged his clothes on in a rush but the expensive jeans, the brand new designer t-shirt, and the softest, finest leather espadrilles from Milan looked expensive and stylish. He hadn't shaved or brushed his hair; he looked tousled, sleepy, masculine, sexy, and rich. He seemed to have completely blanked out the night before.

"Your bloody gardener!" he spat at her, leaning over the table in a fury. "Your bloody gardener! How dare she! I want her sacked! She's been screaming her head off at me!"

"Really? What have you done to her?"

"She put a bloody great dent in my car! Deliberately! Kicked the door in!" He thumped the table with his fist, making Dolly run for cover. Rupert's hackles went up and Sooty started shivering.

"I told you not to upset the dogs," said Rosie. "Sit! Shut up! Get down, dogs!" Suddenly turning her attention away from them all, and ignoring Flo completely, Rosie stood up and went forward with a wide smile. A shy-looking, frail woman with a fat spaniel on a lead had just appeared round the corner saying, "Bonjour?" in a breathy little voice.

"Madame Lavall, bonjour!" Rosie already knew all about Fanny the spaniel's pregnancy problems, but as Flo disappeared into the house, she sat down at the table, poured out two cups of coffee and prepared to listen to them all over again. She nodded understandingly and scratched Fanny's ears as the woman talked on and on, until finally, Madame Lavall went off looking tremulous and begging Rosie to phone the minute anything happened. "Tout va se passer très bien, Madame," said Rosie. "Je vous assure!" and Fanny's owner finally left.

Rosie turned round and saw Flo scowling from the back door. She suspected he was more outraged by Nicole shouting at him than kicking his car. He really didn't know his place in the pack, that was his problem. He needed to learn that he wasn't top dog.

"Coffee?" she said, calmly. He stomped out of the doorway and started complaining again. "Your gardener has just attacked my car and probably done about two thousand pounds' worth of damage, and you're offering me cold coffee. Don't you realise..."

"Nicole's a communist. Doesn't like conspicuous wealth. Are you having coffee? Or not? Don't tell me that monstrous phallic symbol isn't insured?"

She broke off as Dolly suddenly emerged from the garden firing off a volley of high-pitched barks at Fanny. The spaniel whimpered and tugged at her lead.

"Quiet, Dolly," said Rosie, "Come on, Fanny don't be frightened..." and then suddenly they heard the sound of large paws thundering across the terrace.

"Gently Spike!" shouted Rosie. "Down!" Flo tried to retreat but got tangled in Fanny's lead. As he grabbed the table to regain his balance, Spike was still charging towards them scattering cats and autumn leaves in all directions.

"Don't move," Rosie ordered Flo. "Spike! SIT!"

Extraordinarily enough, the dog's rear end dipped and almost before he'd stopped running, he sat down. Dolly skittered over and sat beside him perkily twitching her ears. "Good boy!" said Rosie giving him a click. "Hey Fanny, now calm down. There, you a good gal. Yes, good gal." Without looking at Flo, she said, "Ignore him. Just relax and start eating something. Don't reward him with your attention."

She pulled some Rescue Remedy out of her pocket and gave Fanny a few drops and within a few minutes the spaniel stopped shivering and lay down. "You want some?" she offered Flo.

"No." He sat down and started putting jam on a chuck of rock-hard bread and she poured him a cup of coffee.

"It's a bit cold now, I'm afraid," she said, nodding at his cup. "Do you want milk in it? This is extracts of flowers, that's all. Really effective. I discovered it when the kids were teething. Works great on dogs."

Not even surprised that it was muddy and sour, Flo drank his coffee in one, and pushed his chair back from the table. Lying a yard away from him, Spike raised his head from his paws and growled softly.

"Don't look at him, just ignore him," said Rosie in a soothing voice. She picked up a piece of bread and tore it into small chunks. "A barking dog is an uncertain dog. He doesn't know whether you're dangerous or not. But in his case, he knows you're dangerous because you've already tried to bash his nose in with a chair, and you're not part of the pack here. So it's not surprising he's feeling insecure. Ah, now I see what's set him off. Here comes Pierre."

Flo swallowed a hasty reply and disappeared into the kitchen but Rosie called him back. "Flo! Come back! Here, Flo! Here! Heel!"

For a split second he wanted to scream. Hadn't she noticed he wasn't a dog? But since his head was killing him and being screamed at was making it worse, he went back outside and tried not to scowl, but Rosie was getting on his nerves.

"This is our friendly local woodman, this is our new guest..." said Rosie and Flo found himself shaking hands with a small, powerfully-built Frenchman glowering at him suspiciously over a handsome moustache.

"Je vais vous ramoner la cheminée!" announced Pierre.

"He wants to sweep the chimney," Rosie told Flo. "It has to be done before we can light the stove. But perhaps today isn't really..."

"Ah! I thought it was you!" said Chris, coming out of the kitchen door with Minnie at his heels, and addressing Pierre in rapid French. "It'll be fine, Muma, just let him get on with it."

Rosie sighed heavily but the three men just stood there looking at her, so she gave up. "All right! Do the chimney!" she exclaimed. "But there's no need, we won't need to light the fire for ages. And there isn't any coal anyway."

Pierre started hauling poles out of a canvas bag.

"So, what are we up to this morning?" Chris asked Flo. "Tackling chapter one, are we? I see your car got stoved in."

"Yes, your gardener was yelling at me..."

Chris grinned. "Nicole? She did? She attacked you as well as the car? I must congratulate her."

"I'm taking it back to the hire place, ok?" snapped Flo.

"Probably a good idea," drawled Chris, "if Nicole's taken a dislike to it. Before you have to return it in carrier bags."

"Stop teasing," said Rosie. "You can see he's not used to it." Then she turned to Flo. "Come on, lighten up. It's only a car!"

Flo choked. Only a car? Hadn't they noticed it was a Porsche? Didn't they care about damaging a work of precision engineering? It was practically a work of art. "Right, I'll be off then," he said grimly, and Chris ducked away as if he was hiding a fit of the giggles.

Flo was still grinding his teeth and muttering to himself as he drove down the road to the village. They weren't just harmless eccentrics, they were criminally loopy. He sighed bitterly. He'd sooner starve in a ditch than spend another minute in that place, whatever Sally said. But Sally still wasn't answering her phone and knowing her, he knew she wouldn't take his calls again for days. Having once out-foxed the press, and put him firmly in his place, she'd leave him to rot until she was good and ready to pull him back out of the hat.

It was a shame he had to give the Porsche back, he thought, but there was no help for it. His moment of lust for a piece of sex-on-wheels could be his undoing and if it attracted the wrong sort of attention, Sally might just refuse to pay for it. Perhaps in a less conspicuous car he could simply drive somewhere else...

What was that on the road ahead? A bundle of clothes? A baby? Flo braked sharply and squinted against the sun. No, it was just a jumper. Or was it a jacket? Whatever. It was a garment. Obviously dropped by some ancient stripy Frenchman on a bicycle with a baguette. Flo could picture him sitting down to onion soup exclaiming "Zut alors, my jacket he is fallen!" Lots of shrugging and red wine.

Signposts, he thought. Don't they have signposts in France? He steered the car carefully round the jacket lying on the road and, just in case there was a half-naked Juliette Binoche look-alike on the loose, went into the next corner more slowly. He wasn't remotely surprised when a tall figure lounged out into the road ahead of him. He couldn't see properly against the bright sun but clearly, here was the owner of the jacket.

Flo braked yet again, and the tyres squealed like hungry piglets. Unimpressed, the figure stared straight through the windscreen, rolled his eyes and put his hands on his hips. He clearly had no intention of getting out of the way. Flo braked harder. The road was narrow and winding, trammelled on either side by crumbling stone walls. Flo pulled a face. The bloody brakes were rubbish. There was a sharp crack and the windscreen crazed. In a panic, Flo jammed the brake to the floor and pushed the glass out with his forearm. Little cubes of glass flew in all directions and the car hit something, skidded sideways across the road and stopped.

The French press must have caught up with him. Any minute now there'd be a posse of motorbikes zooming up the hillside and a Paris Match helicopter overhead. Once again, he regretted having insisted on an open topped car. He'd left himself nowhere to hide, and not being interested in mechanics naturally had no idea how to make the fucking soft top put itself back in place. There must be a button somewhere, but he could just imagine the photomontage of him struggling with a recalcitrant convertible. Sally would flay him alive.

Flo pulled the handbrake on and undid his seatbelt.

"Oh my God! Are you all right?" said Chris, running up to the car.

"Yee ha!" screamed an excited voice, and Sobie emerged from the woods above the road at a canter. Leaning low over his back, Larrie was wearing a black felt tricorn and a mask across her eyes. She wheeled around, her long hair swirling around her head. Sobie reared up, his front legs spiralling slowly as Larrie's hat slid off her head and hung on her shoulders. Then she waved cheerily and urged him down the slope.

Flo gasped. Loose stones skittered under the

horse's hooves as he plunged off the path. Sobie's front legs were thrust out forwards and his back legs were so bent that he was almost sitting on the dusty gravel. His head was arched up over his powerful, straining shoulders as he slid calmly down the bank towards the car. Leaning well back, her stirrups practically on the horse's neck, Larrie was in gales of laughter. Flo leapt out of the car. What in hell? Chris, his arms crossed and his eyes gleaming, flicked him a quick glance and raised one finger.

As Larrie whooped with glee, Sobie's tail swished across the loose scrub sending terracotta clouds swirling round the pair of them.

She's a valkyrie, thought Flo.

"Ata-boy Sobie!" urged Larrie, Sobie sent his long mane flying in all directions, and scrambled down the last section of the slope onto the road. His metal shoes struck sparks on the tarmac making him skitter and jump. Larrie, keeping her seat with absolute ease, hauled a large clumsy-looking highwayman's pistol out of a holster attached to her saddle. It was so heavy that she needed both hands to point it straight at Flo.

"Stand and deliver!" she ordered loudly.

"Are you completely insane?" demanded Flo.

"Stick 'em up!" she ordered. "I warn you this is loaded!"

"Larrie! It'd better not be!" exclaimed Chris.

"I bloody hope it's not," said Flo.

Outdoors, Sobie was even more enormous than he'd looked in his loose box. His hooves alone were the size of manhole covers. His gleaming chestnut coat looked as though it had been dusted with snow, although Flo knew enough about horse-flesh to know that it was sweat.

"Reach for the sky!" ordered the girl, as the horse shifted his weight. "Chris, it is him! You are, aren't you," she said to Flo. "You're whatsisname from Hellraisers, aren't you?"

Chris nodded calmly. "I googled him this morning. It's definitely him."

"You're wrong," said Flo with a disarming smile. "People are always mistaking me for him, but I'm a writer. My name is..." (What in hell had Sally told him? Shit!) "I've never made a film in my life!" he said as humbly as possible.

"Stay right where you are," said Larrie, throwing a great handful of long hair over her shoulder. "And no funny business!"

Flo didn't know whether to lose his temper or laugh. "Is that thing really loaded?" he demanded.

"Well, no actually," she said ruefully. "Of course it isn't. The airgun was, but I haven't got any ammo for this one. But you've still got to stand and deliver, because I'm a highwayman. So stick 'em up and be quick about it!"

Chris was laughing like a drain. Flo obediently stuck 'em up. "Look, I don't know what's going on here," he said, "or who you think I am, but you've definitely got the wrong guy."

"Bollocks," said Larrie, standing up in the stirrups. "He's the Hellraisers guy, Chris! He's been in practically every movie ever made. What IS his name? Dick? Bricky? Picky? Sicky? Kicky? It begins with a C. He's going to be the new James Bond, Chris. Kent! That's it! He's Florian Kent!"

"You're right. He played the drag artist in Tin Of Beans!"

"God, that was a crappy film!"

"I'm a writer," droned Flo, sounding utterly bored.

"Hang on, what did you say Larrie?" said Chris suddenly, his face draining of colour. "About an airgun? Did you shoot that windscreen with an airgun?"

"Jesus Christ!" said Flo.

"Shut up," said Chris. "Larrie, come on tell me the truth."

She shrugged. "Well, I didn't hurt him did I? I just made him stop the car. How else was I going to make him stop? That's what highwaymen do!"

Flo could feel a rising tide of hysteria in his chest. "Don't tell me: it doesn't matter because it's only a car, right? Look, it's a hire car. Now it's got a large dent in the passenger door, a broken windscreen and it looks like substantial damage to the offside front wing and someone's going to have to pay for it all."

"I didn't make you crash the car!" said Larrie indignantly.

"I'm going to deal with you later," said Chris. "Where's that gun now? And where did you get it from?"

"One of the boys in school lent it to me. It's up there," she said gesturing up the hill. "I threw it in a bush because I didn't have a holster for it and I thought I might need two hands to get down the slope. But I didn't! Did you see me? One hand all the way, I could easily have held onto the gun!"

"Just don't let Muma know you've got an air-gun, okay Larrie?"

"God no!"

"You'll have to give it me and I'll... honestly, you're a menace." Shaking his head as if to clear his mind, Chris turned back to Flo. "Right, let's deal with you. Passport!"

Flo didn't bother arguing any more. He'd always thought Sally had been over-optimistic about him not being recognised: "Darling," she'd said, "Rosie's a batty English aristocrat, off her head. I should know. We were at school together. Lives in the 18th century half the time. Provence, big French château, red wine, walled garden, garlic, that sort of thing. There isn't a cinema for 200 kilometres. They don't even have a TV, for Christ's sake. You'll be completely anonymous."

"Make it snappy!" said Chris. "Passport. And no messing otherwise Larrie will run you over with that nag of hers."

"Sobie wouldn't hurt a fly!"

Still reaching for the sky, Flo shrugged and Chris reached into the car and started checking for papers. Sally had obviously not taken this precious pair into account: "Now, listen darling. You're an actor, you can do this, it's a piece of piss. You just play the part: you're a writer, a historian, an academic. So take a pair of glasses and make sure you wear them. No contact lenses. Oh, and for God's sake don't look at the furniture. Rosie hates people noticing the furniture. Not unless it's Roman. Don't ask! Forget it. And while you're there try, sweetie, just try and write a few notes for your autobiography."

If he humoured them, thought Flo, would they keep quiet? Or perhaps he could pay them off?

"Don't be nervous," said Larrie kindly. "Sobie won't hurt you."

"Bullseye, Larrie!" called Chris flicking through Flo's passport. "He's Florian Kent all right."

"Oh my God!" breathed Larrie gazing at Chris.

Flo gave her a sharp look. She sounded truly horrified. Shaking her head, Larrie lowered her heavy old-fashioned highwayman's pistol. "I feel sorry for you," she said, and shoved the gun clumsily back into the holster attached to the saddle. Flo reclaimed his hands from the sky.

Larrie and Chris gazed at each other for one awestruck moment, and then they both looked back at him and Chris nodded. "It's true," he said seriously. "You are in deep cheese."

Larrie clicked her tongue and the horse took a few steps into the middle of the road. Apparently satisfied that Flo wasn't planning to run away, she kicked her feet free of the stirrups, sprang down into the road and fished in the pockets of her jods as the horse nosed her hand greedily. "Isn't he beautiful?" she demanded and Flo realised with a small shock that she wasn't referring to him. She murmured some endearment under her breath and kissed the horse's nose tenderly. "He's my baby!" she cooed.

Sobie drooled dotingly onto her shoulder and flicked his ears at Flo as if to say get lost. For a split second, Flo was furiously indignant. How could she prefer that smelly animal to him? Only last month he'd been voted sexiest man on the planet by US Cosmopolitan, and here this guttersnipe...

"You're basically buggered," said Chris, handing his passport back.

"Totally up to your neck in it," agreed Larrie.

"Muma hates actors," said Chris. "Detests them. Well, all men really. Except me, of course. And the dogs. But even Spike's going down to the vet for the big chop."

"And Sobie, Muma doesn't hate Sobie."

"He's not a man," said Chris.

"He's your baby!" snapped Flo, fed up with being ignored.

Chris laughed. "Crap photo, by the way. Totally greasy. You look like a spiv."

"And what would you know about spivs?"

"Oh, I'm frighteningly well educated," he said casually. "Everyone knows that. I'm older than I look, too. So don't try and patronise me."

"Don't tell me you're a photographer as well."

"He is, actually," said Larrie indignantly. "A really good one. But stop trying to change the subject. What are you going to do?"

"More to the point, where are you going to stay once you get kicked out of the château?" said Chris. "There aren't any posh hotels round here. There's only the Café de la Poste..."

"...and everyone knows they've got rats in their bedrooms," said Larrie gleefully. "Really huge ones with yellow teeth and holly-toes-is! And if you get bitten by them, green poison leaks into your system and you curl up and die shrieking with agony and your guts turn black and explode inside your belly!"

"You'll just have to hope she doesn't recognise you," said Chris. "She might not."

"As long as you don't start boasting about your Oscar and wanting champagne for breakfast," said Larrie. "Or having orgies with starlets. Or inviting the paparazzi to come and photograph you swimming naked in the river or something. Eee-Yuk!" Gathering Sobie's reins up in one hand, she swung herself back into the saddle.

"You're going to tell her who I am, aren't you?"

"Yeah, sorry, Fifi," said Chris apologetically. The fan is pretty much shit-covered as far as you're concerned."

"Don't call me Fifi!"

Chris just laughed.

"And what about that airgun?" said Flo suddenly. "How will she like that, eh?"

"You wouldn't tell on me!" gasped Larrie. "You snake in the grass!"

"Well, I won't tell if you won't," said Flo fiercely. "How's that?"

"Why do you want to stay with us so much? You think it's a rat hole. There's no swimming pool, no champagne bar, no helipad on the roof. So why the hell are you so desperate to stay?" demanded Chris.

"You might as well tell us," said Larrie. "Or we'll torture it out of you. There'll be slugs in your shoes and beetles in your dinner."

"Jesus Christ, the pair of you are mad. To be honest, you've caught me making a getaway attempt." Flo paused, but they just stared back at him and he realised he'd have to tell them the whole humiliating truth. "I've got nowhere else to go. My own fault. The truth is, I need to get out of the spotlight for a while and Sally suggested your mother because no-one else will have me. So I'll have to come crawling back, if you'll let me."

Larrie and Chris swapped looks, and to clear the embarrassment Flo changed the subject. "Why did your gardener attack my car, by the way?"

"She's not our gardener," said Chris. "She's called Nicole. She lives above the stable block, and she gardens for the love of it. She pays her rent in produce. Fruit, vegetables, eggs, chickens, jam... practically everything you've eaten came from her. She doesn't believe in money."

"You really are all mad," said Flo.

"Nope. Just not money-orientated."

"Which is a good thing," cut in Larrie, "Since we never have any."

"It's also a good thing because without Nicole, we wouldn't eat."

"So do we have a deal?" said Flo. "I don't mention the airgun, you don't mention my job or my name?"

"So what are we supposed to call you then?" asked Larrie wrinkling up her nose.

"Flo. That bit was true. My friends do call me Flo."

He and Larrie both looked at Chris but he was thinking. "All right," he said at last. "But only as long as you don't upset Muma. You annoy her or upset her in any way and I'll call the press. Is that understood?"

"I won't upset your mother. Promise."

"Well, if that's settled then I'm off," announced Larrie. "Highwaymen don't hold up men who make bargains. And anyway Sobes is getting hungry and I'm supposed to be coming home on the school bus, so hasta la vista mís amigos! Hup, Sobes!"

The massive horse obligingly reared up on his tree-trunk back legs and waved his outsize clogs in the air. Flo recoiled.

"Jesus! Is she safe on that thing?"

"Probably safer than on the back of some boy's motorbike," said Chris, watching Larrie trot smartly down the road. "Safer than you'll be if Muma finds out who you are."

"Look Christopher..."

"Christian Bellvadere Fitzwilson at your service - and that was Larrisa Caliope Fitzwilson, and don't bother remarking on our names. We've suffered enough. Fifi."

"All right. Pax. Are you really a photographer?" asked Flo.

"Yup," said Chris. "I won a scholarship to study in London but didn't go in the end. I enter photographic competitions but only the ones with cash prizes. Or photographic equipment."

"Do you ever win?"

"About once a month, twice if I'm lucky."

"You must be good then."

"I am. Why are you pretending to write a book on antiques?"

"Antiques?" said Flo, startled. "Is that why she keeps mentioning furniture?"

"No, that's because Sally told her you were gay. Why are you pretending to be a writer?"

"It's called acting," snapped Flo. "It's what I do for a living."

"Not in other people's houses, surely? I thought that was called fraud? And you don't even look like a writer. Not with those sunglasses and I don't know. Your clothes are really not writer-ish. And what are you doing with this car? Everyone knows writers are always broke."

"Can't I be a successful author?"

"Not round here, you can't. This whole mountain is infested with poverty stricken scribes and arty bohos, but successful spivs in red sports cars? Fearsomely not on, old chap."

"Do you always talk like Brideshead Revisited?"

"Bitch all you like. But you've been warned. Even one sniff of your real identity and you'll be dead." Chris leant down lazily and pulled his bicycle up from where he'd left it lying at the side of the road. "I'm not a fool. I'm just hoping that you aren't as disappointing as you seem."

"I'm not," said Flo, blushing. "I don't disappoint people. Not always, anyway."

Chris didn't move.

"It's only a couple of weeks. I just want some space. It's not always easy being..."

"Spare me! All right, I won't say anything as long as you try not to be disappointing."

"Ok," said Flo with his heart sinking.

"See you later," said Chris.

Flo watched him pedal away down the road and wasn't the slightest bit surprised when Chris suddenly turned right, careered off the road and went whooping straight down the hill.

CHAPTER THREE

Flo stood in the road for a long time, gazing into middle distance. Then he got back into the crumpled Porsche and drove slowly back to the château. He would have to get the hire company to tow it away. His shoulders were as hot and heavy as his feet, and although part of him was protesting that it wasn't fair, another part of him acknowledged that he'd screwed up in just about every possible way. Go straight to jail. Do not pass go, do not collect £200.

Perhaps there was a way out of the mess he'd made but if there was, the path wasn't signposted and he was too tired to look for it. He was even too tired to stock up on Scotch. He just retraced his steps, un-packed the car and went back up to his lemon-rind prison. For the next ten days, he stayed in bed most of the time, rarely venturing downstairs except for supper. To all enquiries, he said that he was working.

"I hope he's all right," said Rosie to Nicole in the vegetable garden.

"Bugger all rich aristos!" said Nicole, pulling

up a large thistle. "Let him rot!"

Rosie smiled and watched Dolly bouncing through the long dry grass, enjoying the tickling sensation on her tummy. The big dogs panted and wagged, anxious for their walk.

"Well, I can't say it's not a relief!" said Rosie. "I thought he was going to be under my feet all the time! I must try and kidnap Larrie, she needs new jeans."

"Ah there's no hurry. We're going to have a beautiful Indian summer," said Nicole straightening her back and gazing up at the sky. "It won't get cold for a while yet. You mark my words. That golden aura up on the hills... it's a good sign."

Rosie smiled. Nicole was right, it would be another month or so before they'd need to dig out their coats and gloves. She took the dogs out through the overgrown rose garden, picked a few dead heads and pulled a couple of tennis balls out of her pocket. The dogs could do with some exercise. Poor Flo, she thought. Her withers were slightly wrung, but then she reminded herself that lots of strays sulked when they first arrived at the château, lots of them found it traumatic being plonked down in a strange place with strange people, especially the spoilt over-indulged ones with an overblown sense of their own importance. Left alone, he'd come round. She hurled the tennis balls as far into the undergrowth as she could and the dogs went rushing off.

Up in his room, gloomily gazing out at the

hills, Flo was facing the fact that his hosts didn't give a damn about him. If he went downstairs they gave him food, if he stayed upstairs, they left him alone. He could die, all alone in this horrible yellow room. He counted the days on his fingers. He'd been there since a week ago last Wednesday and it was now Friday. He decided to go down to breakfast the next morning.

But when he arrived in the kitchen with a self-conscious half-smile on his face, there was no sign of breakfast except a pot of the usual acid-mud coffee on the table. Everything else was clean and tidy and Flo was surprised to find Rosie was wearing a full-skirted dress and a pair of black riding boots. She had a scarf in her hair and hoops in her ears too. And make-up.

"Wow!" he said. "You're dressed up."

She pushed a pair of cats off the table. "Oh well, market day you know. Got to make an effort. Are you coming? No, Dolly, you are staying here! Basket!"

"I don't know," he said slowly. "Is it a big market? Lots of people?"

Rosie sighed. "Look, it's just a market. In fact it might do you good to stop moping around in your room and being in bad mood all the time."

"Am I in a bad mood?" he said, pouring himself a very small cup of coffee.

"Well, perhaps just a bit sulky, or bored or something," she conceded. She shoved a shopping list into her straw shopping bag. "You know, what with having to pretend to be writing about antiques all the time."

She picked up a powder compact, added some bright lipstick to her face and smiled at herself. "I'm just going to put the big dogs in their run," she said. "Johnny will be leaving in precisely ten minutes. You can take your coffee upstairs with you if you want to find a jacket."

She gave him a bright smile and he realised that she still wasn't interested. She didn't care. He could stay and rot in her leaky château or he could tag along to her horrible provincial market - and either way it wouldn't make the slightest difference to her. Without a word, he took his coffee and went back off upstairs. He crossed Chris on the landing. "Are you coming to the market?" he asked.

"Thought I might. Any objections?"

"You can't go looking like that," said Chris in a low voice. Pressed close to his knee, Minnie quivered in agreement.

Flo looked at them in surprise. How could the sexiest man on the planet be wearing the wrong clothes? But Chris had disappeared again and suddenly Flo realised he couldn't be bothered. Sipping his stone cold coffee, he went into his room wondering why he didn't simply get himself a coffeemaker. There was plenty of space on the chest of drawers and at least that way he could have hot coffee whenever he wanted. Hot coffee, fresh bread... if anyone had asked him a fortnight ago, he'd never have dreamed that such basic items would seem like un-dreamed-of luxuries. His room was decidedly chilly, and there was a thin layer of condensation on the windows, although outside the sun was already beginning to warm the autumn leaves.

"Okay, you'd better try these on," said Chris coming into the room behind him. He dropped a bundle of clothes onto one end of the bed and flung himself onto the pillows at the other end, rumpling all the sheets up with his bare dusty feet. Minnie leapt up beside him gracefully and curled up. "Blimey, it's cold in here," he said, chattily. "It'll soon be October. Aren't you afraid of contracting frostbite staying here?"

Flo looked at the jumble of tatty garments, glared at Chris's feet, and sighed.

Oblivious, Chris shrugged and said, "No, you're not obliged to try them on. Just well advised to consider it." He pulled an empty Scotch bottle out from under the covers and raised his eyebrows. "If you want company in bed, why don't you let some of the cats in? The fluffy orange one is a good warm sleeper, although Larrie normally nabs him if she can. And you really ought to leave all those smart personal accessories in your room too." He wriggled his feet into Flo's bedclothes and dropped the empty bottle onto the floor beside the bed.

"What accessories?"

"The watch, the wallet, the little leather bag, the posh phone... you can't go to the market wearing all that stuff. You'll stick out a mile. You just look expensive and international, and altogether abnormal."

Flo would have given millions to disagree, but he was an actor. One glance in the mirror and he knew Chris was right. He didn't look abnormal but he did look cosmopolitan and stylish, just the way his stylist had intended. Irritated, he stripped his pure cotton shirt and cashmere jumper off in one easy movement and threw them at the bed. Flo's body was a mass of firm muscle and his skin was glossy and evenly tanned. There wasn't an ounce of fat on his stomach, and his shoulders were as broad and strong as an Olympic athlete's. Gazing at him from the lumpy four-poster bed, Chris raised his eyebrows.

"We have gym membership, do we, Fifi?"

"Fuck off, Chris," said Flo. He snatched a football shirt off the end of the bed and hauled it over his head.

"Not bad," said Chris, pulling Minnie's ears gently. Flo looked in the tarnished mirror. The shirt had once been yellow and green stripes but the colours had run and the collar seemed to have disappeared. It was large and shapeless and the yellow made his olive skin look sallow rather than sexy.

"See?" said Chris. "Normally, you're just too well dressed. You look like a rich person. Like a star. All these well cut, beautifully designed understated clothes of yours. What's this jumper made of?"

Flo shrugged, and Chris looked at the label. "Silk and cashmere, dry clean only." He laughed suddenly. "Better keep that out of Muma's way. She boils everything. That's why every item of clothing in this rat-hole is like cardboard." He sat up, pulled the sweater on and knelt up on the bed so he could inspect himself in the mirror. "Wow," he said softly. The sweater was slate grey but made his eyes look blue, and on Chris's thin frame, it fell into folds which in some extraordinary way made him look as if he had gym membership too.

Flo shrugged. Chris was a good-looking kid. Tall, graceful, dark brown floppy hair, big eyes, thin face, intense expression... He wasn't in the slightest bit surprised at the transformation. That was the whole point of paying a couple of hundred for a sweater: it made you look good. The kid was quite pink with pleasure.

"Wear it if you like," he said suddenly. "One of us had better look human and I'm obviously doomed to look like a dead wasp."

Chris's thin face broke into a grin and he suddenly looked younger. "You sure? You don't mind?"

"Take whatever you like," said Flo. He had already realised that if he wanted to go unrecognised, Chris's awful, worn out, faded, boiled-stiff wardrobe would be the perfect disguise. Especially without his trademark stubble and Ray-Bans.

"And don't stand like that," said Chris, watching him from the bed. "You look like a person who knows they're beautiful and is expecting to be photographed."

"I do?"

"Yes, there's an kind of invisible tension at

the back of the neck keeping the head erect and balanced with the chin just slightly down, and your shoulders are too straight."

"I don't want to be papped looking like a slob."

"But if you look like a slob, you won't be papped, will you?"

Flo looked in the mirror again.

"Stand like a slob," said Chris. "Stomach out, spine relaxed, head all no-how like you aren't aware of what your neck is doing."

Flo followed his instructions and his reflection in the mirror suddenly looked shorter, fatter, less impressive. Chris was right. Without turning his head, he shifted his focus so he could see the kid through the mirror. "How do you know all this? About my posture and clothes and stuff?"

"I look at people, that's what I do. I try and see them in the same way as a camera does."

Flo looked at himself again. It was amazing how accurate the kid was. In his new-acquired horrible old clothes and patchy haircut, he hardly recognised himself. "I know you're thinking that as an actor I should know how to do this, but I never play ordinary people," he said with a touch of defiance. "Producers hire me because I'm sexy, I bring glamour..."

"Well you won't be needing that here," drawled Chris. "In fact, the less of it you bring anywhere, the better it will be for all of us. Particularly you."

Minnie hopped off the bed and onto an armchair standing in a ray of sunshine. She curled up neatly and put her head on her paws. Flo gave himself another look in the mirror. If he could ever persuade someone to cast him in this type of role...

"You could easily buy some normal clothes in the market," said Chris, slipping into one of Flo's jackets. It was dark cranberry suede lined with fine alpaca. "You know, they have jeans for a tenner in SuperU. And t-shirts for just a couple of euros." He picked up a shirt which Flo had left over the back of a armchair. "Do you mind if I try this shirt on?"

Flo looked at it. It was about $500 dollars' worth of raw cream silk with oyster-shell buttons. "Sure, you can borrow it if you like," he said. Chris had obviously never had any decent clothes in his life and designers sent Flo expensive clothes all the time. He went into the bathroom and began to shave in the lukewarm water that came out of the hot tap. "Does your sister make a habit of holding people up?" he asked, raising his voice so that Chris could hear him in the other room.

"I do apologise for that," said Chris coming to the doorway and looking guilty. "I promise you, I've confiscated that gun. Are these real Levi's? Can I try them on too?"

"It wasn't the first time though, was it?"

"With the airgun it was. But no. If you want to know, she likes holding people up. She says she's practicing to be a stunt rider. I don't know, perhaps she just likes scaring the life out of people, but there's no point in holding up the locals because they don't take any notice of her and some of them are even liable to complain to Muma."

"Well, I'm not surprised your mother doesn't approve," said Flo, patting his face dry with a bone-hard, balding towel. He went back into his bedroom where Chris was trying the Levi's on.

"It's not that," said Chris. "She hates films, she'd rather die than let Larrie anywhere near a film set."

"Why?"

There was a slight pause and then Chris said "Too dangerous."

"Is that really why?"

"You know what? If we're going to the market, we'd better get a shift on." Chris turned away from the mirror with a completely new image of himself. Flo's clothes had turned him from a scruffy clodhopper into a sophisticated, cosmopolitan adult and, although he knew it shouldn't make any difference, he was thrilled.

Flo looked at him. The transformation was good, but his clothes were too big for Chris, and they accentuated his thinness. If he ever remembered, perhaps he'd ask his stylist about getting hold of some smaller sizes.

"You can come and see my studio if you like," said Chris hesitantly. "You won't find it on your own, but I could take you. It's over the other side of the château."

"I would love to," said Flo with a nice smile

and no intention of ever going to look at the boy's amateur snaps.

Chris smiled back at him. "Here, Minnie! Heel! I don't let many people in there," he confided. "You can come to the market with me, if you like. Rather than driving that ruined red thing. I mean, it's pretty conspicuous." Minnie scampered over to Chris's side and stood with her head leaning against his knee.

"I think someone called John is driving us actually," said Flo.

Chris burst out laughing and followed him down the stairs refusing to say what was so funny. "You just wait at the gates," he said, with a big grin. "I'm going to shut Minnie into the kitchen, then I'll go round the back and get the Renault. And I'll make sure that er... John is on his way!"

He was still laughing when he got round to the stable yard where the family left their cars. "He thinks Johnny is a chauffeur!" he told Larrie.

She let out a loud guffaw.

Behind her, the not-so-trusty Toyota pickup had its bonnet open. "Are you coming with me?" called Rosie from the depths of the engine compartment. "Essaye!" she yelled at Nicole, who was sitting in the driver's seat, and the engine sprang to life. Black smoke belched out of the exhaust pipe and the whole machine began vibrating from side to side.

"No, I'm taking the Renault!" yelled Chris over the din. "Come on, Larrie, hop in. Let's get out of here before we get stuck behind Johnny all the way to the main road."

His Renault was painted pale brown - practically the same colour as the extensive rust growing up from the chassis like brown ivy. They rumbled over the cobbles to the gate, Johnny roaring and choking behind them.

"I wish I could see his face when he realises he's got to go in that," giggled Larrie.

"Oh you never know, he might take it better than you think," said Chris.

Johnny crashed down the lane behind them, frightening rabbits for two kilometres in every direction until they reached the main courtyard gate, when instead of following Chris down the driveway to the main road, Rosie drew up. "You'll have to get in the back, Flo!" she called. "Don't worry about Spike, I've put him in a crate. Just open the bottom half of the door, the top is jammed shut!"

"I think I'll walk!" said Flo, horrified.

"As you like, but I'm not waiting!" yelled Rosie. "Do you know the way?"

Of course I don't know the way, thought Flo. He'd been incarcerated in her bloody château for nearly a fortnight without going anywhere, so how could he possibly know the way? Was she being deliberately obtuse?

"Can't I ride in the front?" he said.

"Non!" screamed Nicole over the roar of the diesel engine, and spat on her palms menacingly.

Barely able to breathe through the exhaust

fumes, Flo hauled himself, sweating and swearing, through the narrow gap between the tailgate and the rear window into the back of the monstrous vehicle. There were no seats, just a corrugated metal floor, some old newspapers, a pile of wooden crates containing vegetables, two unsanitary-looking cold boxes and a large collapsible metal cage containing Spike.

Rosie tossed him a cheery remark over her shoulder as Johnny lurched forward, but he couldn't hear a thing over the terrible din of the engine. Spike lifted his chin and began to howl. The car rocked from side to side like a fairground ride, every dip producing an ear-splitting shriek and a new bruise. Rosie pulled a face at Nicole, firmly sitting in the passenger seat, but Nicole just shrugged. Et alors? Why should she move over just because he was so indulged he'd never before ridden in the back?

At the market, Rosie flung Johnny up onto the pavement outside the vet's surgery, hauled on the handbrake and jammed her hand on the horn.

"Come on," she shouted at Flo, "Push the back door open!"

Sweating horribly, Flo shoved. The lower half of the window opened with a soul-searing screech and he was liberated. Nicole grabbed the cold boxes, kissed Rosie on both cheeks and staggered off towards the stalls.

"Why are you wearing Chris's clothes?" asked Rosie, momentarily distracted. She looked at him curiously as he brushed bits of straw off a pair of brown corduroys that had seen better days. "I thought that stripy sweatshirt was in the ragbag," she said. He looked peculiar, somehow misshapen and ordinary. You'd never know he had beautiful long legs. Her stomach turned over and she made a mental note about getting a doctor's appointment.

Firmly refusing to look at any part of Flo, she leaned into the car and hauled Spike's crate towards her. Terrified, he threw up, splashing Flo through the bars. "Poor baby," she said. "Never mind. Muma make you better soon." She turned to Flo, "Can you just take the other side of the crate. I don't want to take him out of it because you know what he's like."

A fortnight earlier Flo would have been outraged, but now he just resigned himself to smelling of dog vomit and helped drag the crate into the surgery, where Rosie dosed Spike with Rescue Remedy and muzzled him. The vet, who had obviously met Spike before, approached gingerly and gave him a preliminary injection.

"Move!" said Rosie and the vet pushed past Flo without a second glance. Spike whined momentarily but then his eyes started to droop. The vet gave Rosie a nod and produced another, larger syringe. "Wouldn't want him waking up half way through," said Rosie with a grin. "I think we can go now."

They left Spike to the vet's tender mercies.

"Why?" said Flo as they got back out onto the pavement. "Why castrate the poor bastard?"

"It'll make him less aggressive and easier to train, it'll prevent any mini-Spikes being born and abandoned, mishandled by stupid owners like his, and you never know, it might even prevent some child being bitten by one of his foul-tempered offspring," said Rosie crisply. "It'll also prevent prostate problems later on."

Johnny was still in mid-lurch on the pavement but Rosie walked straight past. "Everyone knows it's my car and it'll make life so much easier for picking Spike up when we go home. Shall we go round the market?"

It suddenly hit Flo that in Moisson, Rosie was the star, not him. He looked around as he trailed after her. The town seemed almost dead, the sky was flat, hard and blue, the plane trees were starting to lose their leaves and most of the houses seemed to be throwing off their plaster in sympathy. The pavements were uneven and the flowerpots were empty. The sun was shining determinedly, but it was a far cry from Cannes or Paris.

"Come along," said Rosie brightly, "chip chop!" She led him down a small side street into the market square which was packed with stalls selling mounds of fruit and vegetables, goat's cheese, wine, huge slabs of bread and ham, whole sausages, strings of garlic and apricot tarts. Every stall was surrounded by people, and more of them were milling about between the stalls, shaking hands, exchanging kisses, calling loud greetings across the crowd. Flo was amazed. He hadn't realised there were so many people in the area.

"Everyone comes into the market," said Rosie. "I don't really come to buy anything; I mean the stuff they sell here is really good quality, much better than in the supermarkets, but so are the prices. And of course, we're lucky. We grow or produce practically everything we need. Or at least Nicole does."

With Flo tagging along behind, she sauntered past stalls overflowing with glossy chestnuts and bright orange pumpkins, exchanging kisses with people and chatting and patting dogs' as she went. The jewellery, the hard-woven shawls, the organic flower-scented soap, the wall hangings from Africa; none of them attracted more than a fleeting glance from her.

Walking in her footsteps, Flo wasn't surprised that she was on first-name terms with every dog and dog-owner in town. She was obviously a local oracle when it came to canine affairs. Having only managed one cup of Rosie's sour coffee since the night before, his stomach was rumbling loudly. He stopped slouching for a minute and looked over the heads of the people. "Oh look!" he exclaimed in-between social greetings. "Rosie! The van over there. Shall we get some sushi?"

"Oh no!" she said, and then relented. "Well, you can if you want. Can't be bothered with it myself. Doesn't fill you up enough. Bloody expensive, too. Anyway, we'll have lunch when we get home." Her eyes brightened as she saw her daughter weaving through the crowd towards her. "Ah, Larrie, where's Chris?"

"Oh, I don't know," said Larrie. "Can we go to the Halloween Fete in Moisson? It's free, you just have to contribute a dish. I could make stuffed eggs. Everyone's going. It's fancy dress! Can I have some pizza? I'm starving!"

"We'll have lunch as soon as we get home," said Rosie. "But I was thinking we might treat ourselves to a coffee..."

"I wouldn't mind some pizza," said Flo, "unless it's forbidden?"

Larrie' eyes sparkled, she started dancing up and down on the spot, and Flo winked at her. Rosie looked at him in surprise. Did he really like pizza? Or was he just trying to be nice to Larrie? "No, of course I don't mind," she said. "Go! I'll save you a place at the Bon Coin."

Watching them stroll off together, she wondered when they'd got so matey, but at that instant Pierre came sailing through the crowd towards her. "Mon coeur," he said in a low, intimate voice, and kissed her on both cheeks, tickling her with his moustache and trying to get as close as possible to her mouth. "How are you? Coffee, I buy you a little coffee."

"Behave yourself," she said sternly. "How's your wife?"

"Just one coffee? How can you refuse?"

"All right but I must just get some lemons and I need cloves, too."

"Excellent!" he said ushering her towards the spices stall. Once she'd completed her shopping, Pierre insisted on carrying all the bags and they wound up at a table outside the café. They ordered coffee and Pierre hooked more chairs towards them with his feet, asking if she'd lit her stove yet. Rosie saw Nicole sitting on the other side of the terrace with a big animated crowd, getting chummy with the local mayor, and waved at them.

"Muma! Look what Flo bought!" exclaimed Larrie bouncing up to the table. "A whole pizza! Not just portions! A whole one! With ham AND mushrooms. And he got a bread machine. It's in that bag there."

Rosie looked from Larrie to Flo. There was something hopeful and appealing in his dark eyes, almost like a retriever with a muddy stick in his mouth. Sweet. "A bread machine, eh? That should keep you busy then," she said. If she'd had a clicker with her she'd have given him a click, but as it was she rewarded him with a smile.

"You don't mind, do you?" he asked.

"Of course not!" she said and had to stop herself patting him on the head. "I'm just going over to talk to Nicole for a minute."

As she walked away from the table, Larrie extracted a large floppy slice of pizza from the box and started blowing at it and licking her fingers. Flo followed her example and pushed the box over towards Pierre, but Pierre was watching Rosie as she threaded her way through the crowded tables, smiling and joking, touching this person lightly on the shoulder, slapping that one firmly on the back.

"She is beautiful," said Pierre reverently, "Rosie is a pin up!"

Larrie choked over her pizza, but Pierre was on a roll. "And she deserves the best but will not let me help her. She works too much." He rounded on Flo. "You hurt her and I kill you."

But Flo didn't speak French. "You wouldn't know where I could buy some decent wine, would you?" he replied, and Pierre rolled his eyes, because he didn't speak a word of English. Flo pulled a face and spoke louder. "Wine, yes? Rosie's wine? Horrible!" he said. "Vinegar! Larrie, what's the French for disgusting?"

Larrie fired off a volley of French and Pierre replied in suit, and then translated. "He says what sort of wine do you want to buy?"

Flo was about to say "anything decent!" when his guardian angel changed his mind: "I'd like to buy something nice for Rosie," he said. "To say thank you for having me. A couple of crates of red."

Larrie gave him a huge sunny smile and Pierre looked approving. "Eh beh..." he began, but Flo cut him short. "Smooth, no acid, some fruit but still dry and a nice deep bass note," he said.

Once Larrie had translated, Pierre sucked his teeth and Flo was about to say, "the price doesn't matter" when once again he thought better of it. "And a reasonable price, mind you!" he said, trying to sound authentic. And humble. At that moment, his slice of pizza collapsed and a large bit of oily ham fell into his lap.

Larrie and Pierre laughed, Pierre ordered a beer and Larrie took a second slice of pizza. Around them, people milled around carrying rush baskets stuffed with root vegetables, and wooden crates of figs for making jam. A scruffy busker in a faded clown's costume was playing a flute further up the pavement and suddenly the sun came out from behind the mairie, illuminating the scene like an enormous arc light. Flo suddenly realised he was having a good time.

"Sorry about that," said Rosie, coming back to their table. "Is that my coffee?"

Behind her back, Pierre was clumsily miming a zipped mouth and a telephone. Swallowing a laugh, Flo nodded and tried to clean up the mess on his cords with a serviette. He noticed that no-one seemed in any hurry to leave, and the waitress wasn't hovering for payment or another order. She didn't even seem to mind them eating takeaway pizza at her tables. Civilised, he thought. Very civilised.

"Well, I suppose we ought to go and collect Spike before he wakes up," said Rosie finally. "Thank you for the coffee, Pierre."

Pierre finished his beer, twirled his moustache, got up and bowed courteously. "C'est moi!" he said, and went off towards a fruit stall with the look of a man determined to pinch the pears before he bought them.

"Are you going back with Chris? Where IS he, Larrie?"

"Trying to impress that stupid Lily girl with his new clothes," said Larrie in disgusted tones. "As if that'll work! She's such a pillock!"

"Why is she a pillock?"

"She eats horse meat!" said Larrie, tears springing into her eyes. "She says it's all they're good for and she doesn't care about their suffering, I mean a horse can feel a fly landing on its back, Muma, so just imagine what they feel..."

"Obviously a pillock, then," said Rosie quickly. "But there's no need to cry about it. You just work hard at school and then you can get into government and change the law!"

"Yes!" said Larrie angrily, her face going red, "I'll make the punishment for eating horses being hung up by your feet and having your throat cut slowly while you're..."

"Quiet!" said Rosie. "That's enough. Sorry Flo."

"Not at all," he said. "I can think of various people I'd like to hang up by their feet. Is all that pizza finished?"

They left Larrie polishing off the rest of the pizza while she waited for Chris, and walked back through the remains of the market to the car, Rosie weighed down with carrier bags and Flo carrying his bread-making machine as tenderly as a baby.

The vet had already got Spike back into his crate so it didn't take long to load him up into

Johnny. As Rosie pulled out her chequebook, the vet waved his hands at her and winked. No charge. For a second Rosie looked like she was going to argue. "I'd prefer to castrate him than be ordered to destroy him for biting some kid," said the vet. "And at least now I won't ever have to destroy his puppies." He shook hands with Rosie and she came back to the car glowing with pleasure.

"People are so kind!" said Rosie. "Come on, Flo. In you get. Chip-chop. Johnny might start, it's worth a try anyway. Just get in my side and slide over." She climbed in after him and turned the ignition. Nothing. Just a small click. "Shit!" she said and fished around under the dashboard. "Wretched wire's come loose again. Ah! Here we are, that should do it. Let's try again. Cross everything!"

Flo watched her, thinking what a nightmare it must be to have such an unreliable broken old car. But this time the engine roared into life when she turned the key and Rosie smiled. "Right," she said putting the emergency lights on. "Let's get out of here!" She pulled out into the road, apparently taking it for granted that everyone would stop for her and they did. "Johnny's such a mess, no-one wants to get in his way. They know I won't care about a few extra bumps and bruises," said Rosie. "And the brakes haven't worked since Noah got off the ark."

"Where's the gardener?" said Flo. "Isn't she coming with us?"

"She's not the gardener, she's called Nicole. And no, she's getting a lift home later."

"Why doesn't she eat with you, with us?" he asked.

"Doesn't want to," said Rosie with a grin. "She does sometimes, but she prefers to cook for herself, says we eat weird stuff at weird times. She's very French. Has to eat at precisely midday and 7pm. Doesn't approve of stir-fries or crackling or curry, and says corn on the cob is chicken food." Steering Johnny onto the main road out of town, Rosie put her foot down and Johnny accelerated, swaying from side to side like a monstrous goldfish, and sounding as if he was panning for gold. Holding onto the dashboard, Flo looked at the speedometer but they were only doing 60.

"Brakes are crap," yelled Rosie over the din. "But he goes all right." Flo tightened his grip.

Back at the château, Dolly and Minnie dashed out of the house and pranced around them as if they'd been gone for years rather than one morning. The big dogs bit each other's ears and ran in circles. Together they unloaded Spike, still in his crate.

"He might still be a bit woozy," said Rosie opening the cage. "Just hold Dolly, we don't want her jumping all over him."

Flo looked at the little white dog bouncing up and down at his feet. She looked rather dirty. "Pick her up!" ordered Rosie. Flo picked Dolly up, trying not to get too covered in filth. "You'll drop her!" snapped Rosie. "Hold her tight, close to your chest so she can't get away. Then she'll stop struggling. Pat her, for God's sake! Say something nice!"

Flo tried to obey and got a sharp little claw in the face for his pains. He hugged the dog tightly to his chest trying to keep his nose out of range of the rank and noxious fumes coming from Dolly's jaws. Dolly wriggled and panted, happily belching old dog dinner into Flo's disgusted mouth.

"Come on, Spike," said Rosie gently. "Atta boy, out you come." Spike staggered out of the cage and Rosie took his muzzle off. "You wouldn't bite anyone, no..." she crooned, "Spikey's a good boy, isn't he?" With her fingers under his collar, she walked him straight across the yard, and through the kitchen into the east wing.

Flo looked at the cage and wondered if he ought to try and fold it up. Or should he close the back of the Jeep? Or would the door jam if he did that? In the end he didn't do anything. He just put Dolly down and watched her race away after her mistress. Then he took his nice new bread maker into the kitchen where he could unpack it and start reading the instructions.

"I've just got to go out and check on Fanny," said Rosie coming back into the kitchen ten minutes later with a metal dog bowl in one hand. She had changed into her jeans and her hair was back in its usual ponytail. "Can you fill this and give it to Spike? No, sorry. That was silly. You don't know where he is and Spike might... right, I'll be back in a jiff! Just get some lunch on the table."

"Who, me?"

"Yes, you. Lunch! On table! Chip-chop!" She

filled the bowl at the tap and disappeared, leaving him sitting at the table apparently paralysed at the thought of opening a fridge door all by himself. Going back to Spike, she realised what a stupid thing she'd said, and almost went back to the kitchen. Flo was quite obviously completely useless for all practical purposes. Except one, said a naughty little voice in her head. Behave yourself, she replied sternly, he's useless, worse than a baby. He'll probably burn the place down. Or blow it up. Well, I'm not going back indoors, she thought.

In the kitchen, Flo had a pretty accurate idea of Rosie's thoughts and his pride was stung. It couldn't be that difficult. She hadn't asked him to cook anything, after all. Just put food on the table. He started opening cupboards and drawers, finding things like oil and strange dark red bean things, but nothing edible. He found some mustard and put that on the table, added a handful of tarnished silver teaspoons and filled the kettle on in the vague belief that they might want tea or something. Finally he opened the fridge and there were lots of things in there.

Twenty minutes later, Rosie came back into the kitchen. "I think I'm going to have to stay with her," she said and stopped short in the doorway. "Oh!"

Larrie and Chris were sitting at the table watching Flo energetically grating a cabbage. "He's already grated a box of mushrooms, two red peppers, a whole cucumber and nearly all the carrots," said Larrie without taking her eyes off Flo. "And he wants to know if we've got any dressing. Bottled island dressing."

"Grated mushrooms?" said Rosie.

Chris raised his eyebrows but Flo didn't raise his eyes from the grater. Going over to the table she looked in the massive bowl he'd chosen.

"It's salad," said Flo. "Lunch." He had that Labrador look in his eyes again. Where was her clicker when she needed it?

"We don't have bottled dressing but I could make some mayonnaise," she said. "Chris, why don't you boil some eggs or make an omelette or something? Larrie, lay the table. Put that mustard away. Where on earth did those teaspoons come from? Get the bread out, darling." She got the olive oil out and an egg and began whipping.

"How's the spaniel?" said Chris.

"Not good. I gave her some Rescue Remedy but she's walking round in circles and I'm worried that she won't settle. Sorry, I'll need the mustard out again. Spike's all right though. Bit woozy, but I put him in the green drawing room; he's on his own in there so he can get some rest this afternoon. I should think he'll be fine by din-dins. How are those eggs coming on? Have we got any bread?"

"There's a bit left from yesterday," said Chris.

"I can make some this afternoon," said Flo. "With my bread machine."

Behind his back, Larrie was gaping, rolling her eyes and pointing at the price tag on the box.

Rosie blinked. All that, on a whim! Holy crap.

"Eggs are up!" said Chris. "Here we go!"

Rosie ordered the dogs out of the kitchen, dolloped mayonnaise onto the salad, tossed it and served everyone with her big metal spoon. It was different but very nice, she had to admit.

"We met Pierre in the market," said Chris. "Says you work too hard. Wanted to know if we're going to the Halloween bash. I think he's hoping to kiss you under the spider's web."

"He's in lurve with Mummy!" said Larrie and snorted into her plate. "Kissie, kissie, kissie!"

"Nonsense!" said Rosie going pink, and Larrie giggled so hard that carrot went up the back of her nose and she choked. "He told everyone in the Bon Coin she's a beautiful woman!" she said, with her eyes streaming.

Chris grinned. "The faithful swain breaks cover," he said. "So he's finally declared his passion, has he?"

Red in the face, Rosie stood up and grabbed a piece of bread and cheese. After a minute's indecision, Dolly prepared to follow her pack leader. The grated din-dins didn't smell like proper food anyway.

"I am going to the dogs," said Rosie with dignity.

CHAPTER FOUR

As the door slammed, Larrie burst out laughing. "Going to the dogs!" she sniggered. "She's been barking all her life! Is there anything I could have for pudding? I'm starving."

"Aren't there any apricots left?" said Chris. "I brought a whole basket of them in from the orchard only the other day." He slipped a bit of cheese rind to Minnie and got up to clear the table.

"Can I set this up in here?" asked Flo. "I got some packets, all you have to do is put them in somewhere and then you have to fill it up with water, but all the instructions are in French. Can you read them?"

Together they cleared the table, went through the instructions, set the bread machine up, and flicked the switch to set it going. Two tabby cats sat on the work surface twitching their ears with curiosity, keeping watch over the new human weirdness.

"I hope it doesn't use too much electricity," said Larrie.

"It should be all right, there's nothing else

running is there?" answered Chris.

"Is electricity that expensive?" asked Flo curiously. "I mean surely it won't make that much difference to the bill?"

"No, it's not that," said Chris. "It's the wiring. We have old wiring, which only gives us access to a limited amount of electricity. If we try to use more, the trip-switch jumps and all the power goes off."

"And what about the gas?"

"That's just expensive, and the bottles are heavy," said Larrie. "That's why me and Muma share one deep bath rather than have two shallow ones."

"Larrie!" snapped Chris and shook his head.

"What?" she said. "What have I said? It's true!"

Flo looked from one to the other. Larrie was baffled, but Chris was pink with embarrassment.

"Any chance of a coffee?" asked Flo. "Is the kettle still hot?"

Neither of them answered, they were still making faces at each other behind his back.

"I'm going out for a ride," said Larrie, stuffing stale bread into her pockets. She picked up an apple and strolled out of the back door giving Flo a cheeky wink over her shoulder.

"No guns, no knives, no fireworks!" called Chris after her. "Wear your hat, don't canter on the road!"

"Keep you hair on, nanny," she called back breezily.

"Well, I've got to do some work," said Chris, and Flo raised his eyebrows. "If you weren't so busy you'd come and look at my work," said Chris. "Then you wouldn't scoff."

"I'm not that busy," said Flo. The truth was that after two weeks of sitting upstairs on his own, attempting to write notes for an autobiography he had little intention of ever writing, he was bored stiff. "Lead on."

"Allo!" called a male voice from the doorway. "Fifi? T'es là?" And then there was the sound of elaborate bumping and puffing. "Voilà!" said Pierre, emerging into the kitchen dragging a messy homemade trolley behind him. "Le vin!"

"I'll have coffee upstairs," said Chris, and promptly disappeared, leaving Flo to deal with the four large wine cases stacked on the trolley. For a moment, Flo almost called him back. What did the little sod think he was doing, dumping him in it like that? What if he couldn't understand the man? Unfazed, Pierre was unloading his trolley and stacking the cardboard cases in the corner. Four dozen of the best, as round and soft as you could hope for, he knew Rosie would love it, Flo would never regret such an investment.

Flo had no idea what he was saying but correctly interpreted it to be a general commentary on the wonderfulness of the contents, his own brilliance in sourcing and delivering it so quickly, and Flo's general undeservedness in the whole business.

"I say!" came another voice at the door. A woman's voice this time, old school, upper class, with flat vowels and precise consonants. "Shop!

Anyone at home?" She came stooping through the door into the kitchen, a great, gaunt woman with cheekbones that sparrows could have roosted on. "You must be the ghastly house guest!" she said without a smile. "Is Rosie around?"

"In the kennels," said Flo. "With a spaniel. Having puppies."

She gave a bark of laughter. "Ha! Her, or the dog? Doesn't matter, don't answer that." The laugh died and her face was as grim as before. "How do you do? Lotta, heroine's best girl-pal, ex-estate agent, ex-drunk, all round social outcast with heart of gold." She thrust her hand out, switching into French and talking to Pierre as she shook Flo's hand. Her face was leather-brown and her hair was a mass of unruly, iron-grey curls. Her nails were dirty and broken. Flo was offended. How dare she stick her hand out at him and then not pay any attention to whether he shook it or not? Rotten woman! He took a deep breath, humble-be-humble, and shook her hand.

"Well done," she said, flashing him a look and suddenly he wondered if she'd recognised him. "You have to pay this chap here, you know. He says you ordered all this wine this morning. He'll take a cheque."

Flo pulled a slim fold of euros out of his pocket. "How much?"

"Two hundred, and he says you're robbing him blind at that price, although I expect that's an exaggeration."

While Lotta went rattling on in French, Flo gave Pierre the money and allowed himself to be heartily slapped on the back. Lotta finally shut up and Pierre gave a great peal of laughter, made a few more comments and punched Flo's arm a couple of times before finally taking himself off, calling "Salut, Fifi!" over his shoulder.

"He says there's more where that came from," said Lotta, dumping her bag down on the kitchen table. "And if you don't like it, he'll sell you something else. You don't mind if I put the kettle on, do you?"

"No, why should I?" said Flo, glancing at the door.

"Don't run away. I want to talk to you," said Lotta. "What are you doing here? Do you want some tea? What IS this monstrous machine?" She gazed at him sternly and Flo felt like a six-year-old in primary school.

"It's a bread-maker," he muttered.

"Yours, is it?"

"They never have fresh bread," said Flo, stung. "And I..."

"Couldn't be bothered to go to the bakery for it?" interrupted Lotta, throwing a teabag into a cup. "Or you thought this would be cheaper?" She shuddered slightly.

"Whatever," said Flo. "Does it matter?"

"Absolutely not," said Lotta, pouring water into her mug. "Hardly anything really matters." She gave him another piercing look. "Except friends.

Making them, keeping them, protecting them from harm. So what are you doing here?"

Flo was stumped. She obviously wouldn't swallow a lie and yet he could hardly tell her the truth. "To be honest, I don't know," he said and she looked fractionally less disapproving. "Are they really that broke?" he asked suddenly. "I mean, the not buying bread and not turning electrical equipment on and saving gas and eating vegetables all the time?"

Lotta sat down at the table with her tea. "Yes," she said simply. "Yes, they are. They've got nothing. Not a bean. I can only suppose that's why you're here. You must be paying Rosie a fortune, because she certainly can't afford to feed an extra mouth."

"So... but why? I mean couldn't Chris...?"

"Get a job? There aren't any jobs around here. And in any case, he has a job. He's a photographer. A good one. And he teaches a bit. But this place eats money. Just the taxes on it every year are crippling. Without Chris, they wouldn't manage. So don't underestimate him."

"No, I..."

"And don't mess Rosie about. If you upset her you'll have me to deal with." She fished her teabag out of her mug and slopped in some milk, and Flo felt like banging his forehead with his fist. He was getting sick of Rosie's supporters warning him not to upset her.

"I'm not sure what I could do to you, but

I'm sure I'd find something," continued Lotta and he believed her. She looked exactly like the type of woman who wouldn't rest until she'd killed someone. Apparently indifferent to heat, she swallowed her tea in a gulp, and Flo noticed that the backs of her hands were covered in scratches.

"I garden," she said, finishing her tea. "Keeps me off the gin. You can call me if you ever need to." She fished in her pocket, pulled out a scrap of paper and scribbled a phone number on it.

"Thank you so much," said Flo automatically. Why on earth would he ever need to call her?

Lotta rinsed her mug in the sink and put it upside down on the draining board. "You might need to confess," she said and Flo had no idea what to say, but apparently she didn't expect a reply. "Must go. Tell Rosie I was here and ask if she wants some suet. Don't forget. Shredded suet. For the Christmas pudding. I think I can get her a packet, all right? I'll swap it for a worming tablet. Don't forget to tell her. Salut, Fifi."

"Don't call me Fifi!"

Feeling thoroughly ruffled, he watched her stride out of the kitchen and heard her footsteps retreating along the terrace. She must have parked at the front of the house. Meaning she must have a car that wouldn't withstand the lane. Another poverty-stricken, yellow-toothed, Froggie-lover.

He looked at the timer on the bread machine. It wouldn't be finished for another two hours. Hardly noticing his surroundings, he slammed out of the kitchen and mooched around the house with his hands in his pockets, not entirely sure where he was in the huge rambling corridors. He kept looking out of the windows to get his bearings. At one point he saw a small flock of what looked like miniature sheep gambolling in a green space beyond the barns. Until a fortnight ago, he wouldn't have given them a second glance. Now, he realised that they were dogs and they must be the same breed as Dolly. He smiled, thinking they looked like flying sausages with their funny little legs and fat curvy little bodies.

Finally he looked out of a window and saw the courtyard in front of the east wing and after that, he found his room quite quickly. Having stripped off the horrible dead wasp outfit that Chris had foisted on him that morning, he shivered and pulled a thick creamy Aran jumper on over a fine silk and cotton t-shirt. Now that the sun had gone down, there was a chilly edge in his room. He'd have to get a heater. Surely Sally could organise it for him?

In his head he could hear Chris jeering at him. "Can't organise a heater by yourself, Fifi?" He shook his head at himself in the mirror. He was obviously going as loopy as the rest of the inmates. He sat down and turned his laptop on, but made no pretence of working. He couldn't even cook. He only knew how to grate because that irritating bloody trainer had made him do it every day at lunchtime.

He almost opened a file called "autobiography notes" but in the end he just flung himself onto his bed and lay there on his back, trying to remember all the prizes he'd won for being handsome, talented, witty, sexy, and marvellous in every way. He must have dozed off because the next thing he knew, Larrie was bashing on his door. "Come on, come on, come on! Hurry up or they'll be none left! Didn't you hear us calling?"

Blinking, he rolled off the bed and scampered down the stairs after Larrie. In the kitchen, Nicole was presiding over the table. The room smelt wonderful, and he realised he was starving. "Your bread machine worked!" said Larrie. "We forgot about it but then when we came in to make supper it was there with the green light on and this yummy smell. I nearly ate the whole loaf because it wasn't very big. I mean it's not like the ones from the baker's. But we're going to put it on again. We can, can't we? And guess what?"

"Sit down," said Chris. "Just ignore her. Do you want some quiche?"

Nicole was standing at the head of the table with one hand on her hip, waving a knife in Flo's direction and giving him a grim scowl. Thinking that if provoked, she was quite capable of feeding his share to the dogs, he immediately passed his plate. Rosie might be off men, but Nicole had obviously never been on them in the first place. She had decent French notions about portions. She gave him a massive helping and topped it off with several enormous, extremely fresh, bright green lettuce leaves.

"Here, this is your bit," said Larrie, passing him a mangled chunk of soft warm bread.

Flo ate and his spirits lifted. Decent bread, decent salad and the best quiche he'd ever tasted. Soft and deep, crammed full of bacon, leeks and cheese. If Nicole could cook like this, she could be as grouchy as she pleased. He gave her a look of admiration and she returned it with a grim nod. He wondered if he could persuade her to teach him to cook, but the idea died almost at birth. Nicole would never teach him anything. While they ate, she stacked a large tray with food.

"Muma won't come in," explained Larrie. "She'll prolly be out there all night."

Once supper was over, Chris slid away again, Nicole stamped out into the darkness with a laden tray for Rosie, and Flo was left with Larrie who showed him how to clear the table, stack the dishes in the sink and put the kettle on, all the time talking about her horse. "The thing is, he was probably handled all wrong right from the beginning. I mean the way he is about plastic bags. You've read Monty Roberts, haven't you, so you can see that he's been frightened in his life which means he needs extra care, and lots of love and he misses me if I don't spend all day with him. He isn't just an animal, you know, he's a person too and horses have feelings."

"Why won't your mum let you be a stunt woman?" said Flo, turning the taps on.

"You've missed a bit on that plate," said Larrie pointing at the washing up. "It's none of your business."

"I just wondered, that's all."

"Well don't! I'm going to bed. You're just impossible, you know that? I was talking to you and you simply weren't listening!"

"I'm sorry. I was listening."

"Stow it. I'm tired anyway," said Larrie and stalked out of the room, slamming the door behind her.

Flo was tempted to fling the plate he was rinsing back into the sink. Bloody girl. Bloody place. What the hell was he doing here anyway? He really didn't have to put up with all this crap. And what was Rosie doing anyway? He was a guest, wasn't he? A paying guest, at that. So she ought to be in the house making sure he was all right.

He dried his hands and went off across the yard looking for Rosie. Having tried various doors, he found his way into the kennel block and followed the dim light until he found Rosie sitting on the floor in a large caged off area. She was humming almost inaudibly. Beside her, in a large basket, Fanny was lying so still that she almost looked dead. On her other side lay Dolly, with her head on her paws, and her eyes fixed on Rosie.

"Don't come any further," said Rosie in a soft, sing-song voice. "Stay outside the run. What do you want? I can't deal with you now. I'm busy." She looked up at him and her face was milky white and tear-streaked. Her grey eyes were large in her face and half her hair had come out of its ponytail.

Her hands were stained with dried blood. Even Flo could see that it really wasn't the right moment to complain.

"How's it going?" he whispered awkwardly.

"Two dead," she said in a low voice. "But the last one was ok, it's alive."

Flo didn't know what to say.

"I think it's a miracle," whispered Rosie. "This dog has never produced a live puppy before. Look, it's suckling now." A stray tear rolled down her cheek but she brushed it away with the back of her hand, leaving a bright red smear across her face. She gave him a wobbly smile and suddenly his heart contracted. She was completely mad, but she was also brave and compassionate and beautiful. There she sat with her huge eyes and her beautiful cloud of golden hair, and nothing except her own physical presence and a small bottle of Rescue Remedy between a litter of living puppies and another tragic failure.

"What can I do?" he asked and was amazed to hear a slight wobble in his own voice.

"You can take those away, I suppose," she said nodding at two small newspaper parcels lying on the ground. He eased the door open and bent down to pick them up, and Dolly raised her head and gave him a warning look. In her view, this business was girl-dog business. Man-dogs had no place around it.

"What do you want me to do with them?"

"I don't know," she said and her voice cracked. "Nothing. Leave it. I'll deal with them later."

A fortnight ago he would have taken her at her word. Now, he picked them up and tucked them under one arm, not even thinking that the newsprint would come off on the cream wool. He just felt stupid for having asked such an idiot question.

"Sorry," he said, "Don't worry. I'll deal with it."

"It's my fault. I should have called the vet," she said.

"I think you're doing fine," he said. "But I'll call the vet if you want me to. I'll pay. Whatever it costs."

"No, I think she's ok now. Can you just find something for Dolly to lie on? She's shaking with cold. Look in the feed store down there on your right. There should be an old sleeping bag in there."

Feeling numb, Flo crept silently out, retrieved the sleeping bag and then found himself dismissed.

"Thanks. You'd better go now. You're just being distracting. Fanny's never going to deliver the rest of this litter with you standing there." Then she just went on in the same low tone, "Here Doll-doll. Lie on this." She didn't even look at him and for a split second he thought about going and sitting next to her. "Go!" she whispered fiercely, "Basket!" And he went.

Outside, he gazed around him. What should he do with two dead puppies wrapped up in newspaper? Was he expected to bury them? Could he throw them on the dung heap? Should he put them in the bin? In the end he took them into the kitchen, wrapped them up tightly in several plastic bags and put them carefully into the dustbin. After that he didn't know what to do. It was barely nine-o clock but the château had gone to bed. He had never felt so alone and so ignored. Perhaps this was a good time to go and find Chris. He set off along the corridors, and then on a whim went up a narrow set of stairs to the first floor where he found himself in what must once have been a handsome picture gallery.

There were only a few paintings left on the walls and he guessed that the frames were probably worth more than the canvasses. Most of them were so darkened by dirt and time that they just looked like black oblongs. Dim light filtered in through the louvered shutters making soft stripes on the floor. He walked along the room, opened a door at the end, and was surprised to find himself in a music room.

A grand piano stood on a low dais, a huddle of music stands were clustered round a stack of cardboard boxes, and there were various chairs standing against one wall. He went over to one of the windows and after a struggle, managed to open one of the shutters. A ray of moonlight flooded across the faded threadbare carpet and he saw that the piano stool looked reasonably solid.

He sat down, opened the lid of the piano and touched the keys gently with his fingers. It was years since he'd played anything, and it probably wasn't in tune. He gently pushed a key down and was amazed at the sound, rich and true. He touched another one. And then, with his foot on the soft pedal, played a scale. The dampers needed attention but in fact the piano was remarkably in tune with itself.

He played the first few notes of Misty with his right hand and suddenly his left hand remembered the rest. The music was like a caress, a sweet comfort from the past and his fingers started to warm up. When he finished, he played Für Elise. The music filled the room and he forgot about playing softly. It was all coming back to him... he moved on to Eine Kleine Nachtmusik, playing from memory.

Outside in the kennel block, Dolly heard the piano being played and cocked her ears up. Rosie heard it too and was comforted. Fanny lifted her head, gazed at the pack leader with maternal pride and relaxed again. Everything was fine; it was relaxy noise. She already had two puppies suckling greedily and there were more coming. She felt warm and soft and kind, sucky and lovely. Puppy, puppy, puppy...

Flo closed his eyes and started a piece of Mozart, melodic and romantic. It had definitely been too long since he'd played. Perhaps he ought to get the piano tuned? He'd have to ask Pierre about it. In the meantime he let the music wash over him, body and soul.

In her cold and tightly-tucked bed, Nicole listened and sniffed loudly. Just because he was a musician and an artiste who could make you dream of loveliness, it didn't make him less of an evil rich bastard. Down in the kitchen, the big dogs snored and, oblivious to the outside world, Larrie dreamed about cantering Sobie along a beach.

In his studio, Chris heard Flo playing the piano and opened the door to let the music in. "Well I never," he murmured to Minnie. "Not such a Barbarian after all."

CHAPTER FIVE

Flo played for a long time, until he had played everything he could remember and, by the time he had finished, the moon had moved away, the room was in darkness and the house was silent. He stacked the music carefully and closed the lid of the piano. Then, hoping he'd be able to find the music room again, he walked slowly back along the picture gallery. From one of the windows, he saw a dim light still burning in the barn. Rosie must still be in there, patiently sitting up with her neurotic dog. Suddenly, for the first time in weeks, his phone rang. He snatched it out of his pocket. "Yes?" he said, his pulse racing.

"Where have you been?" snapped Sally. "I've been calling all day! Don't say it! Don't say a thing. You are in such deep shit, I think I've fended it off for the moment but if this one gets out, we're finished. I don't see how you'll ever rehabilitate yourself! You are so..."

"Why? What are they saying now?" asked Flo. He hated being judged by a pack of lousy hacks every time he moved his little finger.

"Just after I've finally finished sorting out that hotel room fiasco in Saudi! For God's sake, Flo! Public Love Rat No 1? I'm just so fed up with this shit. Why can't you ever do the right thing?" ranted Sally. "Why do you always fuck up? Especially as the Bond announcement is so soon!"

Flo couldn't even be bothered to ask what had happened. Obviously some scandal rag had run a story about him, and whether it was true or false everyone would believe it. He realised he didn't even care.

"Look, I've sorted it out for now, but I tell you, you're going to owe me big time. You stay there, be good, make them all believe you're a writer. Unless you've already blown it? Don't tell me you've blown it already?"

"They don't know! It's fine. Promise!"

There was silence; Flo could just hear Sally dragging at her cigarette and swigging gin from the bottle.

"All right," she said finally. "But this is the last time. The absolute fucking last time, do you hear me?"

"Don't worry, I'll be good."

"Hmmm," she said suspiciously. "Well in that case, it wouldn't do you any harm to write a few notes, for an autobiography. Just in case by some miracle you do get Bond - I could make you an extra million on a book deal. You won't even have to write it, just chat to someone about your life and they'll do all the actual writing."

For the first time in over a week, Flo wished he hadn't run out of Scotch. Why the hell hadn't he got some while he was in town? "I'll make some notes," he said, and after a bit of post-explosion venting, Flo slid his phone back into his pocket and walked slowly through Sleeping Beauty's palace back to his room. There, he drank a glass of brackish tap water and flung himself down on the bed where he lay staring at the ceiling. How had he got here? Finally he slept, but woke a few hours later with a shudder. His room was freezing. He groped for his watch. It was 6am and dawn was extending long silver-blue fingers into the world.

Shivering, he pulled a series of jumpers over his sleep-rumpled clothes and set off through the silent, frozen château to get some coffee, or tea. Anything hot to drink. From one of the windows, he saw that the light was still burning on the other side of the yard.

Out in the kennels, Rosie surfaced from sleep very slowly. She hurt all over, and someone was tugging at her fingers. She opened her eyes and closed them again and suddenly remembered. "The puppies!" she gasped and struggled upright. Everything was fine. Dolly was curled up on her sleeping bag snoring peacefully, and Fanny was lying serenely in her basket nursing a pile of soft little slugs.

"How many are there?" said Flo kneeling down beside her.

"Five," she said and shivered violently. "I think it's five. Unless she had another one." Her teeth were chattering and every joint ached.

"I brought you a coffee," he said. "I saw the light was on." Her face was luminous with exhaustion and she had huge tear-stained shadows round her eyes. Her hair was tousled and her lips all swollen with sleep. "Are you all right?"

She nodded. "What time is it?"

"About six."

She took the mug of coffee from him with trembling fingers. "Why are you? What? Why are you in here with coffee?" she asked, cupping her hands round the mug. It seemed so strange to her. He hates dogs she thought, and he hates kids. Weird, she thought, very weird. He hadn't shaved and she had a sudden impulse to touch the stubble on his face, perhaps even smooth her fingers along his eyebrows or run them through his badly cut hair. Instead, she looked back at Fanny.

"Is she all right?" asked Flo.

"I think she'll be ok now," said Rosie quietly, and drank some more coffee. She staggered stiffly to her feet and moved a couple of oblong straw bales closer to the basket so that there were no drafts. The minute she moved, Dolly woke up and followed her, looking as tousled and sleepy as her pack leader. Rosie inched carefully away towards the door, but Fanny didn't protest. Her ears cocked up, but then she relaxed again.

"That dog, she's never done that before," said Rosie with a small smile. "She's always been a terribly bad mother. Refusing to settle, miscarriages, stillborn litters, Caesareans, one thing after another."

"So why do they keep breeding her?"

"She's a very valuable dog; but it's not that. Her owner is desperate for a puppy so that when this dog dies, she'll have another one the same."

"Sound bonkers."

"I know. But that's what I do. I deal with aggressive dogs, frightened dogs, neurotic owners, problem owners, idiots, morons and pillocks. No-one brings me a well-adjusted, sane, healthy, properly trained dog. Why would they? Those sorts of dogs don't need me. Neither do their owners." They walked out of the barn together, Dolly valiantly toiling along behind them.

"Yes, but you could make money from proper dogs, couldn't you? I mean like boarding people's dogs? I know peop... I've heard that rich people pay fortunes for good kennels."

"I don't have the infrastructure. Rich people don't pay to have their dogs in kennels that can't be properly sterilised. I mustn't forget to phone Fanny's owner. I hope she'll be pleased."

As they approached the steps up to the terrace, Rosie shivered and he put his arm round her shoulders. He felt warm and strong. For the briefest of seconds, she was tempted to lean against him, lay her head on his shoulder, close her eyes, let him fold her in his arms, warm her up, breath life into her, kiss her. But then she thought how stupid she'd feel if she had another hot flush, so she pulled away and ran up the steps. "I need a shower," she said. "Thanks for the coffee."

She scurried through the house into her bedroom above the kitchen. There, she looked at herself in the mirror, touched her mouth, her cheek, the soft skin of her neck. Her skin was tingling all over, and she felt dizzy and breathless. Tired, she told herself. You're tired. She stripped her clothes off and showered, turning the water up scaldingly hot and to hell with the expense. Twenty minutes later, wearing fresh jeans and a thick jumper, she went back downstairs to find Flo inspecting the stove.

"How does this thing work?" he said pulling one of the doors open. "Is it heating oil or what? Is this where you put water, or cook? How do you turn it on?"

"It's solid fuel," she said, getting a loaf of bread out of the bread bin and cutting herself a thick slice. She wondered where the bread had come from; it didn't look like something from the local baker. "You can't turn it on, you have to light it. With matches. You need twigs, and then wood and some coal, but I'm not sure Pierre finished sweeping it. He couldn't get up on the roof."

"So when is he coming back?" he said.

"For God's sake!" she snapped.

Contrite, he held his hands up and moved towards her as if he was going to take her in his arms and hug her. In a panic, she grabbed a large wooden laundry paddle and ducked away behind the table.

"Don't you start that again," she said. "And pass the jam. No, just put it down there!"

"I'm really sorry," he said with his Labrador face, "I didn't think."

"Look, it's 7am on a Sunday morning," she said, refusing to look at him. "Why don't you go back to bed? Wrap yourself up in towels if you're cold and Chris'll find you some more blankets later. But right now, I have a lot to do. I need to walk Spike, deal with the bichons and get back to Fanny before she goes neurotic again and starts eating her puppies."

The thought of going back up to his room and sitting there all alone, bored out of his brains with nothing to do, made him shiver. He was sick of being a useless burden. "I could help," he suggested. "I could make tea."

"No! Basket! Go over there and stand by the door. I'll deal with you later."

Flo gawped at her. She really, truly didn't like him, she didn't even trust him to make tea. He was just another task on her list.

"Get to the door! And stay!" she ordered gesturing with the paddle, and he obeyed her in a daze. She glared at him, kicked the stove door shut, finished her bread and jam and made a pot of tea. He didn't say a word, just watched and took note. When she stomped out of the kitchen towards the new part of the château with her tea in a plastic bottle, he followed. She stopped and glared at him again. He took a pace back and raised questioning eyebrows. She raised a warning finger, and then set off again. Keeping his distance, he followed her to the once-handsome drawing room where Spike had been incarcerated since the day before.

She opened the door cautiously and as she went in, Spike launched himself towards her, his poor stumpy little tail jerking from side to side, his red tongue trying to lick her face. "Come in and shut the door. Ignore the dog. We'll just wait for him to calm down and then I'll take him out."

She yawned, drank some of her tea and leaned on the mantelpiece while Spike capered clumsily around her.

"Please let me do something," said Flo, genuinely humble for the first time in his life.

Rosie made a mental note that he was starting to realise that he wasn't top of the pecking order, and gave him a click. So he wanted interesting activities, did he? She drank some more tea. "Fold those blankets up if you like, bring those bowls," she ordered Flo. "And see if he's done a poo anywhere. Don't forget the water. Come here, Spike."

Spike obligingly trotted over and Rosie inspected his rear end. It was covered in silver wound spray but she could see that the stitches were fine, he hadn't been pulling or picking at them and there didn't seem to be any inflammation. She patted him on the head. "You good boy, aren't you?"

Flo swallowed nervously. "That's what you do to aggressive dogs? Castrate them?"

"Yes, but you also need proper training for it

to work," she said. "He's had to learn that he's not top dog, and he's had to stop some bad habits like snapping at people to get their attention."

"So how did he learn that?"

"I don't have time to teach you dog training right now," she said. "Just bring all that stuff. Don't forget to wash that dog bowl. Spike! Heel!"

She walked out of the room with Spike trotting happily beside her and trailing along behind, Flo winced at Spike's poor silver bottom. But perhaps it was better than being put down.

In the kitchen, she gave him Spike's lead. "Take him out but don't let him off. If he pulls give just one firm tug so he knows you mean it. Then let the lead go slack." His heart thumping, Flo led Spike onto the lawn so that he could water a handy rose bush, but the animal was perfectly docile. So feeling more confident, he led him back to the door for a drink, after which he and Spike followed Rosie back to the kennel block. Flo had a sense of complete unreality. Spike seemed to have undergone a complete character transformation, and as for himself - what on earth was he doing out of bed at dawn leading a castrated boxer around a derelict château? Had he also had the chop?

"Okay, put him in there," said Rosie, pointing at a small outdoor run. "I don't want him doing too much exercise today. Give him some dog biscuits, just a half ration. They're in the bin."

She clicked her teeth at Spike and his ears pricked up in response. "Good boy," she said, and went in to see how Fanny was doing. Left alone, Flo didn't know whether he was supposed to give Spike the biscuits all at once or feed them to him one at a time. What exactly was half a ration? And was he meant to take the lead off or what?

But Rosie wasn't paying him any attention. She was peeking through the wire door at Fanny. No need to worry. Everything was fine. The dog was completely calm and the puppies were all suckling. Closing the wire door firmly behind her, she went in for a closer look. Moving quietly, she picked up all the bowls and plates scattered around the floor and went to the door where she was surprised to find that Flo was there to take them from her. "Get a bowl of clean water," she said. "She might be thirsty. Tap in the courtyard."

She watched him obediently trotting off down the barn for a second before she called, "Rinse the bowl before you refill it!" Then she went back and bundled the dirty newspaper into an old coal sack. A few minutes later, Flo came back with the water, and then having given Fanny a double ration of food, she made up a clean basket. Fanny's ears were twitching but her eyes were calm and although she kept watching Rosie, she also kept on eating. "You good girl," soothed Rosie. Very slowly, she put her hands under the top layer of newspaper, gathering all the puppies up in it, and transferred them to the new basket. Fanny instantly climbed into the clean basket, sniffing possessively.

"Okay, we'll just leave her alone now. She'll

finish her food when we've gone." She picked up the vegetable crate containing the remains of last night's picnic and the untidy bundle of dirty newspaper.

"Time for breakfast?" said Flo helpfully.

Rosie wanted to smile but then firmly told herself not to. It might encourage him, and that would never do. "Bichons next," she said sternly.

"What are they here for? Who do they belong to?"

"They're mine. I breed them. They're Dolly-dogs and in theory should make a lot of money but the overheads are enormous. And I can't bring myself to sell them to idiots." She went out through the back door of the barn, sensing that Flo was walking just behind her, his broad shoulders swinging slightly, his long legs moving in time with hers. She knew she ought to make him back off again, but she just kept on walking.

He followed her into another more modern farm building with a concrete floor. As soon as she opened the door the yapping started, and it got louder as they went through two wire mesh doors and into a large run containing a flock of little white dogs, who all frolicked around Rosie as if they had been locked up for years. She waded through them to yet another door and the dogs all surged after her, bouncing and wagging and yapping. She opened the door and they all rushed outside.

"That's a lot of dogs," said Flo.

"Mmm. Fourteen all together. But three of

them are retired; they've been spayed. And one of them just doesn't seem to breed, but what can you do? I can't just have her put down." Rosie closed her eyes and leaned against the door. Lack of sleep was starting to catch up with her.

"Why don't you go to bed?" said Flo. "Surely there's nothing that can't wait."

"I'm too tired to go to bed. I have to check their water."

He smiled at her. "I'd offer to carry you if I didn't think you'd hit me with a bread knife or something."

She gave him a smile then. "Sorry, was I a bit rude?"

"No, not a BIT rude," he said, pulling a stupid face and at that she did laugh.

"Oh I'm sorry," she said. "I just hate being mauled about."

"Perhaps I could push you in a wheelbarrow?" he suggested. "Then I wouldn't have to touch you at all."

Rosie blushed. "No, I'll be all right," she said, and went outside, where she refilled the water drinker. Walking back towards the house she said, "If you really want to help, you can let the big dogs out. They're in the little laundry room behind the stove. Take them out, give them a drink and then when they come back, make sure you wipe their paws if they've been down to the stream. OK? Once you've done that, they get one biscuit each and they'll probably just lounge around on the sofas."

"What about your dog? Dolly? Where is she?"

"Oh, she'll have gone to bed in Larrie's room. I shouldn't think either of them will get up until at least lunchtime."

They got to the kitchen and Rosie noticed that Flo was making an elaborate show of keeping his distance. So much the better, she told herself firmly. She definitely didn't want him taking advantage of her, touching her, holding her, kissing her exhausted mouth, slipping his hands inside her clothes...

"I could make you a cup of tea?" he said. "Coffee?"

She shook her head. "Damn," she said, "we left the picnic stuff in the barn."

"I'll get it. Go to bed!" he said.

She wondered what it would be like to hear him say, "Come to bed," and realised that she was hallucinating with fatigue. Going slowly up the stairs, she wished she had the courage to smile at him, bat her eyelids, leave her door open... Going mad with exhaustion, she stripped her jeans off, crawled into bed and fell asleep.

It was the start of a gruelling few weeks. The harder Rosie drove Flo, the more he insisted that he wasn't tired, wasn't bored, was perfectly ready to do a bit more. He got soaked with water trying to groom the bichons, snapped at by Fanny, learned the hard way how to put Dolly's coat on, cleared up acres of puppy poop, scrubbed the bichon run daily with a yard broom, walked Spike until both of them were out of breath, watched classes in obedience and agility, learned how to lead-train a dog, and washed up dozens of dog bowls and plates every day. Rosie was secretly impressed, and Flo was openly amazed at the amount of work involved in keeping a few mutts happy and healthy.

The favourite part of everyone's day was playing with Fanny and her puppies. Once they started weaning, Fanny was happy for them to tumble around in their large outside run. Larrie loved every inch of them, from their soft floppy little ears to their crazy helicopter tails. "Pup-pup-puppies!" she would call in a high-pitched voice and they would all scamper after her, falling over their paws and squealing like furry piglets.

And then Spike discovered the puppies. He froze on the spot, obviously unsure how to react. Flo threw his head back and laughed but poor Spike was backing away in terror.

"Hey, boy... good boy, come here," said Flo, reassuring him and petting him before Rosie even had time to intervene. She was amazed. What had happened to the man who hated dogs? As he bent over the huge boxer, she could see the fine strong lines of his neck and shoulders and a patch of soft skin where his jumper had ridden up. He seemed to have an all-over tan. Mentally disciplining herself with a willow switch, she retreated to her study and started drafting an advert for the local paper. One of the gals was pregnant and she really ought to try and find homes for the Granny Bichons.

Life with Flo was an unexpected revelation. Sally's cheque had been a life-saver, but Flo was turning out to be even more useful. Although the whole family teased him for being a gadget-head, obsessed with buying crazy kitchen machines on Saturdays, he had taken over much of the physical slog in the kennels. "I don't know what we ever did without you," she said one day mid-October.

He gave her one of his disturbing, twinkly smiles. "Oh you were just waiting for me to come along, weren't you?" he teased.

They walked back to the house together. "There's somebody coming to see the Granny Bichons," she said. "I'm not sure whether to give them away completely or retain legal ownership in case something goes wrong and I need to take them back, you know?"

They walked into the kitchen and she broke off short. There was a strange girl sitting at the table with a snivelling child on her lap. The girl was very young; pale and tear-stained with a soft pink mouth, and large, cloudy-grey eyes surrounded by smears of black make-up. She was wearing a multi-coloured 50s frock with Doc Martens, and her jet-black hair stuck up in all directions round her head. The child on her lap was the ugliest boy Rosie had ever seen. He was small, and dirty with large ears, a flat nose, bottle-bottomed glasses and a shaven head covered in stitches.

But if Rosie was surprised, Flo was transfixed. "What are you doing here?" he managed at last.

"He's your son," said the girl and burst into tears.

CHAPTER SIX

Rosie stared at Flo, trying to imagine what had possessed him to seduce this child, but apparently paralysed, he was just staring at the girl with horror. "I think we need tea, don't you?" she said, and filled the kettle.

"Sylvia threw us out," the girl told Flo, scrubbing her eyes with one fist. "So I went to your agent's office and she said you were at Château Moisson in the south of France, but she wouldn't give me a phone number. Just said thank God Moisson wasn't on the map and sent us back to Sylvia's, but then we got thrown out again."

"Jesus Christ!" said Flo, his fists clenching involuntarily. "That's what Sally was ranting about."

"It's bercos I'm unperpossessing," said the little boy in a cracked whisper, "and dirty." He shivered, and buried his head in the girl's shoulder.

"No, you're not," she reassured him, and hugged him closer.

His face drained of colour, Flo went and kneeled down beside them. "He held his arms out, but the boy shrank away. "Daisy, what the hell happened?" he asked. "Where have you been all this time? Are you all right? Are you hurt?"

Rosie put a large mug of tea at Daisy's elbow.

"I'm all in," she croaked. "But we're all right."

"Are you hungry?" asked Rosie. "What about your little boy? What does he eat?"

"He only really eats tinned sardines, but I don't think he'll eat anything now."

"What about some milk?" asked Rosie, and the boy's head nodded. "Chocolate milk? I'm afraid we haven't got any fizzy drinks."

"Choclit," said the hoarse little voice.

"Okay, we can do that," said Rosie putting a mug of tea on the table. "Sit, Flo. Sit up to the table, and drink your nice tea." She turned back to the girl. "What's your son's name, dear?"

"Oh, he's not mine," said Daisy. "I'm just the au pair." She had a faint, soft American accent. "Sylvia is his mother, but she threw us out."

"Are you serious? This child's mother threw you out of the house? Both of you?" Rosie was utterly shocked. She knew people would be callous about animals, but it had never occurred to her that some of them could also be cruel to children.

Daisy nodded. "She was always doing it."

"And does she know where you are now?"

Daisy shrugged.

"But Sally knew what was going on?" interrupted Flo. "I am going to kill her. Why didn't she tell me? Why didn't Sylvia ring me, come to that?"

"She doesn't like you much, neither of them

do," said Daisy, shifting the boy to the other knee. "I don't think anybody does."

Flo went ghostly pale and Rosie automatically patted his shoulder. "I do," she said. "I like you. You're a very good boy."

"I figured you couldn't be any worse than Sylvia, but I couldn't find your number. I looked through her papers when she was out but the only useful thing I found was his passport. I was just so sick of being locked out." She blushed and then continued quickly, "So when she threw us out again, I went back and got it while she was at the gym. And I took some cash too, to pay for the train."

"But how on earth did you find us?" said Rosie, reaching for the Rescue Remedy.

An exhausted tear ran down Daisy's face but she brushed it away. "I googled "Moisson" and found the village, so we got the train to Aix and then I took a taxi. The driver knew exactly who you were. Said you helped train his dog."

"What's this about her throwing you out all the time?" demanded Flo.

"You know what?" said Daisy in a fading voice. "I..." She flicked a meaningful glance at the boy on her lap.

"Yes, of course! We'll discuss it later," said Flo pulling himself together with a huge effort. "I'm so sorry. Drink your tea!"

"Anyway, we're terribly glad to see you," said Rosie brightly. "I hope you're staying because we've got puppies and we need someone to help us find names for them." She smiled at them encouragingly, but neither the little boy nor his nanny responded and she raised mental eyebrows. What sort of children didn't like puppies? She was used to dealing with waifs and strays, but these two were so young. She wondered where she could get a tin of sardines at this time of night. Perhaps Nicole had some in her store cupboard?

"Hot or cold chocolate milk, angel?" The boy's shoulders twitched. "You can have it hot if you like," she said. "It's no bother." The little head nodded again.

"You wanna come and sit on my lap?" asked Flo, but the little boy still shrank away from him.

"He's wet," said Daisy. "Accident in the taxi. He was sick too."

"No problem. This hot chocolate's nearly done. Perhaps you'd like to bring him upstairs with me and we'll get you both cleaned up," she said. "What's his name?"

"Sebastian," said Flo.

"I'm a dirty nuisance," came that hoarse little voice again.

"I never called him that," said Daisy, picking him up. "I call him Steve, after Stevie Nix. Don't I, Steve? Stevie the Wonder Boy?"

He nodded.

"His mom calls him Sebastian, but he doesn't like it."

Steve stuck his tongue out and Rosie winked at him. "Well, we can call you Steve, if you like," she said. "What do you think, Flo?"

"Don't ask me!" he said. "I've got a girl's name!"

"Why?" said Steve.

"Because I looked a bit girly when I was a kid. All the men in our family are a bit weedy as kids. But we usually hit six foot in the end. I expect you will, too."

Steve looked thoughtful for a moment, but then he shook his head. "No, cos I'm a runt."

Rosie poured the hot chocolate into a mug, picked up a packet of Jaffa cakes and led the way upstairs. So Flo had a son. Were there any more offspring? And what about this child's mother? As far as she could gather, the woman sounded criminally negligent. But faced with a pair of dirty, starving exhausted children - Daisy looked hardly older than 16 - she didn't have time to worry about Flo. These youngsters needed to be warmed and dried, groomed and fed and popped into a nice clean kennel and, once they'd had a good night's sleep, she would see what could be done for them.

While Daisy and Steve were washing in the bathroom, she unpacked the rucksack which Daisy said was Steve's luggage, piling things on the table in her bedroom. There really weren't any suitable clothes in there. Everything was torn and dirty and in any case, too lightweight and completely impractical. It was nearly November; he would need proper warm winter clothes. Especially in the unheated château. Daisy's luggage seemed to consist of a fraying patchwork nosebag containing a make-up kit, a phial of patchouli oil and several boxes of loose love beads.

She dug out some of Larrie's spare clothes, and left Daisy changing Steve. Down in the kitchen, she found him furiously jabbing at his phone and swearing. "Nobody's fucking talking to me! Fucking Sally's got her phone turned off!"

"Who's Sylvia?" ask Rosie. "Don't you think you ought to tell me what's going on? How many children have you got?"

"Just one. As far as I know. The bitch, the cow, the fucking..."

Rosie reached into her pocket for the Rescue Remedy. "Open up," she said holding the dropper in front of his face.

"Fuck off, Rosie. I'm busy."

"It's your choice. If you want to deal with this like an idiot in a blind rage, carry on. If you want to calm down and behave like a rational adult, open sesame!" A second later, he opened his mouth and she dosed him up. "Good boy," she said. "Now drink your tea and just tell me the story from the beginning. Who's Sylvia?"

He took a deep breath. "It's not a great story. I'm not proud of myself. It... Sylvia, she was a one-night stand. A club, what does it matter? The point is she got pregnant. I'm usually pretty careful about that stuff but she said she was on the pill. Maybe she lied, maybe it was a genuine accident. Anyway, a year's worth of legal expenses and a DNA test later,

I ended up paying her a fortune in maintenance but with less access than the postman."

"Really? And why was that?"

He blushed and shrugged. "I was going through another court case at the time. Public disorder. Brawling. Drunk and disorderly. I hit a policeman. The judge said I wasn't fit."

Rosie couldn't help laughing. "And Sally told me you were a withdrawn, gay, half-blind, Woolworths-loving writer specialising in antique maps! But you're clearly some sort of psychopathic millionaire playboy on the run from the mob. Just why are you here?"

He gazed at her for a long moment, and then suddenly decided to tell her truth. She would find out eventually in any case, and he'd to feel bad about lying to her. He nodded, and took a deep breath...

"Muma! There's someone in your room!" said Larrie bursting into the kitchen. "The light's on and I saw them through the window when me and Sobie came back. But I don't care about that. Guess what? The Halloween Fête is going to have fireworks!"

"Those jods are filthy!" said Rosie. "Off with them!" Larrie obediently started undoing the zip. "Not in here, idiot! Go into the laundry room and change; there are clean jeans in there. And if there aren't, call me and I'll find some!"

Larrie dropped her anorak on the floor and went off still raving about fireworks, "We can go, can't we Muma? We'll have to take Johnny cos I can't ride over if they're letting off fireworks. Do you think they'll have rockets?"

"Put some thick socks on too!" called Rosie. "I don't want those paws getting cold!" She turned back to Flo. "What do you think? Does Stevie normally share with Daisy?"

Flo shook his head. "I don't know. We'll have to ask them."

"I think the rooms on this side are more cosy. They are nearer the kitchen and they could wake me if they needed to in the night. And they wouldn't get lost."

"I'm really sorry," he said. "I never meant this to happen."

"It's not your fault," she said. "But I don't think we've got any sardines. Not until the shops open tomorrow morning anyway."

"He shook his head guiltily. "I didn't know what was happening, I honestly didn't. Listen, Sylvia made this whole big thing of how she was the perfect mother and how I was so unfit and that's why I should pay so much, so she wouldn't have to work and could devote herself to the baby... and the judge agreed and the social workers pretty much ordered me to leave them alone. I mean I've only seen him a handful of times. I thought he was living the life of Riley."

Flo clearly wasn't really much more grown-up than his ugly little son. "Right now, you peeling potatoes. We'll make some chips for a treat. I'm going to light the stove." Flo meekly rolled up his sleeves.

Lighting the stove was a bit of a battle, as it was every autumn. First Rosie had to unearth the kindling box, and the coal buckets, the poker, the riddling handle, and the shovel. Then once she'd laid a fire she had to use about six matches because the chimney was cold so it didn't draw properly; the firebox seemed to have forgotten what to do and faint wisps of smoke started snaking into the kitchen. But finally the fire roared into life, the chimney drew properly and the stove began to heat up.

At supper Larrie was in her most boisterous mood and Rosie was determined to cheer Steve up so he would eat something. Between them they kept up a non-stop stream of nonsense and Flo made an effort to join in. Steve sat on Daisy's lap and drank half a cup of milk while Daisy wolfed down three stuffed peppers and a huge plate of chips without speaking a word. Chris came in halfway through, but didn't seem particularly surprised to find two newcomers at the table. He was more interested in the chips.

"This is Flo's son Steve, and his nanny Daisy," said Rosie.

"Good show," he said, shoving a ginger cat off his chair. "As you'll have realised, we don't normally have fried things," he told Flo. "Muma won't cook them because she says they're unhealthy and Nicole won't because she says it's cultural colonialism. Is there anything else, or is it just chips? Not that I'm complaining."

"I'm sorry darling, I thought you'd gone out," said Rosie. "There were stuffed peppers but they've all gone. But I've got lots of eggs..."

"I guess I ate your share," said Daisy in a low voice. She was as pale as her empty plate and kept yawning.

"Chris was doing kissie kissie kissie!" announced Larrie gleefully. "With Lily Lipstick! In town!"

"No," said Chris. "You're wrong. She says she wouldn't be seen dead in a Renault 4, especially not with me." He gave them a twisted smile. "She went to the cinema in Aix with that Duchère clown."

"Not Alain!" gasped Larrie. "You know in school they say he eats hedgehogs! Roasted ones!"

Steve's eyes widened. "Real ones?" he croaked.

"Yes, he digs them out of the fields in the middle of the night with an empty skull, and he..."

"Larrie, that's enough!" said Rosie. "You'll be giving Stevie nightmares with your silly stories!"

Larrie pulled a hideous zombie face at Steve, but she shut up.

"So how long are you staying?" Chris asked Daisy. "Are you coming to the Halloween party?"

"I don't know," she said and shook her head, making her earrings jingle.

Once all the chips had been gobbled up, Rosie and Chris went off to drag a second single bed into the spare room next to Rosie's. They also found a couple of little tables and a chair. "We need a working lamp, if we can find such a thing. Just for tonight and then tomorrow we'll see what we can do. I wonder what happened to that mat with all the roads on it? The one you used to play cars on..."

"I have never played cars, either on or off that hideous mat."

"Didn't you darling? I thought you loved it."

Daisy appeared at the top of the stairs holding Steve by the hand. Flo followed them, looking around curiously. He hadn't been into that part of the house before.

"We'll do better tomorrow," promised Rosie. "Now you two, go and get into your pyjamas, while I find some bedding and a rubber sheet... I think I still have one."

"Left over from me before you ask," Chris told Flo, "Larrie's room is that way, Muma's is over there. And don't gloat."

"Wouldn't dream of gloating," said Flo. "Had the same problem myself." He was rewarded by one of Chris's rare smiles.

By the time Rosie had made up the beds, both Daisy and Steve were wearing pyjamas and bedsocks. They went to bed immediately and, although Rosie would have liked to talk to Flo, Larrie insisted on telling her about the fireworks while she washed up, and by the time she'd let the dogs out, the moment had passed and everyone went to bed.

Rosie was woken three hours later by Dolly scrabbling at her duvet and whining. She sat up rubbing her eyes, and suddenly heard another, more heart-rending, noise coming from the other side of the corridor. She got out of bed, and pulling a thick dressing gown on, went to investigate. In the spare room, she found Steve sobbing and choking into his pillow. On the other side of the room, Daisy was fast asleep, her thick lashes brushing her pale cheeks and her breathing deep and regular.

"What's wrong," whispered Rosie.

"Sorry, sorry, sorry," he choked. "I'm dirty horrible boy."

"No, you're not," she said, realising that his pyjamas were soaked. "All my puppies wet the bed every night. It's completely normal. You can do it as much as you like. That's why I got all these spare sheets out. Here, have some Rescue Remedy. Good boy, now come out of bed. Let's have those jimmy bottoms. Have you got any more somewhere?"

He shook his head. "What happened to your head?" asked Rosie stripping his pyjama bottoms off. "How did you get all these stitches?"

"I deserved it," he said. "Cos I'm dirty."

Rosie didn't know what to say. "Have you got any clean pants or shorts?" she asked. "Does Daisy always sleep like that?"

"She sleeps like a mog," he said.

"Like a log?"

"No, a mog. A cat."

He was a funny little kid. "You like cats, do you?"

"Yes, cos they're dirty fleabags too."

Rosie finished stripping the sheets off and remaking the bed. "Well, now let's see you sleeping like a mog," she said. "And if you wake up again, you just come and find me." She showed him her room and then sat and held his hand until he fell asleep, by which time she was wide-awake. Thoroughly shaken by Steve's revelations, she pulled on some thick socks, threw a blanket over her dressing down and crept downstairs to make some tea. She was surprised to find the lights on and Flo boiling the kettle.

"Oh," she said, all of a sudden acutely conscious of not being dressed. "Couldn't you sleep either?"

"You look about 12 years old," he smiled. He was wearing soft charcoal sweatpants, a luxuriously thick dressing gown and a pair of sheepskin slippers. Rosie watched him getting the teabags out and noticed that her pulse was racing. Yet again. Bloody hormones. She went and huddled by the stove.

"Have you been to sleep at all?" he asked.

"No, yes, I er... Dolly woke me up. Stevie wet the bed. He was very upset about it."

"That cow."

"What's going to happen to him, Flo?"

"He's not going back to Sylvia," he said, making two mugs of tea. "No way. But it's going to be a nightmare. It could be lawyers, court cases, every damn thing."

"But if she doesn't know where he is, and hasn't reported him missing, can't you just keep him here?"

"Nice idea, but If I'm going to convince everyone that I'm a fit parent, I'll have to tell her that he's here. Otherwise it will look like I'm irresponsible or heartless or that I kidnapped him or some damn thing. I just hope she doesn't insist on me sending him straight back." He stabbed at the teabags, slopped milk into the mugs and pushed one towards Rosie.

"Would she do that?"

"Who knows? If she thinks I want him, she might. My only hope is that once she realises how badly she'll look if the pre... if people find out that she threw her own son out, then she might let me keep him. Especially if I go on paying. If I stop, she might do anything. But whatever happens he's staying here with me for the time being." He stared moodily into his mug.

"Well he'll need some clothes," said Rosie. "And sardines. And other stuff. It's freezing up there. He needs proper pyjamas."

"Don't worry, I have a credit card. You can buy him anything you like tomorrow."

"Me?"

He came towards her and took one of her hands in his. "Christ, your hands are cold! Rosie, please, please, please can you take my son shopping tomorrow morning and take Daisy along too, so that I can concentrate on ringing foul Sylvia, and ranting Sally and my disgusting lawyer, and try to sort this mess out?

Rosie nodded and gazed at her hand, enfolded in Flo's. Her heart was beating so fast that speech was impossible. She really would have to make an appointment with her GP.

"I will give you my credit card," he went on, "and the pin code. Just buy whatever he needs. Don't worry about prices, it won't matter. Spend whatever you like. Oh Christ, I've just remembered I asked a piano tuner to come tomorrow! Sorry, hope you don't mind." He rubbed her hand between his and then took the other one and rubbed that too. "You're so cold," he said tenderly. She was so adorable all wrapped up in her blanket...

Rosie suddenly had the insane idea that if she moved just a tiny bit, even just a centimetre towards him, he'd take her in his arms. She took a deep breath and pulled herself together. "A piano tuner? You're crazy," she said breathlessly. Her heartbeat was misbehaving. It was definitely a hot flush. "Yes, I'll take him shopping tomorrow!" she croaked, trying to pull away.

"Are you all right?" he said, moving to put his arm around her. She almost looked like she was going to faint.

"Basket!" she gasped suddenly. "Behave yourself! Stop it!"

He moved back instantly, but he had a little smile on his lips. "I expect you want your tea, don't you?" he said. "Would you mind if I come upstairs with you?" The little smile became a broad grin. "Just to see that Stevie's all right, of course."

She could hardly refuse to let him see his own son, so she nodded and watched him pick up the two mugs of tea. He gave her a mug and her knees were jelly. Her legs kept going weak. The menopause was obviously going to be more debilitating than she'd anticipated. "You go up first," she said.

Upstairs, they went and stood beside Steve's bed. He was fast asleep with his thumb firmly stuck in his mouth, making sweet little snoring noises. They crept back out into the corridor and Rosie paused outside her room.

"Well, I'll say good night then," she whispered.

He leaned so close to her that she could feel his warm breath on her skin. His hand reached behind her, opened her bedroom door and pushed it open. She took a tiny step backwards, refusing to look at him. He lent closer to her again and she stood as still as an English setter scenting a squirrel.

"Good night sweet sprite," he said and very, very softly kissed her on the forehead.

She tried to say goodnight but her throat was dry so she only managed a faint croak. Stepped backwards into her room, she quickly closed the door and leaned against it, listening to his retreating footsteps. Dolly, who had taken the opportunity to scramble into the pack leader's bed and curl up on her pillow, opened one gleaming black eye.

"He called me a sprite," said Rosie.

Dolly burped, and a satisfying whiff of half-digested cat sick filled the room. Rosie choked and came to her senses. Booting Dolly off the bed, she climbed back into it and although she felt she'd never calm down enough to get back to sleep, she fell soundly asleep leaving her tea untouched. In the morning when she went downstairs, there was no sign of Flo and she told herself it was just as well. She had a lot to do, dealing with the dogs, making a shopping list, pushing Larrie onto the school bus, and grabbing a coffee before going upstairs to wake Daisy and Steve.

"Do you want to come shopping with me?" she asked him. The little boy didn't reply, just burrowed under the covers so only the top of his head was showing. "I want to buy you some new clothes, and you can chose them if you like." He didn't move. "Would you prefer it if Daisy came too?" He emerged slowly and looked nervously at the heap of Daisy's back as she slept.

Rosie went over to Daisy's bed and tugged gently at her earlobe. "Come on Daisy, get up! Up you get!" She made a mad face at Steve but he still looked dubious. She tugged the covers right off the bed and sang, "Up you get! Rise and shine!" Steve put his hands over his eyes, but Daisy just opened her eyes and laughed. She'd slept really soundly, hadn't heard a thing, and was completely ready to go shopping.

CHAPTER SEVEN

In town, Rosie felt paralysed. With such a long shopping list she didn't know where to start, and Daisy and Steve were no help at all. In SuperU, Steve was too scared to express any preferences and Daisy kept wandering off and exclaiming "awesome!" whenever she saw anything that struck her as particularly French.

Finally she bought half a dozen tins of sardines, two multi-packs of cheap boy's underwear and some t-shirts and jeans. Gathering confidence, she moved on to Intermarché for jumpers and a thick anorak and half a dozen pairs of pyjamas, after which she drove into the centre of town and dispatched Daisy and Steve to the Bon Coin with instructions to buy hot chocolate and pains au chocolat. Then she kicked her way through the falling leaves to the pram shop for a new rubber sheet and while she was in there, bought a beautiful golden brown teddy with a serious face, velvet paws and a cherry-red bow. In the household linens shop, she bought a new duvet cover and some pillowcases. There was no point in buying sheets, she had dozens of old ones already. Feeling that she'd saved Flo lots of money, on the way back to the café she made several more purchases in the toyshop.

She was amazed Flo would just let her loose with his credit card. He was obviously much richer than she'd thought.

"Ah... I see you liked the hot chocolate," she said, going into the Bon Coin to find Daisy and Steve sitting either side of a dark varnished table. She slid onto the red leatherette banquette beside Daisy. "How many pains au chocolat did you eat? More than four each?"

Both of them shook their heads seriously.

"No? You only had two each? Pathetic! Well, I have just one or two more things to buy and then we'll go and find some pizza." If there was one thing Rosie couldn't stand, it was badly fed puppies. Jeanette came over and she ordered an espresso and drank it feeling guiltily extravagant - she only ever bought coffee in town on high days and holidays. Then she whisked her charges off to the shoe shop and kitted the pair of them out with Kickers, Wellingtons and thick slippers. The kids would get frostbite walking round the château in bare feet at this time of year.

Then she thought of a whole list of other things and they had to go back to SuperU for Junior Raspberry toothpaste, a musical toothbrush and a tub of multi-vits. She threw everything in the trolley, added a thick woollen poncho and some pyjamas for Daisy and then insisted on attacking the food aisles.

"And you can ride in the trolley if you like," said Rosie. "Like that boy over there." After a minute Steve nodded and she lifted him right into the main bit of the trolley. He was worryingly light. She'd dealt with lots of traumatised puppies who wouldn't eat and knew that what he needed was tempting. It really didn't matter what he ate to begin with, he just had to get into the habit of putting something into his stomach three times a day. So she let Daisy choose what she thought he might like and then she added her own ideas. By the time they came out of the shop it was nearly lunchtime, Johnny was full of shopping bags, and Rosie was feeling as if she'd stepped into a surreal film. But he had said to buy whatever was required and a 6 year-old boy had a lot of requirements.

"Shall we get some pizza?" she suggested.

"I'm still full, and he won't eat it," said Daisy. "He doesn't like tomatoes. Or cheese."

"Oh well," said Rosie. "Another time perhaps."

As if in honour of the occasion, Johnny started first time and Rosie drove slowly, not wanting the Petits Yoplaits to get crushed and leak all over the new sheets. The sun was shining and the sky was blue but there was a bite in the air, a whiff of winter creeping through the fields, and the multicoloured patchwork of autumn colours on the hills was fading along with the grass. There were pale violet clouds blooming behind the distant mountains. It wouldn't be long before the weather broke.

As she drove into the courtyard, Chris was seeing a strange car off. "Piano tuner," he said, pointing at the man's little blue car disappearing down the track. He raised his eyebrows at all the boxes and bags stacked in the back of the quatre-quatre, but all he said was that Spike's owner had come to collect his dog.

"Oh God yes, I'd forgotten," exclaimed Rosie. "Did he pay? Was Spike all right?"

"He didn't look thrilled, to be honest, and his owner tried to give me a cheque, but I got cash out him."

Rosie knew she would miss Spike, but his departure was well-timed because a traumatised boxer was hardly the ideal dog for Flo's pathetic little son. She would just have to hope the new reformed Spike would settle back into his home without slipping into his bad old ways.

In Steve's room, she unpacked her shopping haul, feeling like the magical Indian servant in the Little Princess. A bright bedside rug, a bedside lamp, new bedding and a series of safety nightlights to plug into the electricity sockets. She stacked new toys and games beside the bed and folded his clothes into a small chest of drawers. On the top of it she ranged the various personal hygiene items she'd bought him along with two new towels - in case he was contagious. Which reminded her she ought to check him for nits and skin infections. Last of all, she smuggled the teddy downstairs to her sitting room and wrapped him up in colourful paper. Leaning through the kitchen door, she signalled to Flo.

"Did you want me?" he said, dropping a drying-up cloth over the back of a chair.

She went bright red. "Yes," she said. "I mean no! Just come with me."

"I'm sure that would be my pleasure," he said following her through the pass door and down the corridor to her study. "Wow, what a nice room!" he said, gazing round at the squashy sofas, the threadbare rugs, the polished oak desk, the doggie books and photos of her children. "How come I've never been in here before?"

"Perhaps you didn't deserve it before," smiled Rosie. "Just be happy you're here now." She leaned on the back of the sofa. "How did you get on with phoning Steve's mother?"

He sighed and a horrible cynical sneer disfigured his face as he stared out of the window. "You know, she had no idea they'd run away. She was in bed with a hangover from some binge or other. I don't think she even remembered kicking them out, and she hadn't the faintest clue that they'd actually left the country."

"That's awful!" said Rosie.

"She says Daisy is over 18, so not her responsibility."

"That's still way too young to be wandering round Europe homeless with someone else's child in tow!"

"Of course, you're right," said Flo closing his eyes. "But the point is now she's got a whiff that I want to keep him, she says she's heartbroken."

"She wants him back?"

Flo gave her a hard look. "As if. She wants what she's always wanted. Plenty of coke, plenty of hard dick and as much money as she can get her hands on."

"That's not a nice thing to say about your son's mother," said Rosie quietly. She didn't like this angry, worldly, cynical Flo.

Standing by the window, he turned round to look at her. "It's impossible for a woman like you to understand someone like Sylvia, because you're different, you're just not like the rest of them."

Rosie could feel another hot flush starting.

"Basically he's up for sale," said Flo. "But while the price is negotiated, he can stay here."

Rosie didn't know what to say. She was glad that poor little Stevie didn't have to go back to what sounded like an awful home, but she still found it hard to believe that any mother could be as negligent and callous as Sylvia. What a horrible world Flo lived in.

Watching her, Flo was surprised to see tears in her eyes.

"Look," said Rosie, giving him the wrapped up teddy bear. "I thought you'd like to give this to Stevie."

"What for?"

"So he has something to hug, stoopid!"

"I haven't got anything to hug," said Flo pulling a sad face, but Rosie ignored him. She really didn't enjoy her temperature shooting up and down. "Pack it in!" she ordered. "It's a bear. I did look for a cat because he said last night that he likes them, but I couldn't find one so I bought this until we... until you, can find him something better."

In the kitchen Steve, sitting on Daisy's lap, was eating sardines from a tin while the others were gobbling down great plates of pasta.

"Hey kid, I got something for you," said Flo, holding the parcel out to him. "Go on, take it. It won't bite." Flo put it on the table in front of him and Steve looked at it doubtfully.

"Go on, rip it!" said Larrie but he shook his head, and Daisy had to help him open it, and show him how to pull the last shreds of paper off. Steve stared at the teddy with amazement. "It's for me?" he asked.

Flo nodded. "It's definitely for you. All for you. It's yours and no-one else's," he said. Suddenly Steve hugged the teddy tight and buried his face in its soft glossy fur. Inwardly, Rosie shook her head. Poor little kid. She could hardly wait to show him all the things she'd bought for his room, but when they finally trooped upstairs, although Daisy and Flo were enthusiastic, Steve just stood by the window clutching his teddy and staring at everything with big eyes.

"And I've got one last thing I think you'll like, stars for the ceiling."

"Those ones that glow in the dark?" said Daisy. "Oh, I love them!"

"Is there a stepladder somewhere?" asked Flo. "We might as well put them up straight away."

While he was fetching the step-ladder Rosie took Daisy aside. "Those stitches in his head, Daisy, how long have they been in there?"

Daisy counted on her fingers. "A week, no, nine, ten days. Maybe a fortnight. He walked into one of Sylvia's plates. A big dinner plate full of sushi and green salad."

Shaking her head, Rosie went back to Steve who was looking out of the window. "I won't hurt, I just want to look at them. You are a brave soldier," she said, inspecting the boy's scalp. He didn't seem to have nits, but she'd better treat him anyway. "These really ought to come out otherwise there's a risk of infection."

"Is there a doctor near here?"

"What for?" said Flo, coming back in with a stepladder.

"His stitches need to come out, but..." Rosie gave Steve a reassuring smile, beckoned Flo into the corridor and shut the door behind them. "The thing is he's in a real state," she said in a low voice. "Physically as well as emotionally, I mean. I don't want to be horrible, but the local GP is very conventional and you don't have any health insurance or papers for him or anything. He might inform the social services. I don't know if they'd actually do anything, but you could find yourself up to the ears in red tape if he does. And if they remove him into care, it would be really bad."

"Oh Jesus, you're right," exclaimed Flo, and sighed. "What are we going to do?"

"I could take them out for you. I've done it loads of times before."

"Dogs?" he said, with raised eyebrows.

"Yes. It might just sting just a tiny bit," said Rosie, "but if he holds still it won't really hurt."

Flo looked straight into her rainwater eyes and knew that she was telling the truth. She was gentle right through to her soul and out the other side. "Well, let's do it," he said, and he wasn't at all surprised when Rosie bribed Steve into sitting still by offering to take him on a teddy bear's picnic. "With honey sandwiches and Jaffa cakes and orange juice," she promised.

"Because that's what bears like best," said Daisy, joining in.

Stevie eyed the three adults up. He knew full well there would be no picnic. If he agreed he wouldn't get into trouble, if he didn't he'd be smacked and sent to bed. But whichever way, there would be no picnic. "All right," he rasped despairingly.

Rosie collected the Betadene and a sterilised pair of tweezers, and Daisy settled Steve on her lap. Picking up the top book on the pile, Flo started reading Pooh Bear. Going as gently as she could, Rosie was amazed at how well Flo read out loud, doing all the different voices and everything. He brought all the characters to life brilliantly, making them all laugh so much that sometimes she had to stop what she was doing and wait for Steve to hold still again. She got all the stitches out, dabbed Steve's head liberally with yellow disinfectant and because Flo was standing too close for comfort, gave him a yellow dab on the nose as well. Steve suddenly hooted with laughter and a second later they all joined in.

"Now we've got two jobs left," said Rosie, once they'd all calmed down. "We have to put the stars up and we have to have the teddy bear's picnic."

"Weally?" asked Steve.

"Absolutely. I'm bringing my teddy, are you bringing yours?"

Deadly serious, Steve nodded at her.

"So, stars first or picnic first?"

"Picnic," he croaked.

"Look, I'll do the stars," said Flo. "It won't take long. Do I have to follow this diagram thing or can I just put them up?"

"Oh, just put them up," said Rosie and he winked at her. In return she wiggled her nose at him. "Time for tea!" she said quickly and led the way downstairs.

In the kitchen, as she boiled the kettle, Daisy helped her put together a teddy bear's picnic. They cut some Jaffa cakes into quarters, and then Rosie remembered she had some biscuit cutters from when Larrie was little so they made bread and butter teddy bears sprinkled with vermicelli, and star-shaped honey sandwiches and by some miracle she found Larrie's Black Beauty mug with the snow storm when you tipped it upside down. She packed everything into a wicker basket.

"Now where shall we have this picnic?"

"A cave," said Steve, stroking a large ginger cat.

Rosie pulled a comic face. "I don't think we've got a cave. Would a willow tree do?" she asked. "It's down by the river and the branches bend right over making a magic green tent. It might be a bit cold outside, but we could take a dog blanket and some cushions? Would you like that?" Steve nodded seriously.

"Is Daisy...?" said Chris coming into the room with Minnie at his heels. "I want to..."

"Hi Chris," said Daisy in her soft drawl. "What do you want me for?"

Chris stopped short and blushed.

Steve smiled up at Daisy. "Spec he wants to take yore photo," he said, hugging his teddy. "Cos yore pretty."

Rosie bit her lip to stop herself laughing out loud.

"Would you let me?" said Chris.

Daisy picked the basket up and nodded. "But not right now, because we're going on a teddy bear's picnic."

"Dolly, Big Dogs, walkies!" called Rosie, leading the way out of the back door. All the dogs rushed after her, and Daisy swung Steve onto her hip and followed. Ginger stretched, shivered his tail expressively, and stalked after them. As long as it wasn't actually raining, he didn't mind going for an afternoon stroll.

"OK, bye," said Chris to the empty room, wondering whether he was affronted or relieved not to be included in this expedition. He went upstairs and found Flo just folding the stepladder up. "Doesn't look too bad," said Chris. "For a kid's room, I mean."

Flo didn't say anything. "Be gracious!" snapped Chris. "We've already established that this isn't Beverly Hills!"

"Sorry," said Flo. "I was just thinking, that's all. About something completely else."

"Well don't," said Chris. "Muma and Daisy have taken Steve on a teddy bear's picnic. Under the willow tree. With star-shaped sandwiches. She's unstoppable once she gets her Mary Poppins hat on."

Flo winced. "Will I be forgiven if I don't join in?"

"I shouldn't think they'll notice one way or the other," Chris assured him, and Flo felt guiltily relieved.

"What are you doing now?" he asked. "Would this be a good moment to come and visit your studio?"

"Walk this way," said Chris with a grin.

Flo followed him through the house into a part of it that he hadn't seen before, behind the wide portrait gallery and through a small door into a strange square hall that led to a spiral staircase made of large chunks of grey stone. He followed Chris into the first room off the staircase. Minnie scampered past him, skittered across the wooden floor, sprang gracefully into a large dilapidated basket chair and curled up. Standing in the low doorway, Flo realised they must be in one of the turrets. The circular room was painted white and fitted with a series of modern trestle tables, office chairs and large flat shelves containing paper. There was a light box, several computers and a large cupboard adorned with notices scrawled with warnings including, "Larrie, touch this cupboard and die" and "Fingers off, Larrie!"

There were modern spotlights on wires, businesslike black blinds at the windows, and a couple of filing cabinets beside the door. There was also a coffee machine. "As you know, Muma can't make coffee to save her life," said Chris. "And anyway, it goes cold before I can get it up here. Do you want some?"

"Yes, great," said Flo absent-mindedly. He was leafing through a pile of large-scale prints on one of the tables. "These are yours?"

"Yup. Sugar?"

"No sugar," said Flo. "These are really good," he said, and meant it. Chris obviously had serious talent. His coffee was good too.

"That's just a competition entry," said Chris handing him an espresso. "This is what I'm really working on." He opened a large portfolio and pulled the top photograph out. It was a black and white study of a girl's spine. The second photo seemed almost the same except there were almost imperceptible leaf shadows. Flo watched as Chris showed him photo after photo, each one taking the study further into the idea of a woman's spine being the central pillar, the tree trunk of a family. The idea wasn't perhaps extraordinarily original but the execution was perfect. Each image was technically faultless and artistically profound; as a series they were touching, uplifting and tender.

"Beautiful," said Flo. "My God. Why are you messing about entering competitions? You should be mounting an exhibition somewhere!"

"Well, perhaps one day," said Chris evasively.

"Why not now?"

"It obviously seems strange to you, but I have responsibilities," said Chris. "I can't just disappear off and spend weeks pretending to write a book. People are relying on me."

Flo flushed, but refused to be put off the scent. "But..."

"My mother and Nicole do their best but they couldn't manage this place on their own, and Larrie's just a kid."

"Only because it's not set up right!" said Flo. "I mean, to make this place work properly your mother needs decent kennelling, proper facilities, webcams, all sorts of stuff. The way it is..."

"I know, Fifi! We all know. But where's that

kind of capital investment going to come from? And don't look at me because even if I could earn that kind of money, Muma would never take it. As it is, she hasn't really a clue how everything gets paid for, and don't you start stirring either. I absolutely forbid you to mention money to her. Or photography."

"All right, keep your hair on!" said Flo. "I was only admiring your snaps."

"They're not snaps!"

"I'm teasing. You should know that. You're a bloody talented photographer and I think you're wasting your time hiding away out here in the sticks." As Chris was about to burst out, he flung his hands up. "All right! I understand. I even honour you for what you're doing. Ok?"

"Ok."

"Very nice snaps," said Flo and this time Chris blushed, nodded and gave him a pleased smile. Flo drank the rest of his coffee and looked out of the windows but it was clear that Chris was waiting for him to go. "I'd better um... I was going to play some scales," he said at last, conscious that he must sound like the lamest of the lame to a young man supporting his entire family by winning photography competitions.

Flo went back down the stairs feeling very small. He'd been so much fussed over as a child, and so much admired and indulged all his adult life that for years he'd believed that he was special, that his every action was extraordinary and fabulous. But compared to Chris... Chris might not look it, but he was the real scaffolding of the household. The image of Steve and Daisy, pale and tear-stained, flitted across his mind and he felt furiously guilty. In comparison with Chris, how had Flo looked after his family?

Heading towards the piano, an even more unwelcome thought came into his head. Here in the doghouse he was just another stray. They humoured him, fed him, put up with him, but he didn't really count. He was just a passing charity case. Suddenly, he wanted to show them that he could be as useful as the next man. Perhaps even more useful. He made a preliminary stab at it when they were organising the expedition to the fancy dress Halloween Fête.

"I'll drive Johnny! I insist!" he said at supper. Everyone variously shrugged, nodded and shook their heads. "The roads might be icy! And I don't mind not drinking," he said heroically. "So I'll drive Johnny!"

"All right, we get the message!" said Rosie, as they all went off to change. When they all reassembled in the kitchen, she was dressed as a witch, in a frilly black petticoat with a black satin corset over the top. Her hair was all teased out and she had lots of black round her eyes and green lipstick. Daisy, more Camden than ever, was head-to-toe in torn black lace, studs, and buckles and Steve was wearing a white sheet with a picture of a pumpkin attached to the front with a large safety pin. Teddy was wearing a black bow tie made from a bin bag. Larrie had put her highwayman's outfit on, complete with mask, and Chris was dressed as a zombie with bright red blood dripping down the front of what Flo recognised as about $500 worth of ripped-up cream silk shirt. Looking from him to Daisy, he had a reasonably good idea who had been Chris's stylist.

"Very gory," he said. "Is that paint?"

"Food colouring," said Chris. "It'll wash out."

Flo knew it wouldn't, but suddenly realised he didn't give a toss. What the hell? It was only a car; it was only a shirt; it was all just stuff. He looked around the people standing around joking and scoffing Halloween biscuits in the kitchen, and thought that any casting director would take them for the perfect family. Mum, Dad and four kids ranging from 6 to 19... only they weren't a family. He and Steve were just two lost dogs.

Rosie, watching Flo looking round at them all, wondered what he was thinking. He was such a weird combination of anger and tenderness, cosmopolitan sophistication and vulnerability. And how funny of him to have painted his face black and green stripes.

"And what are you meant to be?" she asked.

"I'm not exactly sure," he said. "I think I might be a sort of mouldy monster. Shall we go?"

They piled outside, pulling on anoraks and jumpers, and Flo realised he couldn't remember the last time he'd driven a car full of people. Perhaps it was a first? In contrast to Rosie's foot-on-the-floor French driving style, Flo drove slowly, steadily and safely all the way. The village square was packed with cars, and people were milling around the entrance to the village hall with wicker baskets of food for the buffet.

Rosie smiled at Flo. "Not feeling too shy?" she asked, and he shook his head. Nicole snorted to herself and marched off round the back. With Larrie leading the way, the rest of them trooped into the hall together. It was already packed with people in fancy dress, milling around long tables decorated with little heaps of chestnuts in nests of leaves. Rosie and Larrie disappeared into the throng leaving Flo standing with Daisy and Chris, who was scanning the crowd for Lily.

"I say, you don't mind, do you?" said Chris glancing towards a chestnut-haired girl in a silver tutu. Daisy shrugged, and lifted Steve higher on her hip.

"Not at all, be my guest," said Flo, and Chris plunged into the crowd of young men milling around Lily.

Flo looked at Daisy and wondered about offering to carry Steve. She was too skinny to be heaving such a large child around, but Steve was clinging to her like a baby chimp and Flo was afraid he might refuse to come to his father. Then Rosie and Larrie came back from the bar with a tray of fruity cocktails and Lotta came over to say hello to them. She wasn't dressed up at all, just showing all her large yellow teeth in a friendly grin.

"Jolly good turn-out, don't you think? Your

guest still here, is he, Rosie?" She turned to Flo. "They haven't managed to frighten you off yet? Can't remember your name now. Don't mind me, monster-mash for brains, and that's the truth!"

Then a handsome florid man stood up on a beer crate and made a long, slow, tedious speech. Flo couldn't understand a word of it, but he could tell it was boring just by looking at the listening faces, and various souls near the bar were completely ignoring the speaker and quietly cracking what sounded like rude jokes. Rosie, patiently waiting for the mayor to stop droning on, saw Nicole standing on the sidelines gazing at him completely rapt; her eyes shining and her lips half open. She was the only one in the whole room who was following every single word with total attention. One might even say devotion.

Rosie choked and clapped her hand over her mouth. Nicole and the mayor! Ivan the awful prosy right-wing mayor! She looked around for someone to share the joke with but there was no-one. Neither Flo nor Daisy would get it. Then the mayor stopped prosing and there was a general surge towards the food, everyone politely trying to be first in the line without actually trampling their neighbours underfoot. Rosie saw Larrie duck under the table and simply help herself from the other side until a portly man with a red face pinched her bottom and she fled, followed by a pack of other prepubescent girls.

"I'm 86!" screeched Tata Yvette, "and I'm hungry!"

The crowds parted for her and Rosie took Steve off Daisy's hip. "What do you fancy, angel? Shall we get a bit of everything so we can taste it all and spit the bad bits under the table?" Bringing up the rear behind Daisy, Flo grabbed some plates and a tray and wished he could think of things like that. How come she was so good with Stevie?

"Eat as much as you can!" said Rosie looking over her shoulder, and Daisy gave her a blinding smile and dived into the fray. One-handed, Rosie piled the most ridiculous selection of food onto their plates and Steve almost started to laugh. Not quite, but his little face was bright with amusement. "Yore bonkers," he told her.

"Barking, completely out with the fairies!" said Rosie. "Let's get some chocolate biscuits to go with the onion quiche, shall we?"

Flo just followed suit, piling a bit of everything onto a tray and adding a couple of cans of coke. They found some free seats at the end of a table and Rosie held her glass up for wine when Pierre the woodman came round with a large metal jug of paint-stripper red. "I do like parties!" she said, her face flushed. She held a piece salmon tart out. "Here, Stevie, give this to teddy. Teddies love fish!"

Stevie held the savoury pastry to teddy's mouth and then to his own. He took a tiny bite and then a larger one and finally ate the whole thing.

"Does teddy want a cherry tomato wrapped up in salmon?"

Steve nodded.

"You know what, angel, why don't you just take whatever you think teddy might like?" said Rosie, draining her glass. Magically, Pierre was there again to fill it up.

A tall yellow-faced man wearing aggressively oblong turquoise glasses slid in beside them and started gabbling to Rosie. She kissed him on both cheeks, perfectly unnecessarily in Flo's opinion, and introduced him first to Flo and then to Steve. The man took Steve's chin in his hand and looked at him, then he removed the boy's glasses and peered at him some more. Rosie was laughing and cuddling Steve even closer and Flo noticed that Steve didn't mind at all. He wasn't even looking round the room for Daisy. He wasn't surprised.

"Didier says we ought to get his eyes tested," said Rosie. "He doesn't think he's got the right glasses. Says he shouldn't be squinting when he's got them on."

Flo would have answered but he was drowned out by a group of fat locals playing a series of deafening folk songs. A-tonal and ghastly," thought Flo, wishing he hadn't volunteered to be the driver. He could kill for a large Scotch. Looking round the room, he saw Chris earnestly talking to Lily who was looking supremely bored. No use talking to that sort of girl, thought Flo. She was a Barbarian.

Tata Yvette had found a group of toothless ancients and was holding forth about modern morals and her own long dead suitors. Rosie held her glass up and Pierre rolled straight over to fill it up again, taking the opportunity to point out that if they wanted good places for the fireworks, they ought to go out onto the playing field behind the village hall. She got to her feet, slightly staggering, and realised that Steve had got rather heavy. Perhaps it was all the salmon he'd eaten. She gave him to Flo, who gave her his charming lopsided smile in exchange.

Flo was so nice, thought Rosie. Steve was such a honey. Pierre was nice too. So nice to have old friends. She followed him across the hall, threading her way through the people who were all moving more or less in the same direction, until she got outside. They were the first ones out there. She shivered in the cold night air. In the dark, Pierre's arm went round her shoulder. Good old Pierre. She smiled at him. Nice Pierre. But suddenly Pierre's grip on her tightened and he pushed her head round with his hand and his arms were too strong and his moustache went up her nose and his wet lips were all over hers. She tried to pull away but he simply hugged her harder and slid his tongue into her mouth. She pushed his broad chest, but he was too strong for her. And then suddenly Flo was standing beside them with his free hand gripping Pierre's throat, and Pierre slackened his grasp on Rosie.

"Get down," said Flo. "Basket!"

Pierre twisted his head round to see who was speaking to him in a foreign language. Then he took a step back. Flo, carrying Stevie and teddy on one hip, had never looked so menacing or so angry.

"Calm down, Flo," said Rosie and switched into French. "Behave, Pierre! Isn't that your wife?" She turned him away as hard as she could. "Stop making a total idiot of yourself!" she hissed at him in the crudest French she could muster. "You're being a prat. Now bog off!"

As Pierre stumbled away, she turned back to Flo. "Basket?" she exclaimed, bursting into laughter. "Basket?"

Then everyone surged towards the field to see the fireworks. They weren't spectacular. They didn't go off in time to music or against a son-et-lumière background. Some of them didn't really go off at all, but it didn't matter. The skies were full of light and noise, the crowd was well fed and watered, ready to applaud and cheer the slightest thing, and Steve had apparently never seen fireworks before. At the end, the mayor got back up on his beer crate but before he could start talking, someone turned the music back on and people started drifting back inside. The main lights had been turned off and the tables pushed against the walls.

"Dance with me!" said Lotta, grabbing Flo's free hand. "You remind me of someone but I don't know who!"

Flo glanced down at Steve's head, drooping against his shoulder, but at that moment Daisy came up and took him out of Flo's arms. "Come on, Stevie Nix," she said and sat down on a bench by the wall. Stevie snuggled into her shoulder, still holding teddy tightly round the neck, and fell asleep. Lotta tugged Flo onto the dance floor, and Rosie sat beside her watching the dancers. Before long, Flo came back. "Come on, dance with me, Rosie," he said and without thinking, she just took his hand and followed him onto the floor.

From the other side of the room, Lily watched Chris was talking to his weird younger sister, who seemed to be sulking about something or other. Then she watched the sister take the sleeping kid off the American Goth's lap, and suddenly Chris was dancing with the American Goth. Lily was affronted. Just because she was foreign she didn't need to think she could queen it over everyone.

Chris wasn't much of a dancer, so he was glad that Daisy's idea of dancing turned out to be standing almost totally still and swaying from side to side in a trance. "Happy Halloween!" he said idiotically.

"You're cute," she said, and gave him a devastating smile.

"Hey, tell me," said a voice at Chris's shoulder in French. "Who's that bloke? Over there, dancing with your mother? I know him from somewhere."

Chris and Daisy glanced warnings at each other. Without exchanging a word, they both shook their heads.

"No-one," said Chris.

"Just a guy," said Daisy in perfect French.

Chris raised his eyebrows at her and she

smiled. "Daddy is French Canadian," she said. "Who is this lemon?"

"Hugo. We were at school together. I used to teach him photography. He wants to join the paparazzi. Thinks it'll make him rich."

Hugo was dancing from toe to toe trying to pretend they were all dancing together. He was plump, pale and spotty, and his designer jeans were too tight.

"What a gargle!" said Daisy.

"My sentiments exactly."

"You know what?" said Daisy turning to Hugo, once again speaking perfect French. "If you shove off and leave us alone, I might just be able to get this guy here to kiss me."

Both Hugo and Chris blinked, but Hugo obediently took a step back and by some miracle, Chris had the presence of mind to take a step forward. He was rewarded by the fleeting touch of Daisy's sweet lips on his. Coming back into the hall with her lipstick smudged, Lily saw them kissing and scowled.

Rosie and Flo were oblivious. Somehow Flo had managed to dance them into a dark corner, and then the music had changed and Rosie dizzily told herself that it would be ungracious to shove two men in the chest in one evening. So while Rod Stewart wailed that he was sailing, she allowed Flo to pull her so close that the could rest her cheek against his chest. She might even, in the dark, have nestled into his shoulder, but she was so breathless by that time that she wasn't sure.

Rod Stewart finally ran out of steam and she looked up at Flo, just to say thank you for the dance, but for some impenetrable reason he misunderstood her, and their lips met. She had no idea how it had happened. It was blissful but very bizarre and in some strange way she was aware that she might be kissing him back but she didn't care.

Finally, she broke away from him because she was having a hot flush again and needed to get her breath back, and realised that a small crowd was drunkenly cheering them. Nicole and the Ivan the Terrible Mayor were in hysterics, Lotta was chanting, "Flo, Flo, quick, quick, Flo!" and the local schoolteacher appeared to be leading a chorus of cheering children. Horrible Lily and her gang of boys were sniggering, Daisy and Chris were laughing their heads off, and Pierre was clapping really slowly although his wife was applauding like a maniac. Luckily Larrie, Stevie and teddy were all asleep in the far corner. Flo's glasses were completely steamed up and Rosie's mouth was all smeared with green and black face paint.

"Bad dog!" she exclaimed. "Basket!"

CHAPTER EIGHT

Rosie woke up with no hangover at all, just a feeling of massive contentment. The world was obviously born anew and everything in it was perfect. Suddenly she dived back under the pillows and buried her head. Oh my God. She'd better get dressed and start doing the dogs before Flo got up and she had to face him. What an idiot she was. In front of the whole village, too. Thank God Larrie had been asleep, or she'd never hear the end of it.

Ignoring the cold, she flung her clothes on, shoved two pairs of socks onto her frozen feet and ran silently down the stairs. She didn't even bother to check the windowpanes for frost, or brush her hair. Fearing that if she hung around in the kitchen, Flo might come down looking sleepy and rumpled and sexy, she didn't stop for coffee either, just riddled the stove, topped it up with coal, and grabbed an apple on her way out to the large barn.

Larrie, bundled up in a thick padded jacket, was already bustling round the stable whistling as she picked out Sobie's feet. He was tied up to a bar looking half asleep, with his mane all tangled, his eyes half closed, and his night rug still on. He almost looked like he was snoring. Rosie stopped to watch and took a bite of her apple.

"Morning Muma! Don't forget those people are coming to see Fanny's puppies."

"Oh God! Good job you reminded me," exclaimed Rosie. She gave the rest of her apple to Sobie and hurried into the kennels. Her head was protesting at the lack of coffee and her stomach was joining in. Perhaps the combination of chocolate biscuits and sautéd chicken livers had been a bit rash. Not to mention... "Nope!" she informed the tap as she was filling the water bowls. "I refuse to think about it!"

The sky was almost pure white, and a mischief-making little wind was tugging at the last leaves on the trees. She really ought to have a sweep-up or they'd go slimy underfoot. And it was time to get the geraniums off the terrace. Just as soon as the clouds blew away across the valley, the night temperatures would plummet. She looked over the trees at the hills in the distance and could see them pulling on their white, winter mufflers.

The east wing would soon be so cold it would be uninhabitable. Flo would have to... to what? Move into the older part of the house with Rosie and the kids? She shook her head. Certainly not! He'd just have to lump it. And in any case, the farmhouse windows all leaked. At least there were no leaks in his room. She thrust the thought of Flo aside and seized a yard broom. She'd be far better off thinking about the bichons. She had already started letting the dogs' coats grow out for extra winter protection, but she would need to make sure that the barn was at least moderately weatherproof - especially as one of them was pregnant. She had just let the bichons out when she heard Larrie calling "Muma! Puppy people!"

They were a nice looking couple and rather than waste time, Rosie took them straight through to Fanny's run.

"So, are you wanting a male or a female?" she asked.

"Weren't you at the Halloween Fete last night?" said the man, and his wife nudged him in the ribs. Rosie blushed. "Thought so," he said with a broad grin. "You had a good time, didn't you?"

"Let her alone!" hissed his wife but her eyes were dancing with amusement. "Just choose a puppy!"

"Which one do you suggest?" he asked Rosie. "You seem to be able to pick the affectionate ones!"

She was really glad when they finally drove off, having given her a large cheque to reserve a rather dull female with caramel-coloured patches on her chest and back. She was desperate for tea. She stumbled through the back door pulling off her gloves to find Larrie in the kitchen eating a huge bowl of muesli and laughing at Nicole, who was washing an armful of chard in the sink.

"But if you lu-rve him, Nicki-loo," she was saying in French, "why don't you get married or at least live with him? Muma, did you know? Nicole is in love with Ivan the Terrible Mayor!" She went off into peals of laughter, spluttering cold milk out all over the table.

Nicole shook her wet hands at Larrie and scowled. "In my day, cheeky flibberty-gibbets like you knew better than to make fun of their elders! You ought to be in school!"

"It's Sunday, Nicole!"

Rosie put the kettle on and checked the fire. "Eat your muesli, Larrie." She riddled the stove thoroughly, and took the ash box out.

"And Chris is taking photos of Daisy!" said Larrie unabashed. She preceded Rosie out of the back door and took the lid off the metal ash bucket.

And what about Stevie?" asked Rosie, tipping the hot ashes into the bucket. They went back into the kitchen and she dropped a log into the fire.

"Upstairs with Chris and Daisy."

"Well, that's reassuring anyway," said Rosie. She made herself a cup of tea and sat down, jealous that Flo could sleep in. But he wasn't asleep. He was on the phone to Sally.

"Well, I have to say hats off to you for sticking it out this long," she was saying. "Honestly, I never thought you would. But at least you can't be getting into trouble with Rosie! She's never going to fall for you! I mean, Rosie!" Sally laughed. "She's way too tough to give you more than houseroom. You haven't found somebody else, have you? You're not messing about with some native milkmaid, are you?"

"No," he said. He flattened a piece of curling wallpaper absent-mindedly and stared out of the window at the rusting gates.

Sally was instantly suspicious. "What's going on? What are you up to?"

"Nothing," he said, thinking that all the gates needed was paint. "You should be glad. I'm not getting up to anything. I might even be growing up."

"Not Rosie?" exclaimed Sally.

"No," he said in a fit of gallantry, "She won't have me."

"But you're in love with her?"

The suggestion hit him like a wave crashing on the shore. "Sorry, can't hear you, running out of battery," he said, and hung up. Then he just stood there, leaning against the wall, staring into the distance. He closed his eyes and took a deep breath, and it was some time before he could shake off his paralysis and plunge into the corridors of the château in search of Rosie. But she was nowhere to be found. Having drunk her tea, she had suddenly remembered all sorts of urgent paperwork needing immediate attention. It absolutely couldn't wait. None of it. Not even things like filling in registration cards for Fanny's puppies. She was in her study going through a messy stack of papers and concentrating ferociously in order to stop her mind floating off into enchanted daydreams. On top of a handful of smaller stuff, there was a demand to renew her car insurance, a large hay bill, and a staggeringly enormous water bill. Not for the first time, she wondered if it would be possible to collect rainwater from the château roof, or possibly pump water up from the river. How on earth was it possible to pay so much for water when they had the stuff dripping into the house through the doors, windows, chimneys, and roof for free?

Every time images of last night popped back into her brain, she firmly dismissed them. The only trouble was, they kept coming back and the bills kept getting into the wrong envelopes. Or the cheques did. Or the envelopes. Some of them even looked upside down. And none of them seemed at all important. She could still feel Flo's lips on hers, his arms around her body, his breath on her face, and the feeling was making her hot all over.

Downstairs, Flo sighed. Having made some coffee, wandered about the terrace and gazed up at Rosie's study window, he realised that bearding Rosie in her den might be a bad idea. He might get ordered to his basket. She might even hit him with a handy chainsaw. He'd better go back upstairs. In his imposing but desperately shabby bedroom, he pulled on the fingerless mittens Chris had lent him and sat down in front of his laptop. An autobiography would sell; there was no doubt about that. If he wanted cash, that was a certain money-tree. He began typing laboriously with his index fingers. "I was born on a frosty night in Chelmsford..." But then he stopped. What else was there to say? As a teenager, his career had taken off, his parents had died, and he'd been partying ever since. Abandoning his laptop he went off to play the piano, but couldn't concentrate on that either. He played a few tunes and then he just sat, and his mind wandered back to dancing with a witch.

Rosie and Flo finally met that night at dinner and although it could have been awkward, in the event it wasn't at all. Having finished their photo session, Chris and Daisy had spent the afternoon in the kitchen with Stevie, showing him how to make vegetarian cottage pie and pear crumble.

"I smashed the tatoes," said Steve proudly, "an' I did mixin! A lot. Me and teddy mixeded ever-fing!"

Chris rumpled his hair and Daisy blew him a kiss.

"I can cook too," said Larrie suddenly. "I can cook anything, I could even cook a rabbit if I wanted to because I know how to skin them. And rip their guts out, you have to start at the tail and..."

"Shut up, Larrie," said Chris.

"Sobie picked up a stone at the top of the sheep path, and I didn't have a hoof pick with me, and I had to improvise..."

"Hey you know what, we could get an ice cream maker," said Flo suddenly. "That would be fun, wouldn't it, Stevie? Stevie Wonder Boy!"

"I hate ice cream," said Larrie. But no-one was listening to her. They were all pretending not to notice that Stevie, instead of eating sardines out of a tin as usual, was hogging down the spoonful of cottage pie which Rosie had put on his plate.

"Sobie doesn't like ice cream either," she said. "In fact, he's dead." But no-one took the slightest bit of notice. With a thunderous face, she helped herself to a lot more pie and ate it with the back of her knife. Then she brazenly took three apples out of the fruit bowl and lined them up beside her plate. But still no-one took any notice. Scowling fit to give them all the Black Death, she stabbed at her lettuce with her penknife.

"You know, what we should do is build a big bonfire for November 5th and cook baked potatoes in the embers. Does anyone fancy that?" said Rosie. "Perhaps we could do it on Wednesday afternoon when Larrie gets back from school. We might even find some chestnuts to roast."

Steve's fork slowly clattered back onto his plate. "I want to do tatoe-baking," he said sadly.

"But you can," said Flo. "Of course you can!"

"But... what if I am gone home?"

There was complete silence. Everyone was looking at Steve, but he just sat there with his eyes screwed shut.

"Secretly, inside yourself, do you want to go back to your mum's house in London?" said Daisy gently. "You can go if you want to, no-one will be cross."

Steve sat like a statue and looked at his plate.

"Whisper," said Daisy. "Just whisper in my ear. Yes if you want to go back to London and no if you don't." She bent close to him and he burrowed through the multiple scarves and long strings of love beads round her neck. When he'd finished whispering, Daisy said to Flo, "He wants to know what happens if he doesn't go home."

"He'll stay with me, of course," said Flo. "In fact, I have no intention of letting him go back, so this whole conversation... I mean, that's finished. You're going to live with me now, Stevie, forever."

"I can stay here? With all you? For my life?" said Steve, looking round the table.

There was silence, and then Daisy said, "Well honey, I'm not your mom. I'm just the au pair, and when my visa runs out I'll have go back to Baltimore."

"No," said Steve, bursting into tears. "No!"

"But you can't all just move in forever!" said Larrie, bursting into tears as well. "Or we'll never get back to normal! Yore all hell!" She pushed her chair back and rushed out of the kitchen.

"You know what, Stevie, I think you should be mummy and give us all some of your lovely pear crumble," said Rosie. "All you need to know right now is that you are definitely coming to the bonfire with us, all right?"

Flo started to say something and she shot a warning glance across the table at him. It really wasn't the right moment, not when the child had just started eating. She fervently hoped that by the time Flo took him away, she'd have been able to feed Stevie up and stop him looking scared all the time. Smiling reassuringly at Stevie, she noted approvingly that his skin was already starting to look better. There wasn't much anyone could do about his sticky-out ears, but his nose had stopped running and if he would only start eating properly, he'd probably have a growth spurt, she thought, seeing as his father was so tall and broad-shouldered.

"Crumble, Muma?" offered Chris, and Rosie shook her head. What he really needed, she thought was a haircut to even up his old hair with the short new growth that was covering his scalp. She wondered how much new glasses would cost. A lot, probably.

"I'd better go and see if Larrie's all right," she said.

"D'you want me to go?" said Chris.

"No, I'll go," she said and picked up the apples beside Larrie's plate. "Come on," she said, and Dolly bounced enthusiastically off the sofa. The big dogs surged to their feet yawning and wagging but she shook her head at them. "No, not you lot, you stay!"

In his loose box, Sobie was lying down on his side like a cat, with Larrie curled up beside him weeping into his mane. Rosie went and sat down on the thick straw bed while Dolly snuffled busily under Sobie's manger for stray horse nuts.

"Come on baby," said Rosie. "What's wrong?"

"Snot fair!" said Larrie, twisting round to face her. "Steve doesn't have go to horrible, beastly school, no-one makes him do homework and he gets everything he wants. His room is like a shop! And Lily says I'm flat-chested and enfantine and she told everyone in the class not to speak to me!" She burst into a wail of tears. Rosie hugged her close and rocked her to and fro.

"Lily's just jealous," she whispered. "Jealous because you're beautiful and slim and smart and gorgeous and because even in a silver tutu she looks like she was made of leftovers."

"But at least she's got boobs! Look at me! It's true! I'm flatter than a frying pan!"

Damn Lily, thought Rosie. The bloody girl seems on a mission to make both my kids unhappy. "She who laughs last, laughs loudest," she said. "Just you wait. Late developers often end up with a better shape than these early starters. Look at me!"

"Were you a late starter?"

"Until I was fifteen all I had in my bra was cotton wool," said Rosie.

"I haven't even got a bra!" wailed Larrie going off into fresh floods.

"Well, we'll get you one," said Rosie. "And not in Moisson either. We'll go into Aix and get you a proper one from Printemps. A really pretty one. We'll use some of the bichon money and to hell with the water bill! You just have to promise not to fill it out with horse nuts."

Larrie snorted with laughter and Rosie gave her the apples to feed to Sobie. "I don't really care," said Larrie, getting busy with her penknife and sniffing loudly. "I was just jealous of Steve."

"Jealous of that poor little boy with his scabs and his scars and his bed-wetting and night terrors? Jealous of a six-year-old who got thrown out of home by his own mother?"

Larrie chewed her lip and looked sheepish.

"You are the light of my life," said Rosie. "There is nothing more precious to me than you and Chris. You are completely utterly adored in every way."

"I know," whispered Larrie. "I was being stoopid, wasn't I?"

"Nope," said Rosie, getting up and dusting the straw off her jeans. "Just being exactly like me when I was your age. A bit of a loony. Come on now. Time for bed."

They went back across the yard together with their arms around each other's waists but Rosie knew there was a major problem with Stevie, and the next morning when Flo came out to help with the dogs, she said, "you know you've got a problem, don't you? If Daisy goes back to the States, that boy of yours will be lost."

"Yes, I know," he said. "But I don't know anything about kids. I don't know how to make him like me. I just wish I did."

"Don't be pathetic," she retorted. "It doesn't matter whether he likes you or not. You have to learn to like him."

"That's not really what I meant..."

"Look. Kids are not that different from dogs. With normal ones, you put boundaries in place and then reward them for remaining within the rules. With rescue cases, you have to teach them confidence. Poor little Stevie doesn't trust the world. It's bitten him badly and now he expects it'll always bite him. So you have to teach him that you won't bite, not even if he does something really, really naughty."

"I can't imagine him doing anything naughty."

"Exactly, so just spend a couple of hours a day with him."

"Doing what?"

"Listen to him. Listen to what he says and respond. Be interested in what he says. Tell him about yourself, teach him to play the piano, show him how your phone works, read him some stories, make teddy bear biscuits together. It doesn't matter what you do. Just listen, show him you remember what he says. Be consistent, patient and prove that you're genuinely interested in him."

"All right, I'll try," he said, uncoiling the hose-pipe and picking up a yard broom. "You're so good at this. Was Larrie all right last night?"

"She's fine," said Rosie, turning the hosepipe on and picking up a yard broom. "Just a touch of the green-eyed monster, that's all. What are you going to do with Stevie? I mean when you go home? Do you have a house? Or a flat or what? Where is Steve going to live?"

"I don't know," he said turning on the tap. "I think I'll have to go to London and sort it out."

"You're taking him back to London?"

"No, I don't want to." He caught the disapproving expression on her face. "No, I mean I do eventually. But just not this time, I'll have to trail around seeing lawyers and doing practical things like finding a proper place to live. Honestly, I think it would be best for him and Daisy to stay here. Less stressful for them both."

Rosie straightened her back, put her hands on her hips and stared at him. She had been right after all. He had kissed her at the Halloween party but it had been no more significant than buying a bag of chips. He was leaving.

"He needs a bedroom, doesn't he? I only have one bedroom," he lied, and when she didn't say anything, he said, "Come on Rosie, please let him stay here! Just while I sort stuff out?"

She shrugged and got to work with the yard broom. It absolutely was none of her business. She had just got fond of the kid, that was all. And as for Flo, he could live wherever he liked. Even on Mars, if he wanted to. Looking at her stiff face, Flo determined to show her that she wasn't the only person with parenting skills on the planet.

The first indication of Flo's new paternal resolution was the arrival of the promised ice cream machine. Pierre dropped it off, with a new selection of packets to use with the bread machine, and Flo wrote him another large cheque. But ironically enough, Stevie wasn't that interested in ice cream. It was Larrie who really loved making gallons of ice cream every day.

"No more!" said Rosie opening the freezer to find it absolutely overflowing with scarlet and purple striped sorbet. "And no more weird flavours either!"

"Tomato isn't a weird flavour. It's a fruit, you know, people say it's a vegetable but it totally isn't... Muma, do you think horses can learn to read?"

"Larrie. No more beetroot sorbet. In any case, it's too cold for ice-cream now."

The first freezing fingers of winter had started to reach across the hills. Despite bright blue skies at midday, mornings were cold, and drifts of leaves were starting to rot where they lay thick on the ground. Rosie gathered all the green tomatoes and moved the potted geraniums into the barn for the winter. Various people came to buy Fanny's puppies; families, couples, an old man with filmy eyes, a hippy with a bongo and a hunter with a large shotgun. "You don't mind if I take em outside and fire off a coupla rounds," he said breathing Pastis all over Rosie. "It's for my wife but I don't want a gun shy one, do I?"

One glance from Rosie, and Flo was only too happy to escort the gentleman back to his car and inform him that the puppies were no longer for sale. In any case there were only two left un-sold, an outsized monstrous male and one female, the smallest and ugliest of the bunch. "She'll be no good for breeding. Bad genes," said Rosie, looking at her over the gate. "Best if she were sterilised before her first season."

"Isn't that a bit cruel?" asked Flo, standing at her side, gazing at the puppies.

"Why? Do you think she knows she could have babies one day?"

As always, Flo was abashed by Rosie's complete realism when it came to dogs. Of course the animal had no concept of fertility or reproduction.

"Chris is a brilliant photographer," he said as they mucked out. "Really excellent."

"I know. I'm very proud of him."

"I'm serious. He should have a studio in Paris or London or somewhere. So his work could be seen." Flo was wearing his nice warm Arran jumper.

"Why? What for?"

"Well, so that he could make a name for himself, earn some decent money. Get rich and famous, probably."

"Is money that important?" said Rosie. She looked at him seriously. "I mean, I agree that a certain amount of money makes life easier. But rich? Why would anyone strive merely to be rich?"

"Well, a working credit card is handy."

"Absolutely. I agree. Dolly, leave the cats alone! But there's a difference between earning enough to live without worrying, and being rich."

"Granted."

"And as for famous?" said Rosie, locking the door to the run, "I should have thought that was a nightmare. I mean always being followed and stuff."

"How right you are," muttered Flo, walking slightly behind her.

"Why d'you say that?"

He took a deep breath. He'd been waiting for

the right moment and finally it had arrived. It was time to tell Rosie everything.

"Muma!" yelled Larrie running across the yard. "Potty-spuds! Come on! Hurry up! We're all waiting! And I can have matches, can't I?"

They hurried into the kitchen where Nicole had unearthed baskets and gloves and a long-handled frying pan with holes in it. Steve and teddy were sitting at the table watching everyone with glowing eyes, and Chris was kissing Daisy's hand.

"Muma, we are going to roast chestnuts!" exclaimed Larrie. "Nicole's already half done the 'tatoes in the stove. All wrapped up in foil and everything!"

The moment was lost. Rosie plunged into organising the bonfire expedition and they spent the afternoon raking through the golden-bronzed leaves, gathering the last of the sweet chestnuts and roasting them over a bonfire. Daisy produced wonky homemade ginger biscuits, and Stevie sat cross-legged on Flo's lap, proudly holding the end of one of the roasting pans as Flo helped him keep it in the flames. Rosie rewarded Flo for his paternal efforts by dropping a light kiss on the top of his head.

"Guess what? I've got chocolate fingers for pudding!" said Larrie. "That's what you have at midnight feasts with sardine sandwiches and lemonade and tinned tongue!"

"Yuk!" said Flo. "Sounds disgusting! I'd sooner have humus and pitta bread any day."

"Boring," said Larrie disgustedly. "Have you ever had mole in the hole?"

"Toad in the hole," said Rosie, handing out potatoes.

"I think so," said Flo. "When I was a kid."

"What was it like?" asked Larrie eagerly. "Was it black and slimy?"

"Well, no," he confessed. "It's not that exciting. It's actually pork sausages cooked in a sort of cake stuff."

"Now that does sound disgusting," said Chris, handing out hot roasted chestnuts. Rosie looked up at the sky and pulled a face. There was a bank of purple grey clouds on the horizon. "You'd better eat those chocolate fingers now," she said to Larrie. "I'm not sure how long we'll be able to stay out here."

"But it's sunny," said Daisy. "The sky is blue, it's a beautiful day!" She smiled serenely at Chris and he smiled back at her.

I see, thought Rosie, catching the glance that passed between them. Well, I hope she's nicer to him than terrible Lily. Flo was peeling hot chestnuts for Steve, who was ramming them into his mouth and washing them down with hot chocolate from the trusty thermos. Nicole, sitting beside them, was quietly filling his pockets with jellybeans.

"Have some chestnuts," Rosie said, passing some to Larrie.

"I'm on a diet," she said.

"That girl, that one in the common-looking

silver tutu," drawled Daisy, "she said Larrie was fat."

"She means Lily," said Chris with a blush.

"Larissa, you are perfect," said Rosie. "You are not fat, in fact if you were any thinner, you wouldn't look as gorgeous as you do now. Lily's just jealous."

Larrie gave her mother a straight look. Her long hair was pulled off her face in a plait, her face was smeared charcoal from the bonfire and she knew she smelt of horse. "You're kidding," she said flatly. "Either that or you're blind."

"No, she's not," said Flo. "You're beautiful, that other girl just wears flashy stuff. Underneath all that, she's an ugly Barbarian."

Larrie wrinkled her nose up at him, but Rosie could see she was thinking about it. She gave Flo a grateful smile and a click. The sky rumbled again. Nicole filled the mugs closest to her and passed the jug round. "Allez, buvons!" They toasted each other's health and had just about finished off the potatoes when the first drops flung themselves hissing into the bonfire.

"It'll pass," said Larrie optimistically.

"I don't think so," said Rosie.

Chris scrambled to his feet and they started gathering mugs and jugs into the wicker basket, but Rosie was full of cider and chestnuts and, with the heat of the fire warming her front, felt too lazy to move. It probably wouldn't rain that much.

A deafening thunderclap made Larrie and Steve scream. "We'll have to run for it," said Larrie, jumping up. "Run Wonder Boy! Run everyone! Run for the cake!" They all fled in disarray, shouting for the sake of it and dropping things as they went. Flo held his hand out to Rosie.

"I won't dissolve," she said as he pulled her up.

"Oh, so you're indestructible," he said and kissed her. The birds stopped twittering, the sky darkened as if God had drawn the curtains, even the flowers held their breath as the pair of them stood lost to the world, entwined in each other's arms. Bang. Down it came, sheets and sheets of rain. But for a moment neither of them noticed. They just went on kissing. Then suddenly Rosie realised she was wet to the skin.

"Oh my God!" she yelled. "Run for it!"

He ran beside her and when she slipped on the wet grass, grabbed her hand.

You're mad," she gasped, as water started dripping off their foreheads. "We're going to be soaked though."

"Our first shower together," he gasped back.

In the kitchen, everyone was out of breath and laughing, dumping mugs and cushions on the table, stripping off wet clothes and rubbing their hair dry beside the stove.

"Where's daddy?" said Steve suddenly.

"Didn't they come with us?" said Larrie.

Nicole, Chris, and Daisy all went to the kitchen window to look out. Flo and Rosie were standing at the top of the steps leading to the terrace. They saw Flo, with his arms round Rosie's shoulders, saying something into her hair. She smiled and then looked up at him briefly. As the rain slashed down on them, Rosie nuzzled the wet shirt on his chest.

"Hallelujah!" said Nicole.

"Eee-yuk!" said Larrie, craning to see over their shoulders. "They're kissing! That's... eee-ooow!"

Flo was whispering something and then their faces merged again and the people in the kitchen could see was one of his hands caressing her soaking wet hair. His other hand was round her waist.

"Come away from the window!" said Chris firmly. "Larrie, stop it. Is Sobie in his box? Have you checked that the thunder didn't frighten him?"

Larrie forgot her mother's bizarre behaviour in an instant. "Oh my God, poor Sobie! He'll be terrified! The poor poor darling! I'd better take him an apple. Or perhaps two!"

"Wellies!" said Chris. "Take an umbrella and don't go across the terrace! Go out of the side door, idiot!"

Beside him, Daisy was still gazing out of the window, and beside her Steve had climbed up on a chair to see what was going on. Rosie and Flo were standing with their heads on each other's shoulders and their arms wrapped tightly around each other. They seemed completely oblivious to the torrential rain.

"Me and teddy do that," said Steve. "At night, before we go to sleep."

CHAPTER NINE

The next day, Rosie still felt breathless. If she closed her eyes, she could taste his mouth on hers, smell his aftershave on her skin, feel his fingers brushing her cheeks. It was as if her body was indelibly marked by his touch, as if some part of him remained on her body, caressing her, making her senses spin... Perhaps she wasn't menopausal after all. However that may be however, she wasn't about to let her physical senses get the better of her. There was only one thing to do. She picked up the wedges and the sledgehammer and went outside. Time to split logs. Winter had begun and the woodpile was pathetic.

Nicole was already there, oiling a chainsaw blade. "Well, I think you deserve a bit of happiness," she said gruffly, but Rosie didn't reply. She just started bashing a thick wedge into an upturned log with her sledgehammer. Her brain seemed to have gone to sleep. She couldn't think anything coherently; all she felt was a huge bubbling well of happiness inside her chest which made her want to laugh all the time. She wanted to hug the whole world, just to pass on a bit of her own endless joy. But since letting people in on her juvenile secret was out of the question, she just set out splitting logs as if her life depended on it.

"What about you and Ivan the Terrible?" she panted after a while. "Are you going to marry him?"

Nicole practically dropped her chainsaw she was so shocked by the idea. "Are you mad? Women like us don't marry men! He's a worthless hunk, anyway."

"He helps me with the dogs every morning," said Rosie with a dopey smile.

"I'm not talking about your lover boy, I mean Ivan. He's stupid, conceited, dishonest and right wing. He's the worst mayor we've ever had."

Rosie snorted and, with an expert twist of the wrist, threw a log onto the stack so that it landed exactly in the right place. "Who are you trying to kid?" she said, straightening up and putting her hands on her hips. "You're crazy about the guy!"

"I'm a communist born and bred! I can't be frequenting a guy who's practically a Nazi. A lifelong commitment to the people's rights isn't thrown away just on a whim, you know. My poor father would turn in his grave!" exclaimed Nicole, her ears going pink.

"So it's just a physical thing, then?"

"There's no "just" about sex," said Nicole grimly oiling the chainsaw again. She fired it up and drops of glistening oil showered around her. "Sex is a fundamental physical..."

The rest of her sentence was drowned out by the noise of her cutting through another thick branch, but in any case Rosie wasn't listening. She'd gone off into her own world again where hands smoothed over skin, where clothes were beside the point, where legs entwined and eyes met, and where there were no problems, just everlasting ecstasy.

"Oy!" shouted Nicole at the top of her voice and Rosie came to with a start. "What's he like in bed?" yelled Nicole. Rosie went bright red all over and shook her head energetically. Nicole was moving way too fast.

"Let's get these logs stacked," she said, and Nicole choked with laughter. Then she attacked another huge branch, hacking it efficiently into domesticated lengths for Rosie to split.

Shut safely into a dog crate in the kitchen, Dolly tried to bury her head under her tail. She hated wood-cutty noise. Upstairs in Chris's turret room, Minnie could hardly hear the chainsaw. Curled into a neat crescent in her very own armchair, she was watching her boy take photos of the new girl. They both smelt relaxed to her. Good thing, she thought.

Chris was lounging at the foot of his old-fashioned cast iron bed with his camera while Daisy lay propped up on a pile of pillows at the other end of the bed. Her black hair was gelled back off her forehead, and the winter sunlight was glinting silver as she breathed. Their clothes lay about in heaps on the floor, and there was a bunch of grapes on the bedside table. From time to time, Daisy ate one.

"I would say it's time young Steven learned to sleep in a room on his own," said Chris, adjusting the focus. "Don't you?"

"What d'you mean?"

"I want you to move your stuff over here."

"I don't have any stuff."

"Your toothbrush, your patchouli oil and your extensive collection of love beads, then. I want you to bring them here and sleep in this bed with me every night."

Daisy looked at him consideringly. "I just might do that," she said, and pulled a purple silk shawl over her thighs.

"Good. Tilt your head down, leave your mouth alone..."

"It won't do any good though. I mean, it's as well that the little squirt learns to live without me, but there's no point in you..."

"What do you mean? Relax your shoulder."

"I mean, my visa's running out and when it does I'll have to report myself to the Embassy or whatever."

"What for?"

"Because if I overstay, I won't get a visa to come back, but I don't actually have any way of going home. I don't have any money and my plane ticket's in London."

"Don't go then. Just stay here with me."

"Can't be done. I'm not really cut out for a life of felony and law evasion."

"Why haven't you got any money? Weren't you being paid in London? Why is your ticket in London?"

"In the heat of the moment, I forgot it. As for my financial crisis, London's an expensive city. Especially if your employer only pays you every second week, fails to pay you at all for the last three months of your contract, and you end up alone on the streets with a kid who can't help pissing on every bus, tube, taxi seat and bed you put him down on."

"Steve's mother really is 100% unadulterated witch, isn't she?" said Chris. "Poor little runt."

"Rotten to her soul," agreed Daisy. "That's why I took the risk."

"What risk?"

"Coming here, dope. And that was some risk, believe me. It cost all the money I had, I mean the taxi out here from Aix was like 130 euros. But you know, I couldn't just dump him at some orphanage or whatever. I mean, he's ugly and he's a pain in the ass with his food fads and his bed-wetting and his phobias, but you know..."

"Absolutely. I do know. He grows on you."

"Exactly. So I had to risk it, but like, how did I know Flo would still be here? He might have left and gone off somewhere; LA, the Caribbean, any damn place, and even if he was here, I didn't know what he was like. He might have chucked us out. You lot might have chucked us out. It was a serious risk."

"What? You never met him before?"

"Just met him once, at the park."

"You look stunning," said Chris. "Just tilt your head to the right. No, that's too far. Yes! Perfect."

"I hope I did the right thing. You know, if the squirt gets a better ride out of it, then...

"But it's turned out fabulously well," said Chris in a low voice. He put his camera down and crawled up the bed to lie beside her. "Just think, if the squirt's mother wasn't 100% evil witch, we wouldn't be here now, together in bed like this." He kissed her. "And you can see what my mother's like with stray puppies. She can't help herself." He pulled a few grapes off the bunch and popped one in her mouth and then one in his own. Then he kissed her again and she giggled and pushed him off. "You're choking me!"

"I'm going to do more than that in a minute!"

"But not with a mouthful of grapes, I hope!"

"Probably not, but you never know. I might turn out to be a pervy grape chap."

"What about your mom? She doesn't know, does she? About Flo. What's she going to do when she finds out?"

"It's not good, is it?" he said. "I mean before, it was kind of ok given the circumstances, but now..."

"Are you going to tell her?"

Chris raised his eyebrows. "Not me!" he exclaimed. "She'll hit the roof! Flo will have to tell her. I'll have a word with him."

"She'll be angry?"

"She doesn't like liars," said Chris, but Daisy let it go.

"Kiss me, buddy," she murmured and closed her eyes. She really wasn't totally interested in a pair of old-timers who didn't seem to be able to get it on. "Take me to heaven!" she said, running her fingers tantalisingly slowly through his hair.

"I'm going to keep you here," murmured Chris kissing her neck. "If they really want to chuck you out of Europe, you'll just have to marry me and then it'll be hard cheese to them, won't it?"

"Hard cheese!" she spluttered and started laughing like a maniac. "Is that a proposal?"

"I suppose you could interpret it that way," he said making a show of gazing round the room at the furniture.

"You're crazy," she said.

"That's your fault," he said, and pounced on her.

Down in the kitchen Pierre was attempting to do much the same thing to Rosie. "Let me just kiss your hand," he said earnestly. "Because I apologise for the other night. I was stupid and clumsy," he said, and then he added with a cheeky twinkle, "I didn't know you were in love!"

"I'm not!" said Rosie, going crimson. "Look, it's ok. Least said, soonest mended. Let's not talk about it again." His head drooped, he was the picture of dejection. "I have work to do," said Rosie, feeling like Cruella Deville. "You'd better go home to your wife."

He nodded and pulled a bottle out of his capacious jacket pocket. It was wrapped up in a crumpled brown paper bag. "I brought you this," he said holding it out to her. "With my most sincere excuses."

Relenting, she smiled at him and he instantly lunged forward and tried to kiss her. Dolly barked at him and Rosie grabbed his arm and turned him towards the door. "I'm not cross. Nothing is wrong. But you have to go!" she said, with her hand firmly between his shoulder blades. Dolly trotted to the door, exuding waves of puppy poo breath. Once she'd seen fatty off the premises, she might be able to persuade the pack leader into a stroll to the muckheap.

Pierre finally left, and Rosie watched him trail with reluctant feet all the way along the terrace to the corner. When he finally turned out of sight, she went back into the kitchen and saw him, through the window, whistling jauntily and twirling his moustache as he walked back to his car. Shaking her head, Rosie tore the paper bag open. Wow. A bottle of Moët! He must have got hold of a crate on the cheap somewhere.

"What have you got there?" said Flo coming into the kitchen hand in hand with Steve.

"A bottle of Moët," she said smiling at him. "Hello angel, how are you? Ready for some milk? Cheese on toast?"

"Peace offering from your over-enthusiastic swain?" said Flo taking Steve's coat off.

"How did you know?"

"We saw his car on the way up the drive. Did you say cheese on toast? Yes please. Notice anything different?" he said pointing at Stevie meaningfully.

"Oh my God, no glasses!" she said. "What did the doctor say? At the eye clinic?"

"Apparently, your friend Didier was right; he doesn't need them, he needs exercises to correct a slight cast but that's all. The guy took his glasses away and threw them in the bin. Look, he wrote a thing, but it's all in French. What does it say?"

"He says teddy doesn't need glasses eye-ver," said Steve. "Can I have some milk?"

"Help yourself," said Rosie, reading the letter. "It's a prescription for a course of sessions with some ogologue or other, a specialist anti-squinty quack person. What's the magic word, Stevie?"

"Abra-ca-dab?"

"Please and thank you," she said automatically. "Mind your Ps and Qs, put the milk back in the fridge. All joints on the table will be carved. This is great. How do you feel angel, without your glasses on?" She piled cheese on the toast and stuck it in the oven for few minutes.

"My ears is better."

"Really? That's good."

"Them glasses made my ears hurt."

She looked behind his sticking out ears. "Yes, that does look red. Never mind, I'll cream you up tonight and you'll never have to wear them again. Here, sit up properly, eat your nice toast and I'll get the ketchup out."

"My glasses is toast!" said Steve chirpily and bit into a cheesy triangle.

Flo looked at him guiltily and shook his head. Then he rumpled the little boy's short hair and looked at Rosie. "I didn't know," he said. "I swear I didn't know."

"I know you didn't," she said. "Tea?"

"What are you going to do with that bottle of Moët?" he said.

"I don't know," she said, "keep it for a special occasion I suppose."

"Why not tonight?"

"Why? What's happening tonight?"

"That's the point. Nothing's happening," he said. "We could sneak away to your study, just the two of us, build a nice log fire, and drink that champagne together."

"Wouldn't that be a bit of a waste?"

"I don't think so," he said and she stopped making tea and looked up at him. "Oh no, I think it could be very special," he said with a glinting smile. "Say yes," he said. "I dare you!"

"Can teddy have more ketchup?" said Steve.

"As much as he likes," said Flo, passing him the bottle. "Help yourself! Please," he said. "There are things we've never done together."

She didn't know what to say. "What things?" she croaked finally.

"Grown up things that people only do when they're alone together," he said with an unholy hoot of amusement.

"Laying eggs," said Stevie knowledgeably. "In the tummy button."

"Absolutely not!" said Rosie hysterically. "No eggs!" She clapped her hand over her mouth to stop herself from laughing out loud.

"I think we should talk about this later," said Flo wiping his eyes and trying not to laugh. "But a locked door, a log fire, and a bottle of champagne sound like a good start to me."

"Yes," she said.

Flo stared at her seriously. "You do mean that, don't you?"

Her heart thumping and her mouth dry, Rosie nodded. Life was taking a decidedly surreal turn and any minute now she'd wake up.

"Oh NO! No! No! No!" screamed Stevie sliding off his chair. His plate skidded off the table and smashed on the floor.

"What is it?" said Rosie

"What happened? said Flo.

They both bent over Steve where he sat on the floor. "Teddy fell in the ketchup!" he gasped. The top had come off the bottle and there was ketchup everywhere. "I'm bad! I'm bad," sobbed Steve. The table was covered, Steve's clothes were covered, and teddy was a ketchup bear.

"It's all right!" said Rosie picking him up. "It's only ketchup, don't cry." It took time to convince him that bears like tomatoes, and even longer to convince him that teddy didn't need to perish in the washing machine, and by the time Steve was calm, both he and Rosie were covered in ketchup.

"See, Teddy is all clean and happy again," said Rosie, wiping teddy's fur with a damp cloth.

"Teddy is my fren," said Steve sitting on his father's lap eating a biscuit. "Cos he never goes away."

"Hey kid, wanna come and read some stories?" said Daisy, coming into the kitchen looking flushed and pleased with life. "I'm way too tired to go out this afternoon. Why is everyone covered in ketchup? And what happened to your glasses?"

"I doesn't need them," said Steve. "The quacky-man frew them in the bin!"

Over his head, Daisy pulled a face expressing her condemnation of Sylvia's complete lack of parenting skills, but to Stevie she just said "Oh well. You still look like a nice guy to me," and took him off to his bedroom to chose a book.

"I um... Flo, are you busy?" said Chris coming into the kitchen as she left, with much the same look on his face as Daisy. "Can I have a word?"

"Would later be all right?" said Flo. "We were planning to collect pine cones and it's going to get cold later. Maybe around 6? Would that do?"

"Is it important?" said Rosie.

"No," said Chris shaking his head. "I mean it is. But it can wait an hour or so. We'll um... I'll see you later then?"

Flo nodded and Chris retreated back upstairs to his turret.

"What was all that about?" asked Rosie, ferreting about in cupboards looking for some more baskets.

"Haven't the faintest," said Flo. "Do we need gloves?"

"Not unless you're scared of snakes."

"What! Are they poisonous?"

"Only kidding."

Equipped with wicker baskets, Rosie whistled up the dogs and they tramped across the lawn and down a path past Nicole's vegetable garden with the big dogs dashing ahead and Dolly poodling along behind them smelling everything methodically as she went. On walkies, you never knew what might turn out to be edible.

"I've never seen the garden properly," said Flo.

"Well, it could be beautiful, but I have my work cut out just stopping it going into a wild bramble patch," said Rosie. "It really needs a proper gardener. It's completely walled you know. Two acres surrounded by a ten foot wall made of small hand-fired red bricks."

"You sound like an estate agent."

She laughed. "Well, it's while since I went round it, to be honest. I just don't get the time. There used to be a wonderful rose garden down there in that sunken bit but you know, and this avenue is nice. I always think I'd like to canter down it side-saddle, wearing a habit and a veil."

"Do you ride?"

"I used to but I couldn't keep another horse. You've no idea how expensive that animal of Larrie's is. I keep nagging her not to change his entire bed all the time and not to use too much of anything, but it's useless. And she never asks for anything else. I mean, she never wants clothes or shoes or holidays or, you know, CDs, books or anything."

The dogs came rushing back and she picked up a large stick and threw it for them so that they all dashed off again.

"She doesn't like school, does she?"

"No-one does, do they? But she's so imaginative, so bouncy, she just gets bored out of her brains. I don't blame her, I couldn't stand it myself, but she's got to go. I can't do home schooling on top of everything else. And it's good for her to learn to fit in with the other kids."

"Is the school that bad?"

"Appalling, frankly."

"Isn't there some other school in the area?"

"Not really. I mean nothing she could get to on the school bus. And if she went to boarding school she'd have to leave Sobie." There was a pause as they tramped through the drifts of autumn leaves.

"Tell me again why we're collecting pine cones."

"For Christmas. They make great fire lighters. We'll light all the fires we can. It won't make the place warmer of course, but it'll feel warmer and the kids love it."

Flo took his jacket off and put it in one of the baskets he was carrying. "Come here," he said putting his arm round her shoulder. He was half expecting her to wriggle away but she didn't and when they had to stop walking side by side because the path was too narrow, she let him take her hand. "I warn you," he told Rosie, "If anyone except me wants your attention tonight, they won't get it!"

"They won't? But what if there's an emergency?"

"They'll have to wait," he said firmly. "I don't care. Even if the entire house is burning down around our ears, they'll have to wait! Even if some misbegotten cur swallows a whole damn toaster, they'll all just have to wait!" He tilted her chin up with his hand and kissed her. Rosie clung to him as if he was the last puppy on a desert island.

"Come on!" she said finally. "Pine cones! If we go back without them, we'll never hear the end of it. Get gathering!" She ducked out of his embrace and ran off down the path towards the pine trees shouting for the dogs, and they all came rushing up, loping and scampering along behind her.

Flo laughed. She was off her head. Completely barking. But he didn't care. He was crazy about the girl. He raced off after her too, the wicker baskets bumping and cracking against his knees. He caught up with her at the clearing and his baskets clatter to the ground as he flung his arms round her. She lost her balance and they both tumbled onto the dry pine needles. They rolled over together. He kissed her again and tickled her. They were both out of breath and laughing.

"I've never met anyone like you before," he said. "I... I've never felt like this before."

She turned away but he grabbed her and suddenly she kissed him. Really kissed him. Her body arched towards him, and he felt her legs tangling over his. Rosie wasn't thinking, her whole body was on fire and all she felt was happiness surging through her veins. She even forgot to give him a click. He was perfect, and she was in love. "Get off dogs!" she ordered, as they snuffled around the humans on the ground. "Stop it!" she said as Dolly started licking her ear.

"Basket!" ordered Flo clicking his fingers. "Get back!"

Surprised, the dogs sat down and Flo raised his eyebrows at Rosie. She smiled. Dogs could always tell. She reached up to play with Flo's hair as he leaned over her and then he kissed her again and she ran her hands up underneath his shirt.

"I need to talk to you," he said, but a sudden metallic rattle made him jump. "What the hell?" he exclaimed, staring in the direction of the noise, which he had recognised instantly; the automatic clatter of a camera. The dogs raced off barking like maniacs and surrounded an oak tree just on the other side of the clearing, howling like maniacs. Dolly's four paws all left the ground every time she yapped, and the three big dogs clawed at the tree, slavering and barking in fury.

Hugo the fat photographer was sitting in the crook of a low branch clutching a large camera fitted with a huge lens. He went on pointing it at the dogs and at Flo who picked up a stick and flung it at him. It missed and he swore.

"Get down! Stop taking those bloody photos!" yelled Rosie. "What in hell do you think you're doing? This is private property I'll have you know!"

Flo had found a really long stick and was poking it viciously at the photographer's legs when suddenly he fell out of the tree, screaming that someone had shot him. The dogs converged on him, variously licking and pawing at him while Rosie yelled her head off and Flo swore fluently.

"Heel!" shouted Rosie. "Dolly, sit! Rupert, behave yourself. You lot. Down! Get down!" The dogs reluctantly moved away from their prey. "Sit!" yelled Rosie.

"Not you," Flo told the photographer. "Don't move. Or you're dead."

Hugo collapsed back onto the ground moaning, and they heard footsteps racing towards them. It was Chris, waving an air rifle aloft and Nicole, armed with a shotgun.

"Bloody lucky Chris shot you before I did!" said Nicole grimly.

"Sorry, Muma!" gasped Chris. "We saw him sneaking up the drive but I couldn't remember where I hid the bloody air rifle!"

"Stand and deliver!" screamed Larrie, riding

Sobie bareback at a gallop through the trees towards them. "Did you shoot him, Chris?" Her hair flew out behind her in waves as she jumped over fallen tree trunks and Sobie kicked his way through piles of leaves.

"Yes, I shot him," said Chris. "But only with that stupid air gun of yours. Trouble is, I don't think I've actually managed to hurt him. I was too far away. The pellet just bounced off his anorak."

"That's not fair!" she said, boiling fury in her eyes. "Why do you get to shoot everybody when I'm not allowed to? If you'd told me, I'd have got my duelling pistol and shot him right through the heart. In fact, if I go and get it now, can I?"

"No, I got here first. It's my turn," said Nicole, grabbing Sobie's head collar. "It's a while since I used this shotgun; let me shoot him!"

"No!" shouted Chris. "He's mine and I've a good mind to finish him off!"

"Don't let them shoot me," whined Hugo, thin trails of slime starting to run out of his nose. "Please..."

"What's he doing here anyway?" said Larrie. She leaned forward and hugged Sobie's neck. "You're my baby," she murmured.

Flinging the airgun on the ground, Chris snatched the camera out of Hugo's hand and started fiddling with it. "He's been taking photos of these two." He went on fiddling. "Flo, check what else he's got. Any other cameras in that bag? Any phones or other recording devices?"

"Of Muma and Flo? Why? What were they doing?" said Larrie and then suddenly realising, bit her lip and buried her head in Sobie's mane, convulsed with giggles.

"No, don't delete them," moaned Hugo.

"Right, that's gone. Sorry about the firework stuff, but you should have cleared the memory before you came out, shouldn't you?" said Chris. "And for your information, you finally had one shot that was at least in focus. A miracle for you."

"You know this guy?" demanded Flo.

"We went to the same school. He's an assistant at the photography shop in Moisson. Gives the worst advice this side of Marseille. I gave him a couple of photography lessons a couple of years ago but it was like teaching a log to sing. Completely hopeless."

"That's because he's fat, spotty, stupid and pathetic," said Larrie fiercely and Sobie jerked his head as if he'd had enough conversation and wanted to get back to his stable.

"He once tried to kiss Larrie at a Christmas party," explained Chris. "A fatal error."

"He makes me vomit frogs!"

"You won't always say that!" said Hugo.

"Where you're concerned, I rather think she will," said Chris.

"I always knew you lot were connected to the stars. I always knew I'd get something if I hung around long enough," said Hugo.

"Right, that's it. This time I'm definitely getting my pistol," said Larrie.

"Don't bother. He's not worth it," said Chris. "It would be a waste of ammo anyway." He went on deleting photos from Hugo's spare memory card. "He's been following you two for some time," he said.

"Don't delete them all," whined Hugo. "I'll give you a cut!"

"Shut up! Be grateful I don't smash the damn thing over your miserable, worthless, flea-ridden head."

"He's got two other cameras, and a mobile phone," said Flo standing up. A ray of sun shone through his curls, making him look like a Greek god.

"Check his pockets," said Chris, beginning to fiddle with the mobile phone.

"You're sure you can delete everything. He won't be able to retrieve anything later?" said Flo.

Chris shook his head. "Not a hope. Not even a lab will be able to retrieve them."

"But what's going on?" said Rosie. "Why is it so important if he's been taking a few photos? I mean, of course he shouldn't, it's rude and disgusting and a breach of privacy, but it's not like he could have sold them or anything."

"But I could have!" sobbed Hugo in French. "I could have made a fortune! I'd have been out of this dump. I could have moved to Cannes and got a job with Hello magazine."

"You're dreaming," said Rosie. "Chris says you're a rotten photographer. And taking pictures from a tree... well I bet they wouldn't have been any good."

"What!? Pictures of Florian Kent in his hide-away love nest? Snogging his new love interest while he waits to start filming Bond? Florian Kent getting down and dirty in a forest!" yelled Hugo. "I could have sold them all over the world. I could have syndicated them! I'd have made my name! I'd have been rolling in money, I could have had a Porsche like his!"

He scrambled to his feet, and Rosie grabbed at the dogs.

"Heel Dolly! You dogs! Down! Who in hell is Florian Kent?"

For a minute no-one answered. Nicole was obviously as mystified as Rosie, but the others were united in guilt. Larrie was speechless and scarlet, and Flo appeared to have gone deaf. Very pale, Chris cleared his throat. "He's the guy from Hell Raisers, Jelly Bean, Heat at Midnight, and Wave Goodbye. He was the star of the Loverboy Series and he's in line to play James Bond in the next three Bond films," he confessed. "Flo is Florian Kent."

"World famous film star, millionaire hell-raiser, womaniser and second most handsome hunk in the world," said Larrie. "They call him the Irresistible Man. You and Nicole are the only people on the planet who've never heard of him."

Rosie looked at Flo and he gave her a crooked, charming, guilty little smile, like a school-boy caught out with worms in his pockets. The Irresistible Man.

"You knew," Rosie said to Chris. The swelling bubbly happiness in her chest was drowning in a rising tide of all too familiar betrayal and loss. "When did you find out?"

"He recognised me straight away," said Flo, reaching his hand out towards her. "But I blackmailed him. I..."

"Flo!" said Chris, jerking his head towards Hugo whose nose had dried up and whose pallid spotty face was glowing with interest.

"We'd better lock him up somewhere," said Chris. "Until we decide what to do with him."

"Oh please can I shoot him?" said Larrie sliding off Sobie's back. "Please?" Neither of them could quite bear to look at their mother, her face was so drawn and pale. "Give me the airgun. I'll shoot him in the foot so he can't run away!"

"Bouges!" she Nicole, gesturing at Hugo with her shotgun. "Get moving."

"I'll take all this stuff," said Chris, gesturing at the cameras and bags scattered around them. "Get back on that nag of yours and you can take the airgun."

Larrie scrambled back onto Sobie and leaned down for the gun. "Reach for the sky!" she yelled in her best highwayman's voice. "And no funny business! Get moving!" The four of them started tramping back to the house, leaving Rosie and Flo alone in the woods.

"You lied," she said in a flat voice. "Right from

the beginning you lied to me." She felt numb. "You're just another scumbag actor on the make. Just floating through the world playing God in other people's lives until it suits you to pack up and leave them." She was determined not to cry, she simply wouldn't give him the satisfaction, but her face was hot with angry tears.

"Don't be like that," begged Flo, walking towards her.

"I thought you were different, but you're all the same. You and your bloody chip bag sex! Don't touch me! I hate you!" she shouted, moving out of arm's reach. Dolly yapped at him warningly and Rupert's hackles went up. All the dogs milled around looking worried. They weren't sure what was going on but vaguely realised that their pack leader wasn't happy. Would din-dins improve the situation? Or should they give smelly man a good barking?

"You're a liar," she said.

The sun slid suddenly out of sight and the woods were cold and dark. Flo shook his head. "I'm not. I never pretended to be anyone I wasn't. Everything about me is true," he said, walking back towards her.

"Yes, I know. Sex means nothing, it's all just a joke to you because you're a film actor and a star," she said, fending him off.

"Not any more. I've changed." He stood in front of her and out of desperation he gave her his award-winning, million-dollar rueful smile. It was his trademark, and it never failed.

"Bullshit!" she spat. "Stop that mindless grinning. And stop lying!" She wanted to hit him but didn't dare in case it gave him the chance to touch her. She was starting to feel exhausted and faint. It was time to stop arguing and get back into the house. She needed tea. And a flea comb because Dolly would be full of grass burrs.

"I'm not lying!" shouted Flo. "Why do people always think actors are liars?"

"Actors always pretend. It's the only thing they know how to do. None of you know the difference between fiction and the truth. I've heard this all before," she said tramping off towards the house with the empty baskets.

Suddenly Flo understood. "Chris and Larrie's father, that's it, isn't it? Whatever he did to you, I'm picking up the tab aren't I?" He grabbed her arm and tried to make her turn round, but she just pulled away and went on tramping.

"Please believe me," he said, tagging along behind her. "Whatever happened in the past, I'm different. I won't let you down."

"I don't believe you," she said, and he thought she was crying.

"Love means faith," he said desperately. "Taking a leap in the dark."

"What movie does that come from?" she snapped, spinning round to look at him.

He just stood there. What could he say? He had just remembered. It did come from a movie. It was one of his most famous lines.

"I wanted to believe you," she said finally. "Against all the odds, I ignored all the signs that you weren't really a writer; I closed my eyes to everything. But I was wrong. So just tell me one thing. Why did Sally foist you onto me?"

"She wanted me out of the spotlight. Somewhere I wouldn't be recognised and where the press wouldn't find me. She wanted me to keep out of trouble."

Exhausted and empty, Rosie turned and tramped away.

"I never meant this!" he called, running after her. "You have to believe me!"

"Leave me alone. Just go away."

"I can't just go," he said, tagging along. "You know that. There's Steve."

"You are the lowest of the low, total slime," she said, rounding on him furiously. "Using that poor little kid as an excuse."

He looked at her and was shocked. Tears were washing down her cheeks but her face was fixed and solid like a concrete mask. "Just stay out of my sight then," she ordered him. "It's over. Do you understand? The story's finished." She walked away through the falling leaves, the big dogs frisking and scampering around her as if trying to cheer her up. The dark swallowed her little by little and all Flo could hear was Rosie whistling the dogs up.

"Dolly, this way! Come on, baby!" Dolly flicked one contemptuous glance at Flo. Only a fool would upset the pack leader. Then she went cantering off after Rosie, her long furry ears flying and her tail whirling over her back.

CHAPTER TEN

In the disused pigsty, Hugo heard footsteps going past and for a minute thought that he was about to be rescued. He sincerely hoped so because his buttocks were numb from sitting on an upturned, galvanised, metal bucket. Larrie went to the door and stared out. It was starting to get dark. Chris looked at her but she shook her head. "It's Muma," she said. "On her own."

"Not good," said Chris, and turned his attention back to Hugo. "Now, what are we going to do with you?"

"You can't do anything!" said Hugo, but he sounded unconvinced.

"I'll tie him to Sobie and drag him along the road until he's sorry. Or even better, we'll tie one leg to Sobie and the other to another horse and then we'll ride them in opposite directions."

"But we haven't got a second horse," objected Chris.

"Well, we can get one. I'll borrow that Arab from down the road. He looks pretty strong."

"Just feed him to the bichons," said Nicole

quietly. "They're small but they're like piranhas once they get started."

Hugo's eyes widened and he shivered in fear. He wasn't particularly scared of Larrie, but Nicole was a different matter: everyone knew she was a maniac. A second set of footsteps went past, and Larrie went back to the door. "It's Flo," she whispered.

"What?" whispered Chris.

"He looks awful," said Larrie. "Like he's ill or something."

"This is all your fault, shitface!" said Nicole, viciously poking Hugo in the ribs. "How dare you come here with your horrible cameras?"

"There's no point," said Chris. "Unfortunately, he's right. We can't do anything to him."

"But we've got to stop him," said Larrie.

"I'll stop him, the rotten worm scum of a whore of a potato insect," muttered Nicole jabbing at him again.

"We've got to cut a deal with him."

Hugo's piggy little eyes swivelled round to Chris with a faint gleam. "What can you suggest?" he whined.

"I can get you access to a much bigger star," said Chris.

"No!" said Larrie. "I don't want HIM here! No! Don't you dare!"

"That's not what I'm thinking," said Chris shaking his head. "I don't want HIM here either. But we could set up a meeting, say one of us wanted to see him and then send this slime bucket along. What do you say?"

"Who are you talking about?" said Hugo suspiciously. "Is he A-list? Who is he?"

"That would be worth a fortune!" said Nicole, awed. "I mean, are you thinking the whole story? You'd let him have the whole story?"

"What?" said Hugo wriggling about on the upturned bucket. "Tell me!"

"First you have to swear!" said Larrie. "On your mother, on your dog, oh you're scared of dogs aren't you, you pathetic little slime ball. Well swear on your precious career as a tabloid hack and crap photographer, then. Swear you'll do this our way."

Nicole, Chris and Larrie all looked at each other with trepidation and a certain excitement.

"I don't see what else we can do," said Chris finally.

"Time some old scores were settled," said Nicole grimly.

"Well if you think it'll work," said Larrie, "I'll cut his arm!" Larrie got her Swiss knife out and spat on it enthusiastically. She wiped it on her jeans, dried it on her shirt, and advanced on Hugo. "Don't worry, it's very sharp so it won't hurt," she said.

"No!" squealed Hugo. "No blood!" and fainted away. His heavy body thumped down on the floor and the galvanised bucket skittered away into the corner. Chris burst out laughing.

"Coward!" said Larrie contemptuously. "He'll never be fit for a life of adventure!"

"You leave him to me," said Nicole, giving Hugo's unconscious form a metallic little smile. "I'll give him the deal and I'll make sure he sticks to it. Don't worry. He won't double-cross ME. Go and help your mother. I think she needs you in the kitchen."

Chris and Larrie looked at her but the stare she gave them back made her opinion quite clear. They were guilty of aiding and abetting the criminal film star to evade the consequences of his decadent, debauched, aristo lifestyle and that was unforgivable. Dropping his eyes, Chris went bright red. "We thought it was for the best," he said awkwardly.

"He blackmailed both of us about me being a highwayman and having a gun," said Larrie in a small voice. "And skiving off school. So it's all my fault."

"Go and apologise to your mother," said Nicole. She turned back to Hugo, who was blinking and rubbing his head, and cocked the shotgun. "As for you, I'm going to give you a souvenir you'll never forget," she said, and took aim at his camera. She pulled trigger and it exploded into smithereens, tiny pieces of shrapnel flying all over the pigsty.

"Christ!" said Chris jumping out of his skin. "Is everyone all right?" He grabbed Larrie, who was doubled up beside him. She stood up and he realised she was choking with laughter. Nicole lent the shotgun up against the wall in the corner and went over to Hugo where he lay on the floor. She rolled him over with her foot, and then bent down and put her fingers on the side of his throat.

"K.O.," she said in a disgusted voice. "He really has passed out." She looked up at the other two. "Go, go on. I'll deal with him, and don't you worry. He won't tell anyone anything."

"You won't actually kill him though, will you?" said Chris.

"GO!"

Chris nodded and dragged Larrie out of the pigsty. As they walked across the stable yard in the gathering dusk, she said, "What do you think she'll do with him?"

"God knows," said Chris. "She's thick as thieves with his mother. Has been any time this last 20 years, so I expect she'll drive him home and complain that she caught him climbing trees in the château grounds and his mother'll give him hell. And to get us all out of the shit, I suppose she'll tell him something about a certain A-lister of our acquaintance."

They shuffled sheepishly into the kitchen and stood just inside the doorway. Rosie was peeling potatoes and at first glance, apart from swollen red eyelids, she looked completely normal. "Are you hungry, kids?" she asked brightly.

"I'm sorry, Muma. I didn't think it was a bad lie," said Larrie.

"Supper won't be long," said Rosie and smiled, but only with her mouth.

"At the beginning I didn't think it would matter," said Chris. "And then we were all getting on so well... but I was going to make him tell you. Honestly."

"It's not your fault," said Rosie. "I'm not cross with you. Honestly. It's all right. I was just being a bit silly, that's all."

"Oh good," said Chris. He gave her a quick hug and a kiss on the cheek. "I'll just go and find Daisy then," he said. "Twenty minutes, eh?"

Rosie nodded and he slid out of sight. Larrie stood by the door, fiddling with the doorknob. "It's my fault," she said finally. "Because I shot Flo's windscreen with an air rifle and made him crash his car."

"You did what?" said Rosie, the hair on the back of her neck rising. "You weren't... don't tell me you were being a highwayman again? Not after all I've said?"

Larrie nodded and scuffed her toe along the floor. "He deserved it Muma! He was lying, and I wanted to see his passport so I could prove it."

"Well, why didn't you just tell me?"

"Because of the money from Auntie Sally," said Larrie. "I thought we needed it for the tax, and anyway I thought he was just going to sit in the east wing, write his book and pillock off a week later. I thought you wouldn't have to worry about the bills."

"Well, you were right," said Rosie. "And that's exactly what's happened. So don't look like that, there's nothing wrong. You just wash your hands and lay the table for me, and if you're good I'll let you mash the tates, how's that?"

She blinked the water out of her eyes, gave

Larrie a reassuring kiss and chucked her under the chin. "But you're a cheeky monkey all the same and I'll be asking questions about that airgun tomorrow, is that understood?"

Larrie gave her a twinkling naughty smile and nodded. "It was a good shot, Muma!" she confided. "Straight through the windscreen. You should have seen his face! He was terrified!"

"I'm sure he was!" said Rosie. "Wash the salad for me, there's a good girl."

Upstairs, Flo waylaid Chris, dragged him into the gloom of the piano room and shut the door. "Tell me about your father!" he said tersely.

"The last of the great romantics?" said Chris.

"Yes but who is he? I have to know," said Flo. "Please Chris! Because honestly, I'm not really getting this. Why does it matter that I'm an actor?" he demanded. "I mean I lied but actually, only about my job. I mean, I've always been me; I haven't been acting or pretending to be someone else. Your father isn't an actor is he?"

Chris looked at him and raised his eyebrows.

"He is," said Flo slowly. "Who is he? Do I know him?"

"He's Ralph Donnington," said Chris, and Flo's jaw dropped.

"Ralph? Your father's Ralph Donnington! The most-handsome-man-in-the-world-Ralph-Donnington? The leading-Shakespearian-actor-of-his generation, turned silver-fox, screen-heart-throb, and chat show favourite, Ralph Donnington?

THE Ralph Donnington?"

Chris just looked sardonic.

"Oh my God, suddenly you look just like him!" said Flo, leaning against the door. "What happened?"

"I don't want to talk about it," said Chris. "Ask my mother. Excuse me, please. I'd like to leave the room or are you intending to hold me here by force?"

"I never meant..."

"I told you not to hurt her," said Chris. "And now you have and it's all my fault. Stand aside if you please!"

Flo moved out of the way, Chris opened the door and stalked out of the room. Flo dashed out onto the landing after him. "Chris? Just one thing? Please! Lotta's phone number. What is it?"

"You should have told Muma before," said Chris. "I meant to speak to you about it this afternoon, but..."

"I'm sorry, you're right Chris. I should have told her. Also I need to borrow your Renault. Seeing as my car got towed... please, Chris."

Chris stopped and glared at him across the hall. Flo looked genuinely sorry. He pulled his car keys out off his pocket and tossed them over. "I'll text you the number," he said and stalked off to his turret.

Flo let him go. It was a bloody mess, but Chris could wait. First he had to dig out the whole story. He went back into his room and started piling on clothes. Within minutes he was on his way to Lotta's. Chris, standing at the turret window, watched his rusty Renault 4 bounce away down the drive. Then he raised his eyebrows and shook his head. Daisy was sitting at the desk going through a contact sheet. "What happened?" she asked.

"I would say the words shit and fan spring to mind," said Chris. "Did you have a nice afternoon, squirt?"

"We did reading," said Steve from deep inside a duvet-nest he'd made on the end of the bed. "And then we did sleeping. And I had Minnie bercos teddy is on the stove and Minnie loves me nearly as much as teddy. Has he gone? My daddy?"

Chris shrugged, and Steve hugged Minnie nervously.

"Just gone to the shop," said Daisy. "Don't worry, honey, he'll be back once he's bought a new piece of domestic machinery."

"Wass that?"

"Oh you know, toasters, rice cookers, waffle makers, all those little machines that he likes buying."

"Maybe a hot choclit machine," said Steve hopefully. "I like hot choclit!"

"Well I'm just going to find a jumper and then we'd better go down and help with supper," said Chris. "Don't want to rock any boats."

Downstairs in the kitchen they ate aligot, everyone making an effort not to notice Flo's empty chair or Rosie's stricken eyes, but they all felt awkward and ill at ease. All except Stevie who was chattering about hot chocolate and Rosie, who spent the whole meal talking jolly gibberish to Dolly but ate absolutely nothing.

Meanwhile Flo was pacing up and down in Lotta's kitchen banging the back of every chair as he went past. "But what the fuck happened?" he demanded.

"Sit down and stop bashing things about!" said Lotta. "You're giving me a headache. You can have a rosehip cordial if you like."

"Haven't you got any whisky?"

"If you don't want rosehip, I've got fig leaf."

"Sounds disgusting!"

She bared her teeth at him. "Well, it is. Absolutely vile. You're better off with the rose hip, frankly. And I'm not offering you anything else because I'm not sure yet whether I like you or not."

Flo poured himself a small glassful of horrible cordial, and sat down at the table with his head propped up on one arm. Lotta pulled a face and shook her head. "It was the usual old story," she sighed. "Rosie was practically just out of school, had her first job as a set designer, and Ralph had just got his first job in the West End when she got pregnant," said Lotta. "That was Chris. The production was May Thunder."

"I remember that. It was a massive hit," he nodded.

"Precisely. It hit him all the way to Hollywood. He just came back once, to look for Rosie and Chris. Snatched them up and brought them to France where he'd bought that huge great château. He was going to do it up and start his own production company and make hit movies there. Less than a year later - I do warn you Rosie seems to be unbelievably fertile - Larrisa was born and the day after that, he disappeared. Went back to the States and was never heard of again."

"But why?"

Lotta shrugged. "The baby was premature. Low birth weight, strange hip formation, face like a wizened monkey and the doctors thought she might have a heart defect, but they weren't sure it would be worth attempting to operate."

"Larrie?"

"Yes, Larrie. To be honest I think Ralph just couldn't stand the thought of watching the baby die. But Rosie ignored all the doctors and took Larrie home. Sat by her bed, day and night, for years. Didn't sleep, didn't speak, didn't leave that kid's side for a minute, and eventually she just grew out of the irregular heartbeat. And then when she was about five, she had an operation on her hip and now, as you see, she's fine. Just a bit headstrong because Rosie can't say no to her."

"And Ralph?"

"Never came back. Never phoned, never sent word. Not a sausage. He just left Rosie in that derelict château with those two sickly little kids; Chris had one chest infection after another, you wouldn't believe it now but he was a runty, peculiar little thing - but Ralph never came back."

"But he must have paid maintenance?"

"Not a penny. She hadn't got enough money to pursue him across the Atlantic, let alone hire a lawyer to do it. And even now I don't think she's got an address for him. He probably doesn't know whether those kids are dead or alive."

"No wonder she's pissed off with men," said Flo, running his fingers through his hair. It had grown out a bit and was starting to twist back into its natural curls. "But I thought Ralph was a bachelor. I mean, I never heard him mention..."

"Precisely," said Lotta. "She and the kids were just erased from his past. The entire world has read all about his charity work for African orphans, his conservation efforts for American eagles, his loneliness, his work ethic, his films, his endless culture and charm. But Rosie and the kids could have been figments of his imagination for all they appear in his life story."

"Well, I don't suppose Rosie cares," said Flo slowly.

"I don't think she really thinks about it to be honest, no. But Chris cares. He's furious with his father for not acknowledging him."

"What about Larrie?"

"I don't know. She's never met her father, so perhaps you don't miss what you've never known."

Flo dropped his head onto the table. "Oh crapping Christ!" he said. "I hate that bastard. I always have. Bloody, sanctimonious, sneering shit-head."

"As you know, I don't drink," said Lotta. "But I might have a medicinal hash cookie around, if you think it might help?"

Flo raised his eyebrows.

"I'm old, alcoholic and riddled with arthritis, but I'm a damn good gardener," she said. "It's top quality. And I'll make you a nice cup of tea to wash it down. I do find this stuff makes you a bit thirsty."

She got the cookies out and made tea while Flo got up again and ranged around her kitchen tapping and flicking at things. "Is that why she won't let Larry be a stunt rider?" he said at last. "Because of her father?"

"Partly. It's bloody dangerous for a gal with a dodgy hip you know, and I think she's got other ideas for Larrie. I mean she doesn't get on at school, but she's not stupid. She has a very vivid imagination and she draws brilliantly although she's never had a lesson in her life."

"Really?"

"All horses of course, but the point is Rosie thinks she'd be better off doing something creative and keeping riding as a hobby. Also of course, Rosie doesn't have an outstandingly positive impression of film people. Why would she want Larrie mixing with them?"

"Well, she's not far wrong. A lot of them are shits," said Flo, throwing a hash cookie into his mouth and chewing.

"Thing is, that year at the château when Rosie was pregnant with Larrie, the place was full of Hollywood types: glamorous, rich, witty, hard drinking, hard-nosed and all touchy-feely; all of them desperate to pat Rosie's bump and call her darling. Actors, producers, directors, I don't know who they all were. Outlandish clothes, gallons of champagne, pounds and pounds of cocaine, darling you're so lovely, darling we adore your romantic, collapsing château, darling, darling, darling. But when Ralph left, they all went with him. Rosie was still in hospital with the baby, but not one of them stayed behind to look after Chris or feed the dog."

"What a shit!" said Flo. He was guiltily aware that he hadn't been a brilliant father himself, but even he wasn't that bad.

"That's where Nicole came in. Her family have lived and worked at the château for generations - she was born there - of course Ralph had thrown her out when he bought the place, but she kept sneaking back to water the vegetable garden, and then one day she found Chris wandering along the main road, filthy and hungry and crying for his muma. He was only 6 years old."

"You mean...?"

"Exactly. Not one of them bothered to look after him. They just all disappeared back to the States leaving Chris all alone in that great wreck of a place. Anything could have happened to him. Well, of course, once Nicole realised what had happened she moved right back into château with Chris. And then Rex, the dog Rosie had at that time, turned up on the doorstep soon afterwards. He'd been kicked out too of course, but he came back once the coast was clear. Very smart dog, that one. I think that's when the first cats turned up as well..."

"Keep your eyes on the road," said Flo, munching another cookie.

"All right bossy boots. Anyway, while she was waiting for Rosie and Larrie to get out of hospital, Nicole gathered up all the luggage and the clothes Ralph and his pals left behind, and sold the whole lot in the market. Used the money to buy clothes for the baby. And a good job too, because none of them was ever heard from again. Not so much as a postcard. It was like they just vaporised. Although Rosie did try and contact them."

"She must have had a phone number!"

"She didn't. Come on, your memory isn't that short. Mobiles and texts and internet were all only just beginning. Transatlantic phone calls cost a fortune back then. I didn't even have a number for him."

"Why would you have his number?"

Lotta rolled her eyes. "Don't be dim. I was the estate agent who sold Ralph the château. I thought he was bloody marvellous. I first met Rosie when she came in to my office dragging two wailing kids and asking for Ralph's number. But I didn't have it."

"No?" said Flo unbelieving.

Lotta blushed and looked down at her own shaking hands. "You lose track of a lot of things when you're permanently drunk," she said. "I don't know where the piece of paper went." She looked up at him steadily and he nodded.

"Rosie must be the basis of Ralph's famous Frenchwoman story," said Flo. "You know, the mysterious beauty who died giving birth to a stillborn son. Which is why he's always remained single. Out of heartbreak." He gave a mirthless laugh. "I always thought it was too pat myself. In my experience, women who have your children never ever die. They just go on demanding money forever." He stared at the wooden boards of Lotta's kitchen table for a while and then he looked up at her. "I'm not like him. I swear it."

Lotta nudged the teapot his way. "Now you've said that, you can have another cup of tea if you like," she said. "Don't get cocky, I still haven't made a final judgement. I just perhaps don't dislike you as much as I thought I did."

"I'm a nice guy, Lotta, I swear I am!"

"Don't tell me, show me."

Flo dropped his head on the table. "I will try," he said in an indistinct voice. "But I wish I'd known all this in the beginning!"

"You'd better sleep on the sofa," said Lotta. "My back's starting to complain. There's a blanket on that chair. Turn the lights off."

Flo wondered if anyone would miss him, but his limbs were floating and after almost an entire tin of Lotta's hash cookies, he felt lethargic and thirsty. So in the end he drank a couple of glasses of water and went to sleep fully dressed on the sofa. The next morning he woke up with a fit of the glooms, and Lotta was obviously pissed off to find him still mooching around her kitchen.

"Haven't you got a home to go to?" she snapped.

He climbed back into the rusty Renault feeling horrible, but he would have been gratified if he'd known that outside the stable block in the freezing cold, Chris was manfully trying to defend him. "I'm telling you, muma, you can't hate someone just because of their job," protested Chris. "You're wrong. You can't judge everyone the same way. He's his own man, he's not..."

"I have the dogs to do."

"Muma!"

"Darling, it's all right. I'm not cross with you and I don't hate Flo. I was a bit upset yesterday but that's all finished now. I'm perfectly fine about the whole thing!"

"Well I'm glad to hear that," said Flo, striding across the courtyard looking rumpled and stubbly.

"Where have you been?" said Chris.

"Talking to Lotta," said Flo, his glinting eyes fixed on Rosie. "Taking a few history lessons. It always helps you understand the present, don't you think?"

"Well the past is past. If you don't mind, I've got work to do," said Rosie. "I have a new bichon litter to look after and Poncho is here - a terrier with a crooked tail!"

"Allow me!" replied Flo, reaching for the huge old cast iron bolt on the barn door.

"I don't need your help!" she snapped.

"Not a good tactic," said Chris.

"I'll decide about that!" Flo snapped, and Rosie clapped her hands in his face. "Shoo! Off you go! Vamoosh!"

Automatically, he stepped back a couple of paces and trod in a recent souvenir of Sobie's. "Argh!" he yelled. "Damn it!"

"Don't swear at me!" she retorted, looking round for something to throw at him.

"Calm down, Muma!" urged Chris.

Smelling adrenaline in the air, Dolly started racing round in circles barking her head off, and the three big dogs loped into the yard to see what was happening.

"I'll do more than swear in a minute!" said Flo, murderously cross and trying to find somewhere to wipe his shoes.

"Muma," said Chris warningly, but it was no use. She'd backed into a pile of potatoes that had gone rotten in the wet autumn. At that moment Larrie came trotting smartly into the yard on Sobie. "Muma? What's going on?"

"Shouldn't you be at school?" demanded Rosie, her breath misting in the cold air.

"Your filthy, bloody horse," shouted Flo.

Larrie uttered a piercing shriek and made Sobie rear up, which silenced everyone for a minute but when she saw them all standing there with their mouths open, she broke into gales of laughter. "You look so stupid!" she told Flo in between gasps of laughter. "Muma..."

"What that girl needs is a decent English boarding school!" snapped Flo. "And some bloody discipline!"

Rosie bent down picked up a potato, handling it very carefully so it wouldn't explode in her hand, and flung it at Flo. It caught him just on the side of the face, leaving a trail of incredibly smelly freezing cold slime across his cheek before exploding against the barn door.

"How dare you?" he yelled and lunged towards her. Dolly yelped as he accidentally trod on her tail and Rosie pushed him away.

"How dare you kick my dog!" she yelled. Reaching down into a handy bucket, she scooped a handful of water out and hurled it at Flo. He swore and lunged at her and she threw the rest of the icy water at him. It hit him full in the chest, soaking him straight through to the skin but he didn't stop. He just charged straight at her and they both fell into the potatoes. The big dogs started leaping clumsily in all directions and Larrie, whooping like a maniac, wheeled Sobie round and round in circles. Dolly was still yapping her head off.

"What in the hell's whorehouse of Satan is going on?" shouted Nicole, appearing from the vegetable garden with a spade in one hand. "Are you all mad?"

"Muma's gone mad," said Larrie, and made

Sobie neigh loudly.

"They're all barking," said Chris.

Rolling over and over in the slimy mess, which had only minutes ago been a pile of rotten potatoes, Flo suddenly began to laugh too. Rosie looked at him with fury but Chris could see her mouth twitching with amusement. Flo wiped his eyes, flicked a gob of rotten potato off his cheek and kissed Rosie on the only clean bit of her face, which was somewhere near her chin.

"Look, you're right," he said tenderly. "I did lie and it was inexcusable. I have had a lot of girl-friends, I have been in a few fights, maybe I've even drunk a bit too much now and again. But I've changed. I'm not mucking around this time. It's real. I love you, Rosie."

Larrie and Chris exchanged glances, and Nicole pinned her lips together. They all looked at Rosie. Practically lying on top of her, Flo was gazing into her eyes. But her smile faded and she looked away from him. "Get off me," she said.

"Come on Rosie," he said, instantly getting to his feet and pulling her up.

"No hard feelings then," she said refusing to meet his eye. "Pax?"

"Rosie..." pleaded Flo.

"I have to go and change and then I need to do the dogs. Of course you can help if you would like to," she said politely. "I daresay I could show you how to teach agility too if you like. We have a class this afternoon."

She stalked away across the yard, leaving them all looking after her. Then, with various expressions of pity on their faces, Larrie, Chris and Nicole all looked at Flo, where he stood shivering and dripping with rotten potato slime.

"It's no good, is it?" he said. "I'm in the doghouse, aren't I?"

"Minutes away from a trip to the vet," said Chris.

CHAPTER ELEVEN

Three days later, Chris realised just how right he had been. Flo was in punitive disgrace and nothing anyone could say would change his mother's mind about him. Daisy, sitting witch-like on their bed, busy plaiting a complicated bead necklet, advised him not to try. "Don't do it. You'll only make her madder than ever."

"True," nodded Chris.

It was a silent Sunday afternoon. Outside the château, nothing was moving on the lifeless hills and inside, most of the inhabitants were fully occupied in keeping warm. Rosie had already dug out all the extra blankets for the beds, and when Flo simply ordered a huge supply of them from town, she had glared at him furiously. Everyone else had simply dived on the blankets with sincere gratitude. Minnie was lying on Chris's feet, giving them pins and needles. He shifted his legs, noticed she was shivering and dragged some of his thick, new, pure wool blanket over Minnie's shivering grey spine.

"They're supposed to be the adults here," Daisy went on. She lifted her head and smiled at him. "You wanna rub my shoulders while I finish this?"

Down in the stables, blowing into her hands to warm them up, Larrie had also realised it was useless trying to understand why her mother was being so weird. "Grown-ups are so complicated," she confided to Sobie as she combed knots out of his mane. "If only they had horse sense, they could save themselves a lot of trouble! I mean look at you. Look at me. Look at us!"

Wearing his thick winter rug, Sobie was already curled up on a big bed of straw in his loose box, and Larrie now sat down beside him and hugged his neck. "See?" she whispered into his large furry ear. "We love each other but we don't have to have a stoopid spud fight to prove it. Do we, baby?"

Sobie whickered softly and settled his head deeper into the straw with a sympathetic sigh. Larrie took this to mean that he agreed with her. Abandoning the comb, she leaned comfortably against his warm chest. "One day," she said, starting Sobie's favourite story, "one day in the spring, when the sun comes back, we'll go down to the sea," she said dreamily. "You've never seen it yet, but it's lots and lots of water and it's always moving. Swishing and swishing. It's much, much bigger than the river here. It's so big you can swim in it, Sobes. It's deep enough so you can get your feet off the bottom. And we'll go swimming and see the crabs and the weeds and the fish, and when we're tired, we'll get out of the water and there'll be sand, Sobes. Miles and miles of perfect golden sand. And to get dry we'll canter along the beach in the sunshine. For miles and miles. One day soon we'll go to the sea and you'll see..."

Sobie closed his beautiful brown eyes and Larrie decided to give her eyes a rest too.

Outside, stamping down the frozen vegetable garden after a hard session of forking and raking, Nicole muttered mighty strings of expletives under her breath. She didn't believe in love, but that wasn't the issue. The reason she wouldn't waste her breath trying to talk to Rosie was because the scar tissue on the woman's heart was too thick. And secretly she thought it was a good job that Rosie had come to her senses before too much damage had been done. Mind you, she did have a few choice observations for Flo - but since he was a filthy barbarian and didn't speak French, he'd have to live without the benefit of her insight. So Nicole just went on with her self-allotted task of feeding five hungry mouths out of one small vegetable patch. It might be the tail end of the gardening season but there was still horse manure to spread and plants to be mulched before the hard frosts set in. Swinging a large garden fork, Nicole surveyed the garden with grim satisfaction. The chard was doing well.

Dolly, on the other hand, felt grim. It might have been the effects of the contraband saucisson sec that she'd consumed behind the sofa three days ago, but she didn't think so. Not when the pack leader smelt all wrong. That was the problem. When the pack leader smelled wrong, life itself smelt wrong. Dolly couldn't even be bothered to harass the outdoor cats as they moved into the house for the winter, she was so depressed. She stuck ever closer to her pack leader, rolling her eyes and panting anxiously. The big dogs watched her and scratched their ears. If fluffy thing was uneasy, something must be wrong.

Stevie was the only person who was oblivious to the cold winds blowing through the château. In fact, because daddy had even started teaching him to read like a big boy, he was happier than he'd ever been in his life before. And daddy played the piano to him, and daddy showed him about draining water pipes so they didn't burst when Jack Frost came. And daddy ate hot porridge with him every morning. With extra sugar. And daddy said they could go to Disneyland and the Grand Canyon in America one day. Stevie wasn't sure where either of these places were or even what sort of places they were, but Daisy had come from America, so he knew it must be a good place.

He had it all worked out. Daisy was an angel and Rosie was a fairy godmother and together with daddy they would make it all end happily with a magic spell. He and teddy would live happily ever after with all the others. In the meantime, his hair grew out and covered the large and beautiful pink ears that stuck out on either side of his head. He was putting on weight and as a result of eating his five-a-day, his skin was clear. In fact he was glowing with health.

"You wouldn't take him for the same child!" thought Lotta, when she came rattling over the icy roads to try and talk sense into Rosie and saw him playing on the terrace. She secretly thought her mission was a forlorn hope but because she felt she ought to at least try, instead of stopping to talk to Stevie, she followed the sounds of hammering and went to find Rosie. "How's Flo?" she asked, as she walked up to where Rosie was checking the chicken wire fence round one of the bichon runs.

"Oh him!" said Rosie going slightly red and tugging at a loose section of fencing. "Pass that hammer, will you?" She hauled a couple of rusty nails out of the fence post and replaced them with fresh agricultural staples.

"I'm listening!"

"Well, it was just you know..." Rosie waved her hammer about dismissively. "Passing flirtation, nothing serious. Nice while it lasted but quite glad to be getting back to my normal routine again. Oh dear, with the mornings so dark now, the day just seems gone before it's even started. Can you hold this section, move back, keep it taut, yes, that's it."

"That's not what Flo says!" said Lotta, ducking away as a strand of wire bounded towards her. "He says he's in love with you."

"Oh I shouldn't think he is. Not really," said Rosie with a forced smile. "I'm not young enough or pretty enough. He was just marking time. The Irresistible Man and all that stuff. Now, I'm just going to check this, and we can have some tea. It's getting too dark to see properly anyway." She finished checking the fence, gathered up her tools and started trudging back to the barns. Tagging along beside her, Lotta sighed. Rosie's eyes were surrounded by dark shadows and her mouth, instead of constantly tipping into a smile, was a thin straight line. She had lost weight, her skin was starting to look papery and Lotta saw her rubbing the left side of her chest as if she had a pain there.

"Are you sure everything's all right?" she said, nodding at Rosie's chest.

"Indigestion," said Rosie firmly. "A nice cup of tea is all I need. Go and put the kettle on, there's a love. I'll just put these tools away and then I'll be in."

Lotta went into the kitchen, where she found Chris and Daisy huddling round the stove. "Kettle on!" she barked at Chris. "Your mother needs tea!"

"How are you, Lotta?" said Daisy, knitting what looked like a long stripy scarf. "How's your arthritis in this cold weather?"

"Horrible," said Lotta. "End of subject. Too boring. What about you my gal? What are you doing in all this mess? Planning to be that child's nanny forever are you?"

"No," said Daisy serenely. "I'm not his mom, I'm too young to be anybody's mom right now. Later, I'd like kids but I have some life experience to gather yet. I wonder if I should go with pink next? Or green?"

"I see! What sort of life experience?" demanded Lotta.

"I might like to design jewellery. Maybe learn to be a silversmith. But I have to stay around until the little squirt doesn't need me any more. I just hope it doesn't take too long."

"Her visa runs out in the New Year," said Chris getting mugs out and putting teabags in them.

"Oh it does, does it?" said Lotta. "Are you getting it renewed or what?"

"Nope," said Daisy and gave Chris a defiant look. Chris returned it with a gloomy scowl and Lotta mentally raised her eyebrows. So Little Chrissie had the bug too, she thought. Good. Perhaps it would finally propel him out into the big wide world instead of hiding himself away in his mother's house.

"Have you spoken to Rosie?" asked Daisy.

"Yes, but there's no talking to her," said Lotta. If only the gal would scream and smash things, she thought, or weep and moan and pull her hair out. But in the face of Rosie's rigid self-control, Lotta was stumped. She didn't waste much energy thinking about Flo. He'd obviously fallen into Rosie's world like Alice tumbling down the rabbit hole, entirely unprepared for this new reality, completely ignorant of the objections normal people might have to actors impersonating gay, antique-obsessed writers. But he, she told herself firmly, could look after himself.

The trouble was, Flo didn't know what to do either. It was impossible to talk to Rosie because she wouldn't even look at him. If she'd screamed at him or tried to beat him up with a rolling pin he'd have felt better, but faced with her remote eyes and deathly pale face he was at a loss. So he just went on helping; getting up early, hosing down the bichon kennel, mixing huge quantities of puppy food, and putting dog blankets through the washing machine as the night-time temperatures dropped ever further past the freezing mark.

Rosie was polite, even friendly sometimes, but there was no getting near her. She was deaf to any personal comments, and adept at keeping a feed bin or a water trough between them. After a few days of this treatment, Flo was tempted to give up and let her deal with the bloody animals herself, but when he noticed the deepening purple smudges under her eyes, he just picked up the yard broom and got back to work.

The only time Rosie was even halfway normal was when Stevie was around. She cracked silly jokes with him, made him strange combination sandwiches like banana and peanut butter, and even let him visit the new litter of bichon puppies. They were at the slug stage, soft little milky creatures tumbling over each other with fat little tummies and pink licky tongues. Steve desperately wanted one for himself but they had all been pre-sold to approved owners and were just waiting to be old enough to go to their new homes.

"I'm so sorry," said Flo, to Rosie one day. "I never meant to hurt you like this." For a split second, she met his eye, but then she looked away again and from that moment on she sang "Happiness, happiness, the greatest gift that I possess" as loudly as she could: in the stable yard; on the terrace; outside Sobie's loose box; and underneath Flo's window. A few days later, she changed the tune to Fats Waller's "Don't let it bother you!"

"Don't listen," whispered Larrie in Sobie's ear. "She never could sing!"

"Stay calm," said Daisy to Chris, who was red with irritation. "Kiss me, lover boy. Warm me up!"

"Voilà!" said Nicole, cornering Flo one day in his bedroom. She had a sheaf of slightly crumpled papers in her hand. "Et ban, regardons tout ça!"

Flo wrinkled his nose up and shook his head. He really didn't speak a word of French and hadn't a clue what she was trying to say. Nicole grabbed his arm and steered him over to his desk. Pulling the stump of a pencil out of her pocket, she shoved him into his chair and pulled up another one so she could sit beside him. Then she gave him the first piece of paper. It seemed to be a letter of some sort but he couldn't read it. Swearing under her breath, Nicole turned it over and drew a child's representation of a house and then she did a cloud with rain coming out of it and hitting the roof and then she drew some squiggles which looked like snails.

"The roof!" he said. "I get it. She told me about the roof, but... what? This is a quote? A destruction order? What is it?"

Nicole drew a dog and a traffic light but Flo

couldn't even begin to guess what she was trying to convey. She drew a camera and a dog, and then a dog and a computer. Then a dog and a bowl of food. Then she drew euro signs all over the page. She looked furious, as if he was deliberately being stupid, and jabbed the page with her pencil.

"Sorry," he said, and she cuffed him across the top of his head. "Ouw!" he protested. "All right, all right!" Fending her off, he got to his feet and picked up the papers. "I'll read it! I'll get it all translated. Leave it with me! Tray bang! Tray bang! OK!"

Nicole left the room chanting what sounded like another of her long strings of abuse. He shook his head, drew the blanket closer round his shoulders, and stuffed her papers into a drawer. Nicole really was... the phone rang and he picked it up.

"Sally! Yes, what can I do for you? How's London?"

Sally started talking and his mind wandered. Was Nicole just trying to make him put a new roof on the place, or did she have something else in mind? He got the papers out of the drawer again and spread them out on the desk. Completely incomprehensible. Especially the ones in a handwritten scrawl.

"Are you listening at all?" said Sally impatiently.

"Absolutely," he lied. "Glued, glued to every word."

Through the window, he saw Pierre's rusty white van come bouncing down the driveway and turn off down the sidetrack to the stable block. What did he want?

In his van, driving with decision and purpose, Pierre wanted to put things right for once and for all. There was only so much a man could stand before he had to take action and when a man reached that point, action he would take. Alors! He got out of the van, hitched his trousers up, smoothed his moustache into place and puffing mighty clouds of breath into the cold air, went to find Rosie. He hoped she'd be alone in the new barn so that he could say his piece. He grabbed the door handle, slid the door aside and let himself in.

"Shut the door!" shouted Rosie. "Ferme la porte!"

"It's me!" he shouted in French. "I come to see you!"

Rosie appeared from a storeroom holding a pair of plastic buckets in one hand. "What?" she said, "What do you want?"

She was all bundled up in jumpers and anoraks, but in the dim late-afternoon winter light she looked luminous, her pale face more than ever like a Madonna. "Marry me, Rosie," he said. "I'll leave my wife and come to live here!"

Rosie just looked at him.

He spread his hands out and shrugged. "I am in love," he said passionately. "What can I do?"

"Are you crazy?" she said. "Go home!"

"Yes, I am crazy for you!" he declared, and dropped onto one knee. "I think of you all the time, you are in my thoughts, in my heart, in my soul!" He kissed the tips of his fingers and held his arms out to her. If he hadn't had such a big stomach it would have been graceful and possibly even touching. As it was, Rosie thought he might keel over any minute.

"Stop it, Pierre," she said. "I'm too busy for this nonsense right now." She turned away and went off to wash the buckets.

He staggered to his feet and followed her. "But why? You are alone, you have no-one..."

"I have two children, dozens of dogs, God knows how many cats, and a horse, not to mention Nicole and..."

"You have no lover," he said indignantly. "A woman like you..."

"Stop it," said Rosie and a large fat tear rolled down her face. "Just stop it, and go away." Pierre looked her in amazement. He'd never seen Rosie cry before, never. Even when she had to have dogs put down, she never cried. Refusing to look at him, she rubbed her face with one elbow and went on sloshing at the buckets with a floor cloth.

"It's him, isn't it?" he said at last. "You are love with the Englishman, aren't you?" Pierre smiled ruefully. "I knew it," he said. "I knew I should not wait too long."

"I'm not an apple," said Rosie.

"What?"

"I was never just sitting around on a branch waiting to be picked by you. You're a nice man, and you've been a good friend to me and the kids. But I'm not in love with you and never have been. And to be honest, I don't think you're in love with me. You just hate to see good apples going to waste."

Pierre sighed weightily and stroked his moustache. Rosie scrubbed at her eyes with her sleeve and emptied the buckets into the large yard sink. "Now I've got to get on," she said but although she wasn't crying, tears were washing down her immobile cheeks and she didn't have the power to stop them.

"Oh Rosie," he said, and for once he wasn't messing around. He flung his arms round her and she wept into his shoulder. "Rosie, Rosie," he murmured. "Poor Rosie. I know..." She just cried harder and harder and all he could do was hold her and wait. He rocked her from side to side and stroked her hair. "Oh là là..." he whispered and kissed her forehead.

"I wasn't good enough twenty years ago," she choked. "No-one wanted me when I was young and pretty." Pierre shook his head. "So why would anyone want me now? Especially him. He's rich and handsome and sexy, and he can have anyone. He just wanted me because there wasn't anyone else around and he was bored. And now he's pretending because of that little boy."

"You're beautiful," said Pierre. "All men are in love with you!"

"He just wants a decent babysitter for his son," she sobbed, and Pierre just held her closer and kissed her forehead again. Neither of them heard the barn door opening or noticed the lights being flicked on.

"Am I interrupting?" said Flo icily from the doorway. "I thought you might need a hand with the dogs, but I see you already have a willing helper!"

Rosie pulled away from Pierre with a gasp and turned back to the buckets. "What's it to you?" she demanded over her shoulder.

Pierre looked from one to the other and shook his head slowly. Flo jerked his head towards the door, and Pierre held his hands up in the air and sidled past Flo with an exaggerated show of fear. "I cede the floor," he said with a courtly bow. "You are a very lucky man, monsieur."

"What did he say?" said Flo watching Pierre whisk himself out of the barn.

"Nothing," said Rosie, wiping her nose on her sleeve. "Are you going to check the water bowls?"

She refused to turn round but stood stock still, listening intently as Flo marched off towards the bichon run. Yet again she'd made a total fool of herself. She shook her head. It wasn't as if she didn't have anything else to worry about. There was Chris talking about contributing to a photography exhibition and, although it went without saying that she was very proud, just how much would it cost to send him up to Paris for three days? Where would he stay and what about making exhibition-sized prints and mounting them on proper card? It would all cost money and the bichon puppies had all sold but of course the money wasn't pure profit, she had overheads to pay. And as if that wasn't bad enough,

Larrie was saying she wouldn't go back to school after Christmas. Rosie was pretty sure that Larrie's attendance since September had been sketchy, but Larrie was way too young to leave school and it was pointless thinking that Rosie would have the time to help her study anything.

Life was just a bit hard sometimes, she thought. It was getting colder night by night and soon she'd have to start using more coal to keep at least part of the old house warm. It would be months before the sun warmed the château up again. She took a deep breath and squared her shoulders back. No point in feeling sorry for herself, no point in letting the dogs see her bad mood. As for Flo, he would soon find a sexy starlet to fall in love with.

"Happiness," she rasped loudly, "happiness, the greatest gift that I possess!"

Sitting at the table in the kitchen, Chris swore and Nicole grimly bit her nails. Daisy shrugged and ate another grape. Dolly heard Rosie howling and joined in. She didn't know what ailed her pack leader, but something was wrong and Dolly was broken-hearted. Hearing her distress, the big dogs started whining as well.

In the stable block, Larrie and Sobie shuddered, and next door in the bichon kennel, Flo gritted his teeth and made as much noise with the yard broom as he possibly could. Rosie was brilliant at many things, he thought, but she sang like screeching chalk.

"I thank the Lord that I possess, more than my share of happiness," crowed Rosie loudly. All she had to do, she told herself, was keep singing and soon the winter would be over and spring would arrive. Then everything would be all right again. But the next morning, the household woke up to find that Flo had gone. He'd left a letter for Stevie propped up in the kitchen.

"What?" whispered the little boy, his chin wobbling. "What's daddy say?"

With flashing eyes, Larrie snatched it away from Chris and tore it open. She scanned down it and then grinned. "He says, Dear Wonder Boy - that's you Stevie - I had to go and do some work. It was a last minute thing, so I had to leave before you were awake. Keep on reading and being a good boy. Love and kisses, Daddy."

Stevie gave a happy smile all round the table. "He put love and kisses," he said proudly.

"Doh!" said Larrie, "of course he did! Here look, PS I will be back very soon - before Kanga can finish the laundry!"

"Good riddance!" said Rosie. Then she burst into tears and rushed out of the back door.

CHAPTER TWELVE

From then on, the winter really started to bite. The château was almost as cold inside as outside, despite Rosie loading the stove with as much wood as she could chop. They all got colds and Dolly howled so much that Rosie put her into a warm day coat to try and cheer her up. Outraged, Dolly stopped howling and almost strangled herself trying to struggle out of the terrible coat. But once she'd got it off, she realised her mistake and started howling all over again. Meanwhile, the cats were squabbling over the stove, each of them trying to get as close as possible without actually setting themselves alight.

Doors became the focus of Rosie's heating efforts; she dug out all the thick ex-Army blanket-curtains and hung them across all the external doors. In the daytime, the internal doors to the kitchen were firmly shut so that at least one room in the place was warm, and at night time Rosie opened the door to the staircase leading up to the rooms above the kitchen so at least they didn't actually freeze in their beds. She asked Chris and Daisy if they wanted to move out of the turret for the winter, but they refused, saying that Minnie kept them warm at night.

Rosie shrugged. Whatever. "Jolly good!" she said a minute later. "What shall we have for breakfast? Shall we have a hot breakfast for a treat? Porridge? What about mushrooms on toast?"

"Don't worry, muma. He'll be back soon," said Larrie. "He's not a bad man."

"Scrambled eggs!" said Rosie. "What about you Daisy, wouldn't you like some scrambled eggs? I bet you would, wouldn't you, angel?"

"Who is a bad man?" asked Stevie looking from face to face. "My daddy is nice! He's nicerer than yours!"

"How do you know, squirt?" said Daisy.

"Cos my daddy is nicerer than all the other daddies," said Stevie, and of course they all looked at Rosie. But she was unbreakable.

"Absolutely right, angel!" she said with a big smile. "Now, drink up your nice milky and then you can have some soldiers."

She started making toast. There was no point in dwelling on the past, she told herself. The present was far more important - that and remembering to block up the gaps in the window frames with twists of newspaper. There were dogs to be walked, classes to be taught, agility courses to be laid out, articles to be written. She'd promised the vet a one-page handout on house-training dogs, and she still hadn't finished it so now that there were no more handsome actors cluttering the place up, she'd be able to get on. As for missing Flo, pish-posh! Before he turned up, she'd always done the dogs alone. She could manage just fine, and as for when he was coming back, what did she care?

The rain started slowly at first, almost like a light mist enveloping the château roof. But soon it became a drizzle and then a steady whispering downpour that lasted for days and days. The rain sloshed, the dogs barked, more wood had to be chopped. Dolly trod on a piece of glass, and then just to complete the joy, Spike came back.

"He's no good," said his owner, standing on the terrace outside the kitchen door with rain dripping off his hat, and one end of a vicious choke chain wrapped round his fist. "He's gone bad again. He tried to kill a kid in the market."

Thinner, sodden, and covered in mud, Spike rolled his eyes and coughed pathetically.

"He can't breathe!" exclaimed Rosie. "You're strangling him! He doesn't need a choke chain. Just a short leather lead is all that's required, I told you!" She squatted down in front of Spike, pulled the chain off his neck and started massaging the folds of skin round his neck. She could feel several scabs with her fingers. What had the stupid man been doing to the poor animal? "Where's his proper collar?" she said, "with his ID on it?"

"See, he's all right with you," said Spike's owner defensively.

"He'd be all right with you too, Monsieur

Trèsbête! You just have to learn to handle him properly. I've told you before, he's not a dog for an amateur; he needs a proper handling by a person who knows what they're doing. You have to come to our classes. Or just come privately and I'll teach you."

"Nah, I don't want him. He's vicious, he's a bad dog, that's his problem," said Monsieur Trèsbête. "You keep him!"

"But I can't keep him!" said Rosie, straightening up.

"Well, get him put down then!" he said over his shoulder as he splashed away across the terrace in the rain.

"Oh dear," said Rosie, looking down at Spike, who wasn't making the slightest attempt to follow his owner. "Spike, what have you done?"

Spike sat down in a puddle and scratched his scabs with one of his back paws. "Oh well, I suppose you'd better come in," said Rosie. Peeping at him from between Rosie's feet, Dolly's beady black eyes registered disapproval, but Spike didn't care. He was just happy that the pack leader had taken his horrible chain off, and he was ready to follow her to the ends of the earth. Especially if she had bic-bic in her pocket.

Rosie towelled him dry and went back into the kitchen to find Stevie unwrapping yet another parcel from his father. In the past week alone, he'd received a little red truck, a toy train set, an easel, a palette and a box of paints, a selection of child-sized gardening tools and enough books to stock an entire library. This time it was a pair of luxuriously thick sheepskin slippers.

"God it's hot in here!" she exclaimed. "What's going on? Is the stove all right?"

"Take some of those jumpers off, Muma!" said Larrie. "Then it'll be better."

"It's Flo," said Chris apologetically. "He's sent about a dozen kerosene heaters and a cube of fuel to burn in them. And according to the delivery man he's ordered another cube of fuel to arrive in two weeks' time." He handed Rosie a note from Flo, which read, "Sorry, this is the best I could do, but at least there won't be a ventilation problem! Keep warm, see you soon, Flo."

Rosie didn't say anything. She just started stripping off her padded jacket and the thick jumpers underneath. The château had always been freezing in the winter, with ice on the inside of the windows, beds piled high with eiderdowns and duvets, pyjamas hastily dragged on in front of the kitchen stove, followed by a freezing shivering scamper to the bedrooms. Rosie couldn't count the times she'd been unable to take her dressing gown off before going to bed. As for chilblains, coughs, colds, chapped lips and fingers too stiff to move, none of the château's inhabitants even noticed them.

"We thought it was best to light them," said Daisy in her soft voice. She nodded at the back of Steve's head. "He's used to central heating."

"Yes, I see," said Rosie swallowing her pride.

"I hope we did the right thing?" said Daisy,

wrinkling her eyebrows.

"Of course you did!" said Rosie, telling herself to grow up and stop being so childish. "It's lovely and warm. I hardly recognise the place!" And it was true. Over the next week, she had to admit that it was amazing what a difference it made, having heating. Of course, it was impossible to heat the entire château, but twelve heaters meant that most of the kitchen end of the old house was warm, along with Chris's turret and Nicole's lookout post above the stable block.

At least she hoped it was. She'd insisted on Nicole taking a heater and told her that she absolutely must use the fuel in the large tank, and although for herself she had been tempted to tell Flo to stuff his heaters where the sun don't shine, she was guiltily aware that Daisy was right: Steve wasn't used to rough living. Despite being the worst mother in the world, at least Sylvia's house was heated. It would be criminal to deny the children heated rooms when the heaters were sitting there all paid for and ready to go. What was she supposed to do? Heat Stevie's room and ban him from the rest of the château?

So now the château was warm. You could take your coat off when you came in, towels dried in between baths, there was no ice inside the house and you could undress in your own bedroom. Of course they were all revelling in it. She didn't put a heater in her own study however, not until Larrie came in one evening and looked round with dismay.

"It's freezing in here! Why don't you light a fire? Or one of Flo's heaters, Muma?" Larrie looked on the verge of tears and suddenly Rosie couldn't quite bring herself to explain why she refused to burn wood or kerosene paid for by Flo when everyone else was just happy and grateful.

"Why, Muma?" repeated Larrie. "Why are you sitting in the cold?"

So Rosie shook her head and smiled and said, "I don't know darling! I wasn't thinking I suppose. Why don't you go and get a Flo-heater, while I light a fire in the grate? Then we'll soon get cosy, won't we? I've nearly finished this fact sheet anyway."

Larrie went bustling off to collect a heater from the utility room and Rosie knelt in front of the fire she had laid for her, Flo and the Moët. It was still waiting for the touch paper. Well, she wouldn't be drinking Moët with him any time soon, so why not light the fire for Larrie? She struck a match and lit the corner of a piece of paper sticking out at the bottom of the fire. It took, and almost at once there was a satisfied roar from the chimney. The phone rang and Rosie picked it up.

"In God's name woman!" said Sally, angrily. "What have you done to him?"

"Who? Your blind, gay antiques writer?" said Rosie.

"No, I don't mean him! I mean Florian Kent! Don't mess with me, I'm seriously angry with you!" Freezing rage swept over Rosie. Control yourself, she thought. Be civilised. But her fingers were slippery with sweat. "I have nothing to say to you," she said and, forgetting that it was never a good idea to hang up on Sally, slammed the phone down. Then she marched over to the wall and pulled the phone plug out of the socket.

"Who was that? On the phone?" said Larrie staggering into the room with a large cardboard box.

"Just your godmother, Sally," said Rosie and Larrie opened her mouth to say something smart but suddenly closed it again. Feeling like a really bad mother, Rosie decided it was time to cheer everyone up. She left Larrie unpacking the heater and came back not only with enough kerosene to last all night but also with a basket of supplies for a midnight feast. "I've got a pack of milk, a saucepan, some cocoa powder and I found some other stuff too," she said.

"Oh goodie!" said Larrie, her eyes instantly sparkling. "Are we feasting? Is there any peanut butter? Did you text Chrissie? Shall I wake Stevie?"

"Yep," said Rosie lighting the heater, "let's have a party!" She wasn't in the mood but it was a pity to waste all that heating and it was ages since they'd had a midnight feast. Larrie came back in carrying Stevie and teddy all wrapped up in a duvet and settled him on the sofa and Rosie poured the milk into a saucepan and put it on the little shelf at the side of the grate to heat up. Then Chris and Daisy arrived with a packet of marshmallows. "My fav," said Daisy. "Hope you like 'em gluey?" Everyone just looked at her, and she grinned at them with delight. "Oh boy, do you have a treat coming to you!" she said. "Marshmallows in hot chocolate! Let's get feasting!"

Looking round at their happy faces, all pink from the reflected firelight, Rosie had to smile. She shoved Flo firmly out of her mind and sprinkled cocoa into the milk. "I grabbed some nuts and raisins," she said, rattling the jar. Anyone want some?"

They stayed up talking and telling jokes, burning their fingers on toasted marshmallows and, once Larrie and Steve had fallen asleep on the sofa, sipping hot chocolate with a splash of SuperU brandy in it.

"What a difference a bit of heating makes," said Chris. "I never realised."

"I'm so sorry," said Rosie. "I'm an awful mother."

Daisy burst out laughing. "Yeah, right!" she said. "Truly heinous!"

"Frightful!" said Chris, joining in. "Utterly ghastly, my dear!"

"Tell me about the Paris exhibition," said Rosie. "What's happening with that?"

He shrugged. "I don't need to go. Not really. It's just, you know, they like you to be there for the opening to talk to the press and stuff like that, but you know, me and Daisy could hitchhike or something. We could stay in a youth hostel. I don't suppose it would cost that much."

Secretly, he also had another plan. If he could

drag Hugo up to Paris, perhaps he could unleash him on Ralph Donnington. He couldn't imagine Hugo getting very far because a big star like that must surely have a professional security team, but at least if would keep Hugo busy and hopefully buy everyone at the château some time. That is, if Ralph really was in France promoting his new film. Distracted, Chris frowned into the fire. But Hugo wasn't destined to be the most worrying of his preoccupations.

The next day, trundling back from town through the rain in his creaky Renault 4, he found Larrie, soaking wet, lying in the middle of the road. He leapt out of the car and ran through the rain to her side. "Oh my God! Are you all right?" He half expected her to sit up laughing and saying "Gotcha!" but she just half-opened her eyes, and gave him a pale smile.

"I can't stand up," she said, wincing. "You'll have to help me." Her teeth were chattering with cold.

"Is it your hip?"

"No! It's not, I swear! It's not my hip, it's my knee. You've got to help me find Sobie," she said, her eyes full of tears. "I fell off him. Well, I didn't fall off exactly. It was the mud. I was being a Cossack."

"Oh Jesus."

"I can do it, you know, I can mount him even when he's cantering. And off again. Just a saddle pad..."

"You were out here, in the pouring rain, riding without a hat, without a saddle..."

"No! No, I wasn't on the road! I swear I wasn't! I was up there! And it wasn't raining much!" She pointed up the hill to a path that cut through the trees above them. "But I slipped and I fell down onto the road but somehow I've twisted my knee and I can't get up. I'm all wet. Even my vest."

"So what happened to that wretched nag of yours?"

"I don't know," said Larrie starting to shake. "Do you think he's dead?"

"Most unlikely. I should imagine he's probably back in his loose box by now, eating his bed," said Chris. "Come on, just use your good leg, let's get you out of here."

"Don't tell muma, please don't tell her!" gasped Larrie. Chris shook his head quickly. The last thing their mother needed was a riding accident to worry about. He helped Larrie into the car, drove her home and got her upstairs to her room without getting caught, but Larrie was more concerned for her horse than for herself. "Find Sobie," sobbed Larrie. "What if he's lost? What if he's broken his leg?"

"He won't be lost. He'll be back in his stable eating his bed."

"Dry him. Tell him I'm sorry. Make him hot mash. He'll need Rescue Remedy!"

Chris slipped out to the stables, keeping a wary eye out for his mother, and practically bumped into Flo walking round the corner leading Sobie by his bridle. "Thank God for that!" said Chris and explained what had happened. "Where did you find him?"

"I heard him rattling at the back door, and had to bribe the brute with apples. Otherwise I think he'd have marched into the house and helped himself. I was just going to put him back in his loose box and then go out looking for Larrie. How come she fell off?"

"She was being a Cossack."

Flo shook his head. "She's going to have to stop careering about all over the countryside before she really does hurt herself," said Flo.

"Try telling her that," said Chris, taking charge of Sobie.

The next time he saw her, Flo make a brave attempt but didn't get very far. Larrie listened for all of thirty seconds before telling him he didn't understand.

"But if you kill yourself, how can you ever get a job riding horses?"

She shrugged.

"You have real talent, you could be good, but you need proper training, you need proper lessons. You have to show people you're serious."

Tears sprang to her eyes but she brushed them all away. "It's none of your business," she said, flicking her hair over her shoulder.

"I'm only trying to help," he said.

"Well don't."

Conscientiously doing his duty down in the stable block, Chris wasn't having much better luck with Sobie but trying to follow Larrie's instructions was a nightmare. In the first place, it all seemed so complicated and in the second, the bloody horse wouldn't cooperate. For the next three days, while Larrie lay in bed refusing to see a doctor and claiming she just had an upset stomach, he slogged around the stable yard, mucking out, fetching water, making up hot mashes, grooming and picking out the animal's feet and putting his various rugs on and off while Sobie kicked buckets over, sulked, spat mash all over the loose box and spent hours rocking to and fro like a neurotic zoo elephant.

"God, you're more work than a bloody baby," he said putting his hand up to pat the animal's nose. Sobie jerked his head up and showed the whites of his eyes.

"I don't know what's wrong with him, Larrie," said Chris that afternoon. "I mean, I've done everything you said, I can't find anything physically wrong with him, but all he does his bash away at his door with that great clog of his. He just wants to get into the house, he won't hold his head up and if I try to pat him, he acts like I'm the horsemeat man."

"You have to tell him a story," said Larrie, propped up on a pile of pillows. "Your best dream day. You have to start by sitting down with him in the straw and getting comfortable. Then when he goes like this...." She imitated Sobie's softest little whicker. "Then you tell him your best wish for the future. I tell him all about how one day we're going to the seaside and we're going swimming together and afterwards we're going to have a picnic with horse nut sandwiches and crunchy apples."

Chris just rolled his eyes. Larrie was crazier than he'd thought. Thank God the swelling in her knee was going down and she was starting to walk again. But the next evening, once he'd finished all his stable yard tasks, he stopped and looked over the loosebox door. Sobie was standing in the corner with his head drooping and one back leg resting. His tail was a dead rag, his ears looked floppy and his mane looked lifeless. In fact, he looked miserable. Feeling sorry for him, Chris went back into the loosebox. "All right, I suppose you're missing Larrie, you idiot nag. And I can see you're not lying down, but here goes." He went over and stood beside the horse's huge powerful shoulder and stroked his shiny brown chest.

"One day Sobie," he murmured. "One day. When you're at the beach with Larrie, Daisy and me will find a rooftop space in Paris. It'll have large sloping windows and a view out across a crazy kaleidoscope of grey and silver roofs. The sky will be white and we'll live in this huge space together. There'll be wooden floorboards and white walls and under-floor heating and enough electricity sockets that you can plug in everything at once and the electricity still won't blow up on you."

Outside, mildly curious, Rosie paused and looked into the loosebox. Right at the back, leaning against Sobie in a sort of trance with his eyes closed, Chris was talking to him in a dreamy voice. Telling herself that eavesdroppers never liked what they heard, she told herself to walk away. But she was glued to the spot.

"There'll be enough space for Daisy to make silver jewellery and for me to set up as many computers as I want," murmured Chris with a dreamy smile. "And I'll be able to run them all at once. I'll have giant sized prints hanging up everywhere. And just down the stairs on the pavement will be a bakery and an all-night grocery store and a neighbourhood cafe selling cheap couscous and vegetables so we won't have to cook or anything. We can just create things all the time and never worry about anything at all. Not dogs, or kids, or tax bills, or even Muma."

CHAPTER THIRTEEN

The day Flo strolled back into the kitchen, at the sight of him, Rosie's heart leapt, her stomach contracted and her legs turned to jelly. She was hot and cold all over. She hadn't felt like that since he'd gone away. He had caused all of it. It had always been Flo. Her symptoms were nothing to do with the menopause and everything to do with having an inconvenient crush. She hated herself for her weakness.

"Daddy!" said Stevie, flying across the room to hug him round the knees. "Guess what? We had a midnight feast with mushmillies, and Larrie was ill and Chrissie's got to go to Paris and Spike eated up my new slippers!"

"Goodness, you have been having fun," said Flo, swinging him up into his arms, and giving Rosie a friendly grin. She reminded herself fiercely that he wasn't any less of a liar just because he'd had his hair beautifully cut and styled into a careless riot of dark curls.

"How are you, Rosie?" he asked. His skin looked smooth and tanned and he was wearing some sort of soft leaf green sweater that picked out the lights in his eyes.

"Fine!" she muttered, and threw another handful of rice into the water.

"I need to see you later by the way. We have a lot to discuss," he announced enigmatically. "Alone!" Then he frowned. "Is everything all right? You look a bit tired."

"Not at all!" she said brightly. "I hope you're hungry? It's chicken curry for lunch."

"Great," he said and his voice was soft and as intimate as a caress. She scowled at him, but the corner of his mouth just twitched and he said, "we have to wait for wonder boy's US visa to come through."

"We did a mix up!" said Stevie. "For Christmas pies! And guess what, daddy? Rosie says I can stay here for Christmas. It's a pomice, daddy! I'm having a stocking and everything. Just like Sobie. You likes Christmas pies, don't you, daddy? You is staying, aren't you daddy?"

Flo looked the question over to Rosie, and she could have killed him. What right did he have to walk around the world blackmailing everyone with his gorgeous son? And how dare he look like a Greek god? How dare he be so understanding and friendly? And as for that sexy smile of his, it ought to be against the law.

"Daddy is staying for Christmas, isn't he?"

said Stevie, his eyes beginning to fill with tears. "I want him!"

"Of course, darling," said Rosie briefly tickling his ribs with one finger. "If he wants to stay for Christmas, he can!"

"Whoopee!" yelled Steve, trying to jump up and down in Flo's arms.

"Oh God, you're getting heavy!" said Flo putting him down. "And I think you've grown. It'll be you lifting me up next!"

Steve immediately wrapped himself around Flo's thighs, trying to lift him up. Knocked off balance, Flo laughed and held onto the table. Nicole came into the kitchen with a large branch in one hand, saying something in French to Rosie.

"Oh I think it'll be great. We can just dry it out in the barn," said Rosie, but then she realised that Nicole wasn't listening. Nicole had just noticed Flo and was rattling away in French at him: "Well done, hats off to you. It made a real difference, bloody well done! Blind a chicken and hang it on a belfry, you whore's tail, you monk's gizzard of a worm of a rotten goat, I never thought you'd do it, but..." she swore, slapping Flo heartily between the shoulder blades. "Perhaps Jesus was a Communist after all!"

"What's she saying?" choked Flo. "Stop that! Nicole, that's enough! Stop it!"

"The heating," said Rosie. "She says thank you. It was really generous. We're really grateful."

"And the rest? What was all that she said?"

"Roughly translated? She thinks you're a jolly decent chap."

"Nonsense, it was the least I could do," said Flo looking at Stevie. He kissed Nicole's hand gracefully. "I mean you've done so much..."

Nicole blushed and jabbed Flo sharply on the upper arm. "Oh get off, you!"

"Oh you're back!" said Chris coming into the kitchen hand-in-hand with Daisy. He looked radiantly, blissfully happy, his pale face split by a wide grin. Beside him, Daisy looked unusually diffident. "Congratulate me!" said Chris loudly. Rosie looked at them and her heart sank. She hoped to god he didn't mean what she thought he did, but his eyes were shining like torches and underneath her black hair, Daisy was blushing.

"Congratulations," said Rosie slowly. "What are we celebrating?"

"I'm engaged!" he said. "I mean we're engaged!"

"I hope you don't mind," said Daisy hesitantly.

"Well done!" said Flo, jumping into the silence. "How on earth did you persuade her to accept you? I hope it wasn't violent torture?"

"Congratulations, darling!" said Rosie, recovering herself. "Goodness, what a surprise!"

"Now she won't have to go back to the States in the New Year!" said Chris triumphantly. "I'm going to the mairie to arrange everything this afternoon!"

"We won't do it if you don't like it," said

Daisy in a small voice. "My parents want to see me anyway." At her side, Chris was silently challenging his mother. If she managed to ruin everything, he'd never forgive her.

"Not at all," said Rosie, playing for time. "I mean, it's um, just rather sudden! And you're both so young. I think I just need to think about it, get used to it I mean. Shall we have some chicken curry? Where's Larrie?"

"Out with Sobie," said Chris. "Saw her from the window. But don't worry. She was wearing a hat, she was sitting on a saddle, and she wasn't carrying a gun!"

"And I see Spike is back," said Flo.

"Oh yes!" said Rosie. "His owner said I ought to have him put down but..."

"Of course you didn't."

"Of course not! But the thing is, I ran into the wretched man last Saturday in the market and Spike was all groomed out and behaving perfectly and now he wants him back again! And legally, well, Spike is his dog. He's got the papers to prove it. And anyway everyone in the whole district knows Spike belongs to Monsieur Trèsbête."

"Dye him black," said Flo promptly. "Say Spike ran off and this is a different dog."

"I'm not going to lie," said Rosie pointedly, and both Chris and Daisy shot Flo looks that said "Dumbo!"

"Only joking," he said lamely. "What are you going to do? Can I help?"

"I don't know," said Rosie. "It's not like I need another dog, after all. If only the stupid man would come and take some classes so I could teach him how to handle Spike, then it might be all right."

"I might be able to explain that to him," said Flo. "I'd just need a translator, and perhaps a gun, since you seem to have so many of them on the premises!"

"What about being spotted by the press?" said Rosie. "Aren't you still avoiding them?"

"No," said Flo shaking his head. "I don't care. I've got nothing left to hide. They can chase me as much as they like."

Rosie glared at him. What was he playing at now? Her suspicions were running all directions, and over the next few weeks they didn't once curl up in their basket and go sleep-sleep. Flo was definitely up to something. His whole body language was different, she thought, watching him wielding the yard broom. If she didn't know better, she'd think he'd somehow managed to move up a notch in the pack hierarchy. His movements were bigger, more confident, less aggressive. Obviously, something had happened in London.

Not that she cared, and not that a hundred hysterical wolves could persuade her to ask him. After all, what did it matter? He was only waiting for Stevie's visa to turn up and then he'd be off to Hollywood to make another fortune and live happily ever after. And Rosie for one would be happy to see him leave any time he liked. Good luck to him!

She was more concerned about Chris and Daisy. They did seem genuinely in love but getting married to satisfy a bureaucratic requirement didn't seem like the best start - and they were only babies. On the other hand, she was only too aware that her own track record in the relationships department wasn't exactly impressive. So if what Chris really wanted was a child bride and an attic in Paris, well, perhaps he knew best?

"You know what," said Flo, a few days later, "Chris needs some proper exposure. I don't mean he has to move to Paris, although I don't see why he shouldn't," said Flo rinsing out the drinking bowls. "But he needs a real exhibition. He needs some reviews. He needs to be just a tad more out in the world. He doesn't need to be tied down here. I can hold the fort."

"I should cocoa!" said Rosie.

"We'll discuss this later," said Flo giving her little smile. But, when Flo mentioned the idea to him, Chris instantly mounted his high horse.

"Don't go thinking I'm an exploited young carer, responsible for a feckless parent and a dangerously out of control teenager. Far from it!" He stuck his nose in the air proudly. "We are a multi-generational household enjoying mutual support and working together to create a communal home. Very modern."

"Don't snark at me," said Flo. "I'm not interfering, just saying that you're not imprisoned here against your will. You are allowed to go other places. I'll hold the fort and whatever else needs holding. You and Daisy can go to Paris, enjoy the exhibition and see where it leads you."

"Very nice," said Chris. "And you'll text me the day before you get bored and decide to push off back to Hollywood, will you? Or will it just be a postcard from LA?"

Flo nodded in acknowledgement of the hit. "I won't get bored, Chris," he said. "Irritated, humiliated, infected with gangrene or rabies, soaked, covered in potato slime, held up by armed robbers, threatened in my bed... maybe. But bored, never."

Chris grinned.

"Your mother hasn't come round to the idea yet," continued Flo. "But I'm here to stay."

"I beg your pardon!" exclaimed Rosie coming into the kitchen at that moment. "Who says so?"

"I do!" said Flo unrepentantly.

"If I didn't have a training session to run, I'd make you take that back," she said menacing him with a dog bone. "Heel, Spike!"

"I look forward to being disciplined by you," said Flo.

Sticking her nose in the air, Rosie went off outside with Spike to the fenced training ground, Dolly trotting perkily at her heels. The little white dog gave Flo a wag as she went out of the back door; the pack leader was happy now the smelly man was come back, so Dolly was happy too. In celebration, she burped up a lethal gust of decomposing chicken, which made the big dogs behind her almost faint.

They respectfully hung back a pace to let her go first.

Spike's owner was the stupidest man Rosie had ever met. He didn't seem to be able to understand the slightest command, and as for remembering things from one week to the next, he was worse than Dolly. If it had been any other dog, she'd have cancelled the sessions and refunded the money. But as it was Spike...

"No," said Rosie, as patiently as possible. "Monsieur Trèsbête, I've told you before, don't drag on the lead. One sharp tug will do it. Turn left."

Monsieur Trèsbête turned right and fell over Spike who skipped sideways, growled and tried to slip his collar.

"Sit, Spike!" said Rosie. "Good boy! Are you all right, Monsieur? Stand up then. Let's start again. First you have to get his attention, you have to ensure that the dog wants to please you. That's why you've got those squares of dried liver in your pocket."

At which point Spike decided he'd had enough. He pushed his owner over, snatched the lead out of his hand and carrying it in his mouth, bounded to the fence and leapt over it. Rosie watched him go, and then said very patiently, "All right, perhaps we'll start with Dolly. C'mere, Doll! Now, you put the lead on, praise your dog, and then give the command. Sit, Dolly!"

Dolly sat down obediently beside idiot man and panted happily. She knew perfectly well that if she pretended to obey him, the contents of his jacket pocket would very soon be nicely tidied away into her own capacious stomach. She lolled her tongue out at the big boys, lazily ranging the boundary fence. They were debating whether to follow Spike and see what adventures he might lead them into or whether to stay put in the hope of dried liver. Life in their opinion was looking up. The human kennel was warm now instead of being colder than outdoors. Also the squares of dried liver had got bigger, and there were more of them in the pack leader's pocket. And the kitchen had meat in it more often. Sadly they weren't getting extra rations, but the smell was better than the terrible green-food the humans usually cooked up there on the kitchen surfaces. Wagging and milling round in circles, they decided to stay put. Spike was a bit crazy anyway. You never knew what he might do.

"That's better," said Rosie. "Good boy, Monsieur! Now, pat the dog, praise her and give her a treat. Good boy, Monsieur! Now let's see you try walking to heel off the lead."

But she wasn't concentrating. She was thinking that as soon as Flo pushed off, their unexpected life of luxury would come to an end. No more bread machine, no more drinkable wine, no more decent coffee, peanut butter ice cream, or heaters in the bedrooms. No more cute smiles, no more tea already made in the morning, no more beautiful man standing around getting under her feet. It would be...

She caught herself up and ordered her thoughts into line. It would be spring soon and then the sun would come back and it wouldn't matter. The leaking roof, the swollen window frames, the frozen sheets, the drafts and the stale bread, none of it would matter. The leaves would bud, the earth would soften, flowers would push into the spring light and the world would be warm and beautiful again.

"Hang on!" she shouted. "What's happening? You're not supposed to be just feeding Dolly! Those are training treats! She has to earn them you stupid man! Stop! Sit! Down!" Oh, what was the point? Monsieur Trèsbête would un-train Santa's elves. It was unbelievable. Dolly was waving her tail from side to side as she chewed her way through all the liver squares in Monsieur Trèsbête's hand and he was just sitting there beside her looking helpless.

"She wouldn't come. She was just lying down. I thought she was hungry," he said feebly. Rosie glared at Dolly, who shot back a sparkling glance of pure amusement, licked her lips and having ensured that she had indeed eaten everything, emitted such an intensely disgusting smell of half-digested kitty-sick that Monsieur Trèsbête simply keeled over in the mud. In response, the other dogs started running up and down outside the mesh, barking and bashing at the wire with their paws.

"That's the end of that lesson then," said Rosie. "Same time next week?"

"But no!" exclaimed Monsieur Trèsbête, "We

are going skiing in the Alps for three weeks so I will not come until January."

"You're going skiing?"

He smiled at her sunnily. "Well, I don't really ski," he confided. "I go to the spa while my wife takes lessons. She has an instructor. Young bloke. Very energetic."

"And what were you planning to do with Spike?"

"Oh, he takes care of himself when we are away. We leave him outside and someone somewhere always feeds him. It's only three weeks after all."

Rosie managed not to say anything, but while she was conducting him off her property it suddenly occurred to her that Nicole could probably get Ivan the Terrible to intervene. Perhaps if the mayor claimed to have unearthed some spurious by-law about large dog ownership, they could arm-twist Spike's moronic owner into signing the papers and giving him up for good.

She'd deal with it after Christmas. Time to feed the house dogs now - and then she ought to check over her Christmas lists. The rumtopf was delicious. The pudding was done, so was the cake, all bar the icing. The chestnuts were ready, the pine cones too. Courtesy of Pierre there was a large turkey in the freezer and an even larger Christmas tree in the barn. She'd sent out cards and emails to everyone, organised Christmas Eve and even done most of her Christmas shopping.

She made a first batch of mince pies that evening and after supper announced that it was time to put the decorations up. She might feel that the whole world was itchy against her skin, but the children loved Christmas and she would do it properly - especially for poor little Stevie who had apparently never had a Christmas stocking before. So after supper they dragged the boxes out from a dusty room which had once been an elegant breakfast parlour, and opened them up. The smell of dried oranges and cloves filled the room.

"Oooh the fairy!" squealed Larrie.

"You know what?" said Flo. "I think it's time you took your education more seriously. I think you need to grow up a bit, and..."

"What do you mean?" she demanded, going pink. "I am grown up!"

"I'm sorry, I take it back," he said. "I'm not picking a fight, just concerned for your future. If you want to keep on riding, you're going to have to make a plan. Dropping out at your age is a big mistake."

"But what about him?" demanded Larrie, pointing at Steve. "No-one makes him go to school! So why should I?"

"Believe me, he'll be going to school just as soon as the Christmas holidays are over!" said Flo.

"He will?" said Rosie, pricking up her ears.

"Oh yes!" said Flo. "I just need to get him enrolled!"

"But it's so boring," moaned Larrie.

"Yes, it is," agreed Flo. "Unbelievably boring.

That's why I was thinking of a decent English boarding school. Exercise, fresh air, custard..."

"I'm not eating custard!" said Larrie. "And you can't send me away. I won't go and if you make me I'll run away. I'll join a circus, I'll be a knife thrower and I'll come back and kill you." She suddenly burst into tears. "You pig! How dare you send me away!" Rosie held her arms out and Larrie ran into them.

"But you can't go on running wild," said Flo in a gentler voice. "It's dangerous and it worries your mother. What if the authorities decide to investigate? You could get into all kinds of trouble, and so could she. I'm not trying to ship you off to boarding school, but if you refuse to go to the local one, what are we going to do?"

"I'll go to school!" she protested. "I will!"

"And work hard in every lesson?" said Rosie, sitting down on a sofa and pulling Larrie onto her knee. "Even maths?"

"Why? Why have I got to do maths?"

"So that when you're talking to people outside the horse world, they don't think you're a pillock," said Rosie, rocking her to and fro. "Pillocks are people who say stupid things about subjects they know nothing about."

"If you let me stay, I'll teach Stevie to ride," said Larrie her tears stopping as suddenly as they started.

"I don't know," said Flo. "I'm sure he'd love to learn but we're not discussing him right now. It's your education that's on the table. Aren't there any other schools in the area?"

"Of course there are, but they're all the same as the one she goes to now," said Chris. "All state schools in France are the same. It's a matter of government policy."

"There are a couple of international schools down on the coast," said Rosie.

"Really?" asked Flo, and Chris raised his eyebrows and rubbed his fingers together.

"But are they any good?" asked Flo.

"I'm not having you paying for Larrie's education, if that's what you're thinking!" snapped Rosie. "She'll go to school properly, won't you angel?"

Larrie nodded, and Flo decided to let it drop for the time being. He'd have to do some research before tackling the subject again.

Chris looked at him curiously. What was Flo up to? He looked at his mother but she was cuddling Larrie and whispering.

"Perhaps if Stevie had a Shetland?" said Flo.

"Oh no!" said Larrie sitting up and frowning at him. "Very bad idea! The problem with them is they're stubborn, and because they're so small they never get ridden by anyone who knows how to ride; they never get any proper disciplining, so they're completely impossible. They get un-schooled and stroppy!"

"Sounds like someone else I know," said Chris, looking up at the ceiling. But Larrie ignored him. "And they get out," she went on. "I mean, they're all escape artists. I'll teach him to ride on Sobes."

"You know what? We'll do the tree at the weekend," said Rosie. "So it doesn't get knocked over by the dogs before Christmas Eve. So just put all the tree stuff over there, while we put the rest of the deccies up."

"Can I really ride your hoss?" breathed Stevie, and Larrie nodded and pulled a funny face at him.

"Don't you have any lights?" said Flo, poking through the box.

"Yes," said Chris. "There are two sets. In that biscuit tin."

"What you need is some exterior lights," said Flo. "You know, a big star on the roof or something."

"I'm not going up on the roof!" said Chris. "Last time I was up there, I damn nearly fell through it!"

"Well, perhaps some coloured lights, or twinkly fairy lights along the terrace then?"

"Oh that would be magic!" said Larrie. "Can Sobie have some too? A flashing Santa with some galloping reindeer and carols?"

"You're forgetting the electricity," said Rosie.

"That's a point," said Chris.

"What about it?" said Daisy, a roll of sellotape in her mouth and her hands full of crêpe streamers.

"There isn't enough. If you plug too many

things in at once, it just all cuts out," said Larrie. "That's why we..." Her mother was shaking her head. Larrie broke off what she was saying.

"Anyone want another mince pie?" said Rosie. "Is it time for some hot chocolate? Or perhaps a cup of mulled wine? Have we got any cinnamon sticks left from last year?"

Flo didn't say anything then, but later on when all the others had gone to bed he said abruptly, "What's this thing with the electricity, Rosie? Is the wiring shot?"

"No, it's not that. I mean the wiring probably ought to be condemned but that's not it. It doesn't matter. It really doesn't. It's nothing you can fix in any case."

"I'll be the judge of that," said Flo. "You might as well tell me, if you don't one of your fan club will."

"My fan club?"

I'll just ask Lotta. Or Nicole. Or even Pierre."

"There's two kinds of wiring in France," said Rosie, irritated. "Cheap weak electricity which will run lights and a few electric sockets, and expensive stuff which needs proper wiring but which is strong enough to run radiators, washing machines, anything you like, all at the same time. We've got the weak sort. Two lots. One lot in here, and one lot for the outbuildings. So as long as we plug them in one by one, we can run either the washing machine or the kettle at the same time, plus the freezer and all the other stuff like Chris's computers. But if you start plugging in millions of Christmas lights without unplugging something else, the system will blow."

"Why don't you get proper electricity then? Surely if you sorted this place out, you could make money from it. Couldn't you raise a loan, do it up and start a proper business? Boarding kennels or a proper breeding facility or whatever you call it? Or if that's too complicated, why don't you just sell the place? Surely you'd get enough for it so that you could buy somewhere decent to live in?"

"I don't own it, it's not mine. I don't even have a tenancy agreement," she said. "After I came home from the hospital with Larrie, I just never left, and no-one ever asked me to. So I'd never get a loan to do it up, would I? And if I moved out, I'd have to pay rent and that would tie Chris down even more than he already is, because I've never had a proper job. I mean, all I know is housework and kids and dogs. I haven't got a qualification, a cv, or a professional reference. So at my age I don't think I'd ever get a job, do you?"

"So what are you going to do?" Flo asked.

"God knows. Stay on here as long as I can, I suppose. I mean, I've still got Larrie in school and..." she shrugged. "I don't know why we're discussing this!" she snapped. "It's none of your business anyway. You'll be off to Hollywood as soon as Christmas is over and then what do you care?"

"Hollywood isn't on my agenda," he said. "I have other plans."

Rosie was concerned about Steve. "Why don't you just settle down somewhere and give that poor little kid of yours a proper home?"

"I've got my eye on one," he said. "I'm not sure the place is available. But I'm hoping..."

"Don't," said Rosie, turning her head away. "You don't need to do all that stuff."

"It's not stuff Rosie, it's real," he moved closer to her and she felt her pulse starting to race. "I know you don't believe me," he went on, "but I've never pretended with you. Come on, you never really thought I was writing some dusty old tome on antiques, did you? Come on! Did you?"

She knew he was right, but to avoid giving him the satisfaction of saying so, she just shrugged.

"And if I'd really been trying to fool you, I could have done it. I promise you I could have done. I'm an actor for Christ's sake! But I never did. It never crossed my mind to pretend about anything."

He moved a step closer and she could feel his breath on her hair, smell his aftershave; she could almost hear his heart beating. "Come on, Rosie forgive me," he said. "I'm so sorry I hurt you, truly I am..."

Very, very slowly and as gently as if she was a dandelion clock, he put one finger under her chin so that she had to raise her face to look at him. Up close, he saw that her face was thinner, her eyes were shadowed.

"I don't know," she breathed and suddenly Flo couldn't stand it any more. He pulled her into his arms and dropped baby kisses on her forehead, her temple, her cheek, her mouth. He never wanted to let her go and, far from pushing him away or ordering him into a basket, Rosie pressed closer into his broad chest and kissed him back like a drowning woman. Feeling like he'd been reprieved from the pound, he squeezed her close. When they finally pulled apart so that they could stare into each other's eyes, they were both trembling. Flo gave her a hesitant smile. "I want you so much," he said and immediately could have put a choke chain on himself because the cage doors slammed down over her face again and she drew away.

"You've forgotten haven't you? What you said the first night you were here?" she demanded. "Chip bags."

Flo stared at her as it came back to him. "I was knackered, I was pissed, I was stupid," he said.

"And now you're not?"

"I've changed," he said. "I swear I'm not the same man!"

"I don't know what to believe," she said. "Ralph used to say all this kind of stuff and look where that got me!" Brushing a tear off her cheek, she pushed past him and fled. Awakened from her doze on the sofa, Dolly yawned reprovingly, shook her head at Flo and followed pack leader out of the room.

"What do you think, guys?" said Flo, addressing the big dogs where they lay sprawled in front of the stove. "Have I messed up terminally?"

They raised their heads and looked at him.

The smelly man didn't appear to have either a biscuit or a lead in his hand. Their eyelids drooped and one by one their heads flopped back down onto the bed.

Flo sighed. "So the jury's still out," he said.

CHAPTER FOURTEEN

By Christmas Eve the jury was still hiding in the back room and Rosie showed no signs of relenting. She was polite, even friendly, but always distant, as if she were behind a transparent screen. Flo would have been driven to despair except that by now he'd learned that Rosie was essentially kind-hearted. She wasn't capable of holding out long term.

"What do you think?" she said, throwing open the door to the large blue drawing room at the front of the east wing. "I thought it would be nice to have a special room for the festive season. I've been getting it ready."

"Wow!" said Flo. "It looks fabulous. Can I go in?"

"Sure," she said, following him into the room. "It's a surprise for the kids when they get back from Midnight Mass. I thought we could spend tomorrow in here, too. I mean, decorating the whole place is too much, so I just did this room."

"It's lovely," said Flo. "Beautiful. Just like you."

"Basket!" Rosie snapped, turning on him. He blinked and recoiled, and feeling guilty she relented, just a tiny bit. "Look, let's just agree pax until after the New Year. No sweet talk, no compliments, no cutesy-pie intimate little smiles. No cornering me or chatting me up and definitely no kissing. Let's just get through Christmas."

Flo tried to keep his face straight. "OK. But in return, no barking at me. You've got to be nice. No rotten spuds, no cold hosepipes, no leaving me in the dark and no more orders to get in the basket! I'm not a dog!"

She blushed. "All right! But stop with the compliments, ok?"

"But I am allowed to say this room is stunning, aren't I?"

For a moment they just stared at each other, Flo with a hopeful expression and Rosie with complete confusion. She was the first to look away. "Yes, you're allowed to admire the decor," she said at last, and they both surveyed her handiwork. The ceiling was still yellowing, the eau-de-nil and gold striped wallpaper was still tarnished, the kingfisher blue velvet curtains remained faded and threadbare. But Rosie had collected up a pair of salmon print sofas, an inlaid pear-wood table, and a selection of armchairs and occasional tables, and strategically placed, they disguised much of the damage.

The mirrors with their spotted silver backs

had been cleaned, and a selection of bottles arranged on the side table, many of them bearing home-made labels. The room had been vacuumed and aired, and was scented by a dish of oranges stuck with cloves, and several bowls of fresh pot-pourri. There were bright paper-chains, cushions, paper poinsettias and several bowls of mandarins. The fireplace has been brushed out and laid with dried pine cones, there were rugs and carpets on the antique parquet, and between the two full-length French windows stood a gigantic Christmas tree decorated with pink and gold baubles, delicate old-fashioned tinsel and about fifty tiny candles. Underneath it were all sorts of parcels of every shape and size, with exciting little gift tags attached.

"It's stunning," said Flo. "You should be a set designer."

"I was once," said Rosie. "It'll be warmer once we light the fire and bring some heaters in. We can put them out of sight. I mean they're great. I'm not complaining or anything."

"But they're ugly. You're right. But I didn't know what else would give instant heating without having to do installation works. They're not meant to be permanent."

"Oh I know!" she said quickly. "You absolutely must take them with you when you go. I expect you'll need them in Hollywood, and we always used to manage without them. But I see completely that Stevie..."

"Where is the wonder boy?" he interrupted.

"Gone with Daisy and Nicole to a special early Midnight Mass for kids."

"I thought Nicole was a Communist?"

"Yes, but she's Catholic too."

"Is that possible?"

"This is France. Anything is possible. That's her crêche." Rosie nodded at the miniature Nativity scene which Nicole always set up for Christmas. The delicate china figurines had been in her family for generations, and she had even included Larrie's contribution to the scene; a herd of plastic horses.

"Why is the manger empty?" asked Flo.

"Because the Christ child isn't born yet. He's lurking behind the sloe gin."

"Are you going to light all these candles? Won't they be a fire risk?" he asked, waving at the wall sconces filled with candles, and the brass and tarnished silver candelabra standing on every available surface.

"And your heaters aren't a fire risk?" she said, stung.

"Of course they are, we'll probably all be toast by Boxing Day," he said and he was about to give her one of his famous intimate smiles when she narrowed her eyes at him. "You're being charming!" she said.

"Sorry," he said meekly. "I won't do it again." He took a tiny step towards her, but sudden furious hammering on the front door broke the spell. As one, they went to the window and peered out into the dusk, but it was impossible to identify the door basher. They looked at each other.

"Well, it is Christmas Eve," he said.

"Better let them in," she replied.

They went to the front door and Flo pushed the top of the huge swollen door while Rosie twisted and tugged at the door handle. The door moved open a crack and suddenly it was shoved open with some force from the outside. Sally stood on the doorstep steaming with fury.

"Rosie, don't you dare hang up on me!" she spat. "Never, ever do that again! It's taken me DAYS to get here! I need a power socket and phone, my batteries are dead. Aren't you going to close the door?" Stepping into the hall as Flo heaved the front door closed behind her, Sally started raking through her bag. "What the hell have you done to my actor, Rosie?" she demanded. "Damn! Where are my cigarettes?"

Rosie just gawped and Flo, standing shoulder to shoulder beside her, sniggered like a schoolboy at a funeral and nudged her in the ribs.

"Be serious!" hissed Rosie.

"Basket!" he smirked.

"Frankly, I'm bloody furious with the pair of you," ranted Sally. "I thought he'd be safe here! I never dreamed you'd... You've been off men for bloody years! You could have let me know! Doesn't anyone have a damn cigarette? Here you are, living in the arse end of nowhere, in this ghastly demolition site surrounded by mad children and wild dogs; you hate film stars, you hate films, you don't even read film fanzines and yet you have Florian Kent throwing away one of the most successful careers in film history just so he can sit in this dump mooning over you!"

She dragged a little screen out of her bag. "Look at this!" she said, jabbing at it and making the pictures move. "See? These are news clips and celebrity reports; just look what you've done to him!"

"I haven't touched him!" expostulated Rosie.

"He pissing well turned it down!" Sally exploded. "How can you say you haven't done anything to him? He's turned down the bloody Bond franchise! Don't you know what that means?"

She thrust a sheaf of newspapers at Rosie. "He's made the headlines of every TV show and paper in the US. Probably in the world! Look what you've done, for Christssake!"

"It's only money," said Flo. "It's not important!"

Sally reeled back as if he'd hit her with a wet sausage. "What? Only money! Are you completely insane?"

"Barking," he assured her, and Rosie giggled.

"I have to admit," Sally told Rosie, "that when I foisted this idiot onto you I did slightly hope you'd straighten him out, help him walk the line. But I never dreamed you drive him completely over the edge."

"But I haven't done anything to him!" protested Rosie.

Sally just shook her head and turned back to

Flo with the air of a shrink calming a Bedlamite. "Look, the producers realised you were just overwhelmed, they recognise and appreciate the artistic temperament. Bond is still open for you. But you will have to do at least some PR and say..."

Flo shook his head. "Nope. I'm not changing my mind. I don't care about Bond."

"But you've got no choice. You have to do it," said Sally. "You simply can't afford to turn it down. Especially if you're planning to take on this lot."

"Why?" asked Rosie.

"Because he's been running round London, not only getting rid of all his assets, savings and money but pledging all his future royalties as well!" snapped Sally, exasperated. "He's broke, and what's more if he turns down Bond he'll never work again."

"It doesn't matter," said Flo with a shrug. "I can always earn money."

"Not if you turn down Bond!"

"I don't need 37 million dollars!" said Flo. "Who the hell does? I just need enough for..."

"For what?" snapped Sally. "For that brat of yours?"

"Come on, Sally," said Flo. "I'll always be able to earn a living. You and I both know I could pick up a million just from telling Oprah and the rest why I turned down Bond. As it happens I'm going to play the piano."

"But a million is nothing!" said Sally. "And after what you've been doing in London..."

"What were you doing in London?" Rosie

interrupted.

"That bloody kid of his, that's what!" snapped Sally, her face going redder and redder. "He's signed over all the Firebrand royalties to that brat's mother!"

"Which means?" said Rosie.

"Which means he's spent a lifetime's earnings, it'll probably run into millions, paying Sylvia off just so that kid of his won't have to go back to her."

"You did that?" said Rosie, turning to him with shining eyes. "You paid all that so you could keep Stevie?"

Flo nodded, and Rosie smiled tenderly at him.

"Don't let me disturb you but I need a phone!"

Both Rosie and Flo looked at her blankly and she realised that telecommunications were not uppermost in their minds. "I'll help myself, shall I? I know my way!" she snapped, and stalked off in the direction of Rosie's study leaving her gazing tenderly into Flo's beautiful brown eyes. He held his arms out towards her, just inviting her to step into his embrace, and she was about to, when there was more hammering on the front door. Flo groaned and banged his forehead with his fist.

This time, a large bulldog of a man stood on the threshold. He had gelled hair, bad skin, small features and a large skull. He was wearing a black leather jacket, a red t-shirt and black jeans. He walked into the hall and glanced around suspiciously. "Ok, boss," he said, over his shoulder, and a second man strolled through the front door, exuding luxury and glamour.

"What the hell!" exclaimed Flo.

"What are you doing here?" breathed Rosie.

Ralph Donnington, flicking imaginary dust off a pair of expensive pigskin gloves, smiled. "Do I take that to mean, please come in?" he purred, and behind him, a girl in a dark brown wool dress tittered. She looked like a poodle. Being careful not to tread on anything disgusting, Ralph picked his way into the house and signalled at his henchman to close the door. "How nice to see you, Rosie. Flo, dear chap. I had no idea."

"What do you want?" said Flo.

"I don't suppose you have a decent malt whisky?" He strolled across the hall into the blue drawing room, and the others followed. Looking around him, Ralph blenched. "I um..."

"Not quite your style, eh?" asked Flo.

"Perhaps just your outer garment, dear man," said Ralph, and the thug stripped off his leather jacket and spread it out on the sofa so that his boss could sit down. "Rosie, bring me my children," announced Ralph, in a rich theatrical purr. He rubbed his forehead fastidiously with his fingertips. "Let me see them, just once!"

Rosie stared at him. It was Christmas Eve, it was supposed to be a time of good will to all men but all she had on her mind was murder most deserved.

"My babies," sighed Ralph in beautifully rounded tones. "How I have missed them!"

"What? Why do you want to see them now, when you never wanted to see them before?"

Ralph made an eloquent gesture encompassing pain, loneliness and inexpressible regret, and at that moment Chris walked into the room. His face was closed and expressionless, his mouth just a thin line in his face. He stared at his father in silence.

"I knew it was him," he said finally. "Saw him over the banisters. What does he want?"

"Ah," sighed Ralph again, sentimentally this time. "You remind me of myself at your age!"

"I feel sick," said Chris.

"To think what I've missed. My son!"

The poodle-woman suddenly burst into a series of high-pitched complaints. "French paps and hacks are unprincipled liars," she yapped. "They simply don't realise how hurtful it is for an artiste of Sir Ralph's calibre..."

Ralph waved his hand in quasi modesty. "Hush Veronica, dear girl. You embarrass me!"

"Sir Ralph? You have a title?" said Flo.

"New Year's list. So vulgar," sighed Ralph. "One does so hate being summoned to Buckingham Palace."

"So Hugo found you, then?" said Chris, putting all the clues together. "Hugo went to Paris, found you, and told you the whole story. He blackmailed you, in fact? Or was it the other way round? You're blackmailing him in some way?" A tinge of colour crept into his cheeks.

"If Hugo is a ghastly provincial lout with pimples and a Canon," said Ralph, "yes, he found me." A brief smile flicked across Chris's thin face but Ralph was not amused. "I gather he got the information from you, Chris. Apparently, until I persuaded him otherwise, he was planning to sell the story to Paris Match."

"Shoulda let me handle it," said the thug. "Coulda minced him."

"He said you were living in poverty," said Veronica indignantly, and there was a sudden silence as everyone gazed around the room. "It would make headlines around the world..." she said, before she tailed off and bit her lip.

"I don't know what you've done to my beautiful château," said Ralph mournfully. "But in any case it's got to stop. We can't have the press hounding us, can we?"

"Ah" exclaimed Flo. "So you're finally going to pay maintenance, are you?"

Ralph smiled kindly. "Dear boy, always so impetuous, so emotionally available. How I admire your ability to throw yourself into other people's lives!"

Flo went as pale as Dolly after a bath, and a muscle twitched in his cheek, but Ralph ignored him. "Now Rosie darling, you know the agreement was always accommodation rather than some sordid grubby little financial arrangement. All I'm saying is that clearly my beautiful château is just too much for you. I'd like to help you move out... leave this scene of struggle... "

"Why on earth are you all in here?" said Larrie bursting into the room. "Wow, this looks great, Muma. Who are they?"

Rosie blushed. "Larrie darling, this is your father, Ralph, and um his girlfriend Verucca."

"Veronica, asshole!" said the thug.

"Personal assistant, not girlfriend," said Ralph.

Rosie turned on the thug. "And this person is Ralph's artistic stylist," she snapped, and the thug surged towards her with his chest puffed out. "Basket!" ordered Rosie, pushing the palm of one hand towards his nose, and he stopped, visibly taken aback. "Get down!" she said. "Now!"

"Oh. Well, they're not staying, are they?" said Larrie. "The thing is, we've just got back from Midnight Mass and Daisy and Steve are helping Nicole in the kitchen, but I'm making a stocking for Sobie and I was wondering do you think it's okay to put a banana in it?"

Ralph brushed one perfect diamante tear from his cheek. "So beautiful, so innocent, so fresh!" he murmured. "And the poor little lame leg? Do you limp terribly, my child?" He held his hands out to Larrie. "Just one kiss!"

"Eee-yuk!" said Larrie, wrinkling up her nose. "I'd sooner snog stenching Dolly!"

"Oh, how heartless!" exclaimed Veronica. "Don't take any notice, sir!"

"You might go around snogging random men but I don't!" said Larrie, retreating to the door. "I might be heartless but at least I'm not a slut!" She slammed out of the room.

Ralph got slowly to his feet and mopped his brow theatrically. Then he sighed deeply again and spread his hands out in front of him. "I came here on Christmas Eve, the season of love, to see my children, to heal the ache in my heart, to close the hole torn in my life by their absence..."

"And make them homeless?" said Rosie.

"To offer them a new life... My parents, God bless them, have passed on and their house on the south coast is therefore empty and cold. How would it ease my soul to know that my children were warming that sorrowful gap?"

Veronica was gazing up at him from the sofa with her hands clasped fervently at her breast. "Oh Ralph," she whispered, with a lump in her throat.

"Not that bungalow in Clacton?" said Rosie.

"The sea air..."

"No," said Rosie. "It only has two bedrooms, and it has a garden the size of a kennel. What about the dogs? What about Sobie? What about Chris's dark room?"

"You cannot comprehend the pain," said Ralph, and he was so moved by his own performance that he had genuine tears in his eyes, "the searing pain of realising your children have been brought up to hate you. I longed to succour them, yearned for them, loved them from a distance, and yet was prevented from seeing them by you."

"How could I have stopped you seeing them?" protested Rosie. "You've never even tried to! I haven't heard from you, not even once, since Larrie was born!"

"The point is," said Veronica, "the press won't find you in Clacton. And why shouldn't Ralph live in his own château?"

"Sans finesse, Veronique," said Ralph, shaking his head. "But straight to the point." He moved towards Rosie. "We could sign the papers now, save ourselves the bother of dragging this out. By the New Year, you could be in your new home, enjoying the sea breezes on the south coast."

Flo exploded. "How dare you?" he said. "You come here on Christmas Eve in order to evict your own children from their home with some sickly tale about wanting them to live in a bungalow in Clacton once owned by your dead parents..."

Ralph gave him a silky, snarky, snakey little smile. "Well that's one way of putting it," he said, "or we could talk about what you're doing here attempting to seduce the mother of my children. Or is it the other way round? Is she making yet another attempt to latch onto a rich man?"

"Bastard!" exclaimed Chris, standing as pale and thin as a Christmas star. "Barbarians, all four of you!" He took a step forward but Flo took an even larger step forward.

"Rosie is too nice to fuss about being evicted, and she's obviously too nice to fight you for money," said Flo through gritted teeth. "But I'm not! Unless you do the right thing from this day on, every move you make, you'll have a pack of reporters on your heels, because I'll be briefing every tabloid editor I know - and believe me I know them all - about how your children live in squalor while you live in luxury. I'll supply them with all the photos they want, and don't think for an instant that they won't believe me because even a fool can see that these are your kids. See what that'll do for your precious career!"

Ralph gazed at him in horror and all the foppish drawling was gone. "You wouldn't!"

"Believe me," said Flo with chilled menace. "It would be my pleasure."

"What do you want?" said Ralph.

"I don't want anything," said Flo. "And neither does Rosie. You sign this château over to Chris and Larrie, and you give them both an allowance. And not a measly couple of hundred pounds a month either. A proper allowance that reflects your salary. 40 million dollars per film, isn't that what you're earning?"

"This is blackmail," said Ralph, steely-eyed. "How do I know you won't go broke three years down the line and start threatening me again?"

"I won't go broke," said Flo confidently. "I'm going to earn my living playing the piano, and in any case Rosie never wants to set eyes on you again. In fact, none of us want to see you again."

They all looked at Ralph, who was obviously

weighing up his options. "I'll have my lawyer draw up the necessary paperwork," he said finally. "I assume you can wait until the New Year."

Rosie hadn't missed 'none of us' and flashed a grateful smile at Flo. On the spur of the moment, he took her right hand and sank to one knee.

"You're making a mistake, dear boy," drawled Ralph. "She's not worth it. She's only after you for the money."

Without the slightest hesitation, Flo leapt up and smashed his clenched fist into Ralph's beautiful smug face. There was a loud crunching noise as his knuckles made contact, and Ralph staggered backwards onto the sofa. Flo swore and bent double, clutching his hand.

"Well done! You really shouldn't hit people. Are you all right?" gasped Rosie. "Chris, call a doctor, I think Flo's broken his hand."

"No need!" whispered Flo. "It's just my knuckles."

Seeing that Ralph was bleeding artistically, Veronica burst into tears. Flo looked up from his excruciatingly painful hand and winced at the noise.

"Nice," said Chris bitterly. "You should have let me deal with him, Fifi."

"Sorry about that. Couldn't let you murder him," said Flo. "Your mother wouldn't like being a prison visitor."

Chris glared at Ralph. "Leave, just get out and don't come back," he ordered him. "I never want to see you again. None of us do!"

"Fabulous, my boy!" said Ralph, dabbing at his cheekbone with a snowy white handkerchief. "Perfect timing, good clear delivery of the lines..."

"Shut up!" chorused Chris, Flo and Rosie.

"Oh, you're all in here are you?" said Sally, stalking into the room. "Oh my God!" gasped Sally. "Ralph! Darling! How fabulous to see you!"

Flo snorted through his nose with amusement.

"Quiet!" said Rosie. "Basket!"

"If you treat me like I dog I'll start being charming again," Flo told Rosie, and she pulled a face at him. At which moment Larrie came back into the room.

"Can I light the fire, Muma? Please? I've got orange peels!" Ignoring their unwelcome visitors, she took the matches off the mantelpiece and knelt on the hearthrug, striking matches. Before long the fire roared into life, and Larrie piled chunks of coal on it with a pair of long handled tongs. Shivering violently, Veronica pushed past everyone and went to kneel in front of the fire, holding her hands out like the little match girl.

Rosie shook her head. The stupid widget probably wasn't wearing anything under that knitted poodle frock. For some reason, the idea seemed intensely funny. Rosie choked and tried to bite back a hysterical laugh, but the more she tried to keep a straight face, the more hysterical she got. She doubled up laughing.

"I fail to see the joke," said Sally, but Rosie

just waved vaguely around her and laughed again.

"Darling, you are extraordinary," said Sally. "You have two of the world's most handsome men in your house, apparently fighting over little old you. Most women would give their right arms to be in your shoes, but you on the contrary, appear to think it's some kind of joke. What is wrong with you?"

Sally suddenly took a second look at Ralph and blenched. "Oh my God!" she breathed, horror struck. "Don't tell me. Not your face! Please don't tell me your face is damaged!" She then looked at Flo. "That hand had better not be broken," she said menacingly. "You'll need it for typing your memoirs. How on earth else are you going to pay for all this if you turn down Bond? Please tell me it's not broken!"

"I shouldn't worry about him, I daresay he'll make a fortune in his new career as snitch to the scum of the earth," said Ralph.

Flo flushed red, and lunged forward looking exactly like Spike in a bad mood, and Rosie put her hand on his arm. "It's Christmas Eve," she said, soothingly.

"I don't care what eve it is," said Larrie, getting up from the hearth with a gleam in her eye. "If he's going to be horrible to Flo, I'm going to torture him with a red hot poker! You know how the Princes in the Tower were killed don't you? That's how you're going to die, Father Most Beastly!" Brandishing the luminescent poker, she advanced on Ralph.

The thug made a tentative move but was instantly halted by Dolly, who went and sat in front of him with a determined glare. To her he smelt of fear and loathing, and she didn't like either of them.

"Call your dog off!" said the thug, and Larrie suddenly burst out laughing. "You pathetic creep," she said. "Don't you know anything about dogs?" She went back to the fire and thrust the poker back into the flames.

"So they're still looking for a Bond?" Ralph said to Sally, where she sat jabbing at her iPhone.

"Bond? You're way too old!" said Flo.

"But you'd make a fantastic Lear," said Sally. "I could do that for you, you know. Give your career a whole new lease of life, why don't mobile phones work in this bloody château? Listen, give me your number, when are you next going to be in London?"

Rosie shook her head. It was just all business as usual.

"Lear?" breathed Ralph. "My dear girl, what did you say your name was?"

"Sally. I'm Flo's agent, or was until he moved into the doghouse and went mad," she said, still tapping at the keyboard busily. "I could... you know. Perhaps we could get you to direct? Something heavy, serious, worthy..."

There was a quiet knock on the door and a soft American voice said, "Hello, can we come in?"

It wasn't quite the Christmas Eve Rosie had planned but there was no help for it. "Don't you dare say anything in front of Stevie!" she said, as the door opened, and Minnie, Spike and the big dogs all surged into the room.

Daisy, Nicole, and Stevie were standing in the doorway, gazing at the room with astonishment and admiration. They carrying candles in glass jars from Mass, plates of mince pies, and a large jar of rumtoft.

"Come in!" said Rosie.

"Look at my fire!" said Larrie. "Isn't big? Muma, can we light the candles now? Please?"

"The Christ child is being borned," said Steve loudly.

"What?" said Flo. "Who told you that?"

Nicole rattled off a load of French and then made a show of spitting at Ralph. "Scumbag flea's arse of a gargoyle's whore," she said. "If it wasn't Christmas Eve, I'd probably kill you. As it is, I might just settle for permanent and major disfiguration."

"Bravo!" called Chris, recovering some colour.

"What's he doing here," demanded Nicole, shooting poisonous looks at Ralph. "The Christ child is supposed to arrive on Christmas Eve, not the devil, curse the socks of his confessor's snail!"

"You is a bad man," said Stevie. "An' you are not perpossessing," he pursued, staring at Ralph with gimlet eyes.

"Who says?" demanded Ralph, ridiculously stung, and Flo was about to jump in, but Rosie grabbed his arm. Steve was smiling. "I says," he said happily. "I says what goes on cos I am a dog handler.

Watch! Spike, c'mere!"

Spike loped across the floor towards Steve and as he got close to the sofa, the little boy put his hand out with the palm pointing straight at Spike's face. "Sit!" he said and Spike's bottom sank gracefully onto the carpet. "Good boy!" said Steve. Then he jumped onto the sofa and whistled and Spike climbed onto the sofa with him, flopped down on top of his feet and gave Stevie's knees an affectionate lick.

"I will tell Ivan that the dog is too dangerous to be kept by an amateur!" said Nicole. "I promise you, the day he comes back he will make Mr Très-bête sign the papers and the dog will belong to this little man. Trust me, he will do it, because otherwise I'll tell the tax authorities about his lucrative summer gîte business."

"You would do that?" said Daisy, round-eyed. "But I thought you loved him. Back home in the States, true love means..."

"You wait until you're my age," said Nicole. "Then you'll be wiser!"

"With me as a husband she'll never need to be," said Chris, wrapping his arm round Daisy's shoulder and sticking his chin in the air. But no-one took the bait. Flo and Rosie were both gazing at Stevie.

"You are marvellous," Flo told Rosie.

"You really are as perfect as you seem," said Rosie.

"Whose is that monstrous child?" said Ralph

pointing at Stevie. "He's definitely not mine!"

Chris nodded at Flo, and Ralph blinked in confusion. "Are you telling me he's your half-brother?"

Chris smiled. "No, but I suspect he's about to become our step-brother!"

Larrie took advantage of everyone staring at Stevie to open a bag of bacon crisps and stuff a huge handful of them into her mouth. Nicole got the Christ child out from behind the sloe gin, and crossed herself. "Thank you dear Lord, for all our blessings," she said. "Viens, mon petit, put him in the manger."

Signalling at Spike to stay, Stevie climbed off the sofa and for a second, as Larrie watched him putting the little doll onto the delicate china straw, she felt wildly jealous. Putting Jesus in the crib had always been her job, all her life she'd done it. Every Christmas. But then her mother caught her eye and gave her a big wink and suddenly she didn't care. She wasn't the baby in the house any more, she was growing up. Soon she'd be as grown-up as Chris. With a big smile, she reached for a mince pie.

While Larrie wasn't looking, Dolly quietly stole her packet of crisps. It smelt of goodie-goo, and she was bored with guarding fear and loathing. Let Spike do it since he enjoyed growling so much. She settled down happily beside the fire to investigate her good-smelling bag. Stevie went back to the sofa and hugged Spike.

It was the perfect Christmas Eve after all.

The lights sparkled, the flames leapt in the fireplace, the tree twinkled and glittered, and the room was filled with warmth and laughter. Stevie, Spike and teddy were cuddling on the sofa, Daisy and Chris had their arms round each other, Nicole and Larrie were pouring mulled wine out, and in the centre of the room, Flo had finally managed to take Rosie in his arms and kiss her properly. "I love you, and I always will," he told her.

"I thought it might be hormones," she confessed, nestling into his embrace. "But I realise that I've loved you since the minute I set eyes on you."

Flo promptly kissed her again, while everyone twinkled and exchanged pleased looks.

"I feel sick," said Sally rolling her eyes. "This is entirely over-sugared for me. Is that your Merc outside, Ralph, darling?"

Ralph nodded.

"I'll drive," she replied.

The four Barbarians climbed into Ralph's massive, expensive, luxury car and accelerated away to wealth and stardom but no-one cared.

In the doghouse, everyone lived happily ever after.

THE END

ABOUT THE AUTHOR

Samantha David

Samantha David is a novelist, journlaist and translator living in France with her family and a menagerie of animals. When not glued to a computer screen or feeidng sheep, she enjoys flying light aircraft. Connect with Samantha David on Facebook or via her website (www.samanthadavid.com) to get latest news of new books coming soon plus freebies and exclusive previews.

BOOKS BY THIS AUTHOR

I Married A Pirate

Katie Fforde described 'I Married a Pirate' as "A rip roaring ride. Huge fun," and readers consistently love the gloriously romantic happy ending.

When Camilla accepts an email invitation to join The Pirate on a schooner in the Caribbean she walks into a golden cage. Under a full moon, the Pirate is charming, and every time he touches her skin the earth moves. Enchanted, Camilla marries him only to realise that she has surrendered her independence to an irascible, autocratic control freak. Joyfully determined to fight back, Camilla learns to swim, steals a gun, attacks him with frozen prawns... but the Pirate has spent a lifetime yearning for a woman who can match his courage and zest for life. No couple were ever more locked in a more farcical battle of wills. Will they ever admit they are soul-mates?

Buy 'I Married a Pirate' today - and plunge into a world of crystal seas, palm trees and a love that defies all conventions.

Living With Spies

An escapist read, this exciting, quirky contemporary romance set in Brussels, will have you giggling as you turn the pages.

Suzie looks like the perfect wife and mother, but is usually lost in her own fantasy of being Blanche: a glamorous WWII spy in a trench coat, with a miniature gun tucked into the top of her stocking. When she receives a mysterious message from a spy called Agent B, it seems as if her dream has come true. But who is her new contact? A dangerous controller, or the love of her life?

Fast-paced, romantic and heart-warming, you'll read Living with Spies over and over for the joy of the beautifully satisfying happy ending.

Buy 'Living with Spies' today - and slip into a cobbled side street for an assignation with the most romantic man in Brussels.

On Golden Sand

This delicious, sunny contemporary romance set in

Cornwall introduces a friendly donkey and an eccentric, bohemian family...

When Flora's long-lost husband Alec washes up on the beach like driftwood, she is reluctant to believe a word he says. She knows he's hopelessly unreliable, and yet the spell of his easy charm is as strong as ever. Is handsome Al really the love of Flora's life? Will she be able to resist him or not? Meanwhile their grown-up daughters, Toni and Primrose, are navigating their own romantic tangles...

Amusing, romantic and heart-warming, this contemporary romance is set in a world where the sun always shines, the sea always sparkles and the scent of strawberry jam wafts along the hollow lanes behind the cliffs.

If you love Rosamunde Pilcher's books, you'll love 'On Golden Sand'. Buy it today and escape to the seaside of your dreams.

Printed in Great Britain
by Amazon

60289735R00199